T5-AGM-599

PENGUIN BOOKS
AFTERWARDS

Jaishree Misra is the author of the best-selling *Ancient Promises* and *Accidents Like Love and Marriage*. She is presently living in London, working as a film classifier and is in the process of completing a historical novel.

Afterwards

JAISHREE MISRA

PENGUIN BOOKS

Penguin Books India (P) Ltd., 11 Community Centre, Panchsheel Park,
New Delhi 110017, India
Penguin Books Ltd., 80 Strand, London WC2R 0RL, UK
Penguin Group Inc., 375 Hudson Street, New York, NY 10014, USA
Penguin Books Australia Ltd., 250 Camberwell Road, Camberwell,
Victoria 3124, Australia
Penguin Books Canada Ltd., 10 Alcorn Avenue, Suite 300, Toronto,
Ontario M4V 3B2, Canada
Penguin Books (NZ) Ltd., Cnr Rosedale & Airborne Roads, Albany,
Auckland, New Zealand
Penguin Books (South Africa) (Pty) Ltd., 24 Sturdee Avenue, Rosebank
2196, South Africa

First published by Penguin Books India 2004

Copyright © Jaishree Misra 2004

10 9 8 7 6 5 4 3 2 1

For sale in the Indian Subcontinent and Singapore only

Typeset in Sabon MT by Eleven Arts, Delhi-35

Printed at Saurabh Printers Private Limited, Noida

ACKNOWLEDGEMENTS

Much love and many thanks are due to:

Karthika, for long-distance encouragement and conviction;

Daya, Omana, Vijayam, my triumvirate of strong women, for always batting on my side;

Khushwant, for constant reminders in small blue aerogrammes to WRITE;

Ian, for being an unerring pair of 'English eyes' and, Miss Mann notwithstanding, ace grammarian too;

Anshu and Geetika, for reading manuscripts between cricket and safari and on sunny Sundays better spent;

Mishri, Batasha and the two people responsible for all that sweetness, Pavan and Renu, for happy days in Cyprus;

Harji and Amrit, for wheels, for unthinking generosity;

Rohini, for helping me stay mindful of the only really important things in life;

And, as ever, D, who is one of those really important things in my life.

PROLOGUE

It was the letter that first indicated there was to be an 'afterwards'. Large, well-rounded writing, unfamiliar of course, covered almost the entire face of a grubby envelope. My name was followed by the address that included England, UK and finally, The World and The Universe, leaving just enough room for a few smudged fingerprints, an Indian postage stamp and a par avion sticker. My grandmother has told me to write to you … do you remember me . . . she asked, in a strangely stilted, formal sort of way. That wasn't how I remembered her at all. Cocky, yes. Rude, oh often. She certainly didn't know how to write then. But that was over a year ago and she'd have changed by now. As I had. Who would have thought . . .

Back then, though, it was as if everything had been freeze-framed. Into a stark black-and-white picture filled with distorted images and edged with sharp, jagged pain. That was where, as far as I knew, the story ended. I would have laughed then if anyone had suggested that there might be anything more to come.

But here it is now, the afterwards that every story ought to have. The flip side of a Foreword, acknowledging that life isn't like a book, recognizing gratefully that, long after the last page is read and the shiny hard cover is slapped satisfyingly shut for the last time, there will still be more to tell. As I sit in my study, overlooking an overgrown back garden in a small, semi-detached, suburban London house, for the first time in this past year I'm conscious of that sense of starting again. And feel a peculiarly childish pleasure in the coincidence of new crocus shoots emerging from the hard black soil in that sunny patch near the patio door.

I pick up the letter again. These childish words, formed laboriously, a small tongue sticking out no doubt, these are 'after words' too—words that I simply wouldn't have thought possible once. A letter from four thousand miles away, arriving from out of the blue, carrying both past and future within it, as though a happy consensus always existed between the two. There is apparently, always, if not exactly a 'happily ever after', at least an 'afterwards' to every story. However unlikely that may seem at the time.

Where should I begin telling you that story? Considering it's your story too, Anjali, and your father's and your mother's and your grandparents'. No story is ever completely one's own to tell and every version you hear will differ from the next. But, because I know that Maya would want me to tell it to you so you remember her well, I feel I have to tell it carefully, and as truthfully as possible.

They say men don't recall things as well as women do, not with the same amount of detail. Perhaps I'm different, then. I remember everything with a clarity that still hurts. Every tiny detail of that summer. But this is the first time I feel I have the energy to see it through. Record everything somewhere. For myself perhaps. For Maya. For you.

So where do I start? Logically, if this were just your story, I ought to start it in the year of your birth. But let me tell it my way for now, dear child, for so much of it is still impossible to recount. Perhaps someday I'll be able to sit down and tell you the rest of the story. That's when we'll fill in all the gaps. Italicize the important bits. Juxtapose your story and mine and finally work out how they ever came to overlap at all. And maybe, on that more thoughtful day, we can try and understand why.

For now, though, all I can manage is the description of how we met and how we came to part. And, to tell you that, I will have to return, whether I like it or not, to the summer of 1996.

Prologue

Part I
1996

That was the summer they performed Maya's death rites. Three years before she actually died. It was the summer just before the communists came back to power in Kerala; the summer the monsoons failed and Vembanad bund was closed to save water for the paddy fields, turning the backwaters into a sluggish, green canal of stench. The summer we fell in love, Maya and I.

How had she come to imagine that she could get away with it? And begin a new life, without needing to look back, without *having* to look back at everything that had gone before, generations before her. She had seemed to genuinely believe she could change things. Not just the way her family thought about her, but the way they thought about everything else as well.

'They'll change,' she had said, smiling, believing it. 'They'll see how, in the end, it's we who are really important, you wait and see . . .' Confident that their love for her would surpass everything else.

Instead, the eleyathu had been called. A man had been sent to fetch him from his lonely shack on a hillside, travelling a whole day by bus to get to him.

Better to get someone from far away, they would have whispered.

. . . It's more private, we don't want too many people talking about it . . .

. . . The local eleyathu might gossip . . .

. . . And he wouldn't suffice anyway, you really do need one with a special knowledge of these things . . .

It's not like performing the usual last rites, you know. It's different when it's done for someone who is still alive . . .

Maya was alive then. Having escaped six months earlier, when I had found her. Restless and caged, iridescently beautiful, terrified suddenly at her own freedom. But alive—and as happy as she could be under the circumstances. About to start a new life when, back in her homestead—Pulayil Veedu, the family seat of the Pulayil Varmas—they performed her death rites, instead. They would have stood—her parents, her elderly grandmother (who, Maya was sure, would have wept grievously for her), Maya's little brother and the eleyathu—in a silent, condemning circle around a smoking fire. Her brother would have been told to take his shirt off and then sit cross-legged to perform the rituals. It has to be done by someone younger, Maya had explained to me, her voice shaking with the horror of it.

Sticky rice would have been moulded into globules by chubby young hands wearing a palm-leaf ring. A pinch of black gingili seeds would have been placed carefully on top, some sticking stubbornly to fingertips despite small hands being shaken vigorously. Incantations of a hawk-faced eleyathu, repeated in a high-pitched unbroken boy's voice, would have rent the peace of the early morning sky, and hands would have been clapped loudly together to summon the crows to peck at the rice . . . the belief being that they carried the souls of the dead who could not be physically present . . .

When Maya wept, I knew only half her tears were for her own shame. The rest were for the baby brother who, she was sure, did not understand what he was made to do. Couldn't they have just told him that I was gone and that he was to forget about me, she asked piteously, did they have to make him do all those . . . last rites for a sister who still loves him?

I had held her close that day, something I had never done before, feeling her body tremble despite the summer heat of Delhi. I was desperate to show her how alive she still was and tried to make her remember all the reasons for which she had fled, reminding her that she still had her daughter. I was desperate to reach her that night. But her misery had been too deep, too agonized and restless to reach . . . for long afterwards. Until it finally seemed to pass and she was able to turn to me again.

If you asked me now whether she had ever really been able to get over the whole thing, though, I wouldn't be able to say. As the months passed and we moved away from Delhi to England, she started to smile again. Laughing at something I might have said, seeming pleased that we were now in this new place with so many new things to learn and experience. Looking so much more like the Maya I had first been so attracted to. But, if you scan her photographs carefully (which I still do far too often, I have to say), you might be able to spot, like I can, that look in her eyes. A sort of air she always carried with her after that. Her halo of sadness, I used to call it. Like a still, sad pool that could not be rippled, whatever was thrown into it. Almost as if some part of her had, in fact, actually burnt in those fires and died that day. Perhaps that was what death rites are meant to achieve—when they are done for the living, that is.

But, to start at the very beginning of the story, I'll have to first describe the Pulayil Varmas, the ancient illustrious clan from which Maya descended. Because without them, Maya wouldn't have been the woman she was, nor her parents the people they were. Coming from an old family was a particular burden, Maya once said. The ancestors whisper at you down the generations. The Varmas were descended, she thought, from a clan called Kiriyatil of southern

Malabar, a branch of which moved further south into Travancore in the middle of the last century, acquiring minor royal connections along the way and settling finally in the wetlands of Champakulam. She imagined that from then on they would have presided over miles of rice fields, adding acre upon acre with each year that passed. And finally built themselves a grand old house on the banks of the kaayal, just where it opened up and widened, turning from green to blue as it readied itself to meet the sea.

Pulayil House. I remember it as a graceful and rather grand old house from that one glimpse I had of it. Maya had told me that some of her happiest memories were associated with that house and I always felt that would have made it far more upsetting for her to imagine those funeral rites taking place in its compound. *I used to play on those steps*, she had said, imagining her little brother being helped down the greasy steps that led to the water tank where the rituals were always done. *He must have immersed himself in the waters of the tank and then performed the ceremonies in his wet clothes . . . he must have felt cold, he hated being wet . . .*

She told me how Pulayil House had been handed down, following the Kerala system of inheritance, from the eldest uncle of each generation to the eldest niece. Her face had lit up and she got quite animated telling me about the unusual inheritance system called *marumakkathayam* because she thought it far superior to the patriarchal ways of the north. I remember her saying once that Kerala's matrilineal system provided protection for women in a way that no other society did . . . before remembering how cruelly it could let women down, too, if they strayed.

The house was finally inherited by Bhageerathi Amma, Maya's grandmother, who had been married to Vasudeva Varma, chief excise inspector of Travancore State in the year India became independent. Theirs was an unhappily short marriage, Vasudeva Varma having died of smallpox when he was a mere forty-five. Maya had never met him, of course. By the time he died, the

Jaishree Misra

inheritance system of *marumakkathayam* had been abolished, but Bhageerathi Amma had shown her mettle by running the affairs of the house, and maintaining the rice fields in good order, bringing up her only son single-handedly, finally sending him to Bangalore to qualify in law. Wanting him to have the choice that young men were increasingly being given. Not wanting him to become another in a long line of wealthy farmers if he didn't want to. In the end, it was to law that he turned, and a man was employed to supervise the rice fields during the busy months of harvest and planting.

When he was twenty-eight, his mother chose for him a beautiful girl from Tellicherry. I remember seeing a photograph of them—Maya's parents, a good-looking couple, Madhava Varma and Rukmani Amma—taken at their wedding probably. Glowing even in sepia, dressed in their wedding finery, frozen at the moment when Rukmani Amma was about to enter her new house for the first time. Burdened by flower garlands, she had looked uncertain and shy next to the tall figure of her new husband. His head had the kind of proud tilt that can only come from generations of nobility. The picture had been placed on top of Maya's fridge in her dining room and I had looked at it, searching for traces of the dignified elderly couple I had seen over the wall a few days earlier.

I had only just moved in next door. That was in February 1996. The year of that terrible summer. When the monsoons failed and the canals across Kerala lay still and brooding, shrouded in stench. The summer that Maya's parents conducted her death rites in the compound of Pulayil House. Before she had even died.

'Careful with that box, it's got my drums in it!'

The boy obligingly placed the box down gently, and wiped the sweat off his glistening arms with a cotton cloth that had been draped around his neck. It was *blazing* hot; I hadn't expected Kerala to be so hot at this time of year.

'Hot,' I said to him, more gently, smiling and making a show of wiping my brow. I wasn't sure how much English he could understand. He flashed a startlingly white smile in my direction, seeming to know what I meant. 'Do you need help with the suitcase?' I asked, trying to be friendly.

'No, saar, only small suitcase,' he replied, going back outside to collect my Samsonite from the boot of the taxi. So he knows English, I thought with some relief. Funny how often Indians, in India, still had to resort to English to understand each other. I followed him out into the afternoon blaze again, taking out my wallet to pay the driver of the taxi. The driver closed the boot of the car, taking the money from me and counting it with a licked thumb. As the taxi sped off, melting into the shimmering heat haze at the bottom of the road, I waved the boy away and picked up my suitcase with its meagre collection of clothes. That was the best thing about travelling somewhere warm, I thought. Not having to pack all those clothes. The best bit had been handing my fleece jacket over to Kevin in the car at Heathrow. 'Don't think I'll need that where I'm going,' I had chuckled, enjoying seeing him rub his frozen hands together in disgust.

He had been disgusted with everything, old Kevin. With the ease with which I had talked my way into getting six months' unpaid leave. With my efficient organization of everything—tickets, the rental on this house, finding a tutor for the mridangam I had decided I wanted to learn to play.

Kevin was the lead guitarist in our part-time band. I was the drummer. We weren't terribly good or anything like that, playing only in the evenings and on weekends. We only ever played for ourselves as we were never good enough for an audience of any sort, although Kevin could never bring himself to admit that and occasionally lined up his girlfriend of the moment in solitary attendance. Was it any wonder his relationships had always been so short-lived! Even those sessions had started to dwindle somewhat when Kevin's company relocated and he moved away to Leicester. That, and my acrimonious split with Anna, were what had really brought me here, if I tried to analyse things carefully. Then there was the sunshine gleaming out at me from the Kerala brochure that I had found somewhere and leafed through on a drizzly Sunday afternoon. Last year's had been a particularly ghastly winter. Finally, the chance to also brush up my drumming skills had decided it.

I had watched a mridangam player on the television late one night, on some obscure Channel 4 documentary, fascinated at the speed with which his fingers moved. And was gripped suddenly by the desire to relearn my old tabla-playing skills, picked up as a schoolboy while growing up in Delhi. It hadn't been too difficult finding the place to learn mridangam. It had to be Kerala, everybody I spoke to said. And a friendly south Indian voice at the Bharatiya Vidya Bhavan in Kensington had provided me with some addresses. I had about five to choose from and finally decided on the one that had an email address supplied. Everything had been an absolute breeze after that. Pannicker, my would-be mridangam tutor, turned out to be a bit of an internet junkie as well and communication had flowed easily over the miles. He lived in Trivandrum, the capital of Kerala. 'There is an international airport here also,' he had written, still trying to tempt me in the early stages. And, after we had fixed the rates for his tuition, he had swung into impressive action, sorting out a place for me to rent for a couple of months near his own house, a boy to help me clean the house and do the cooking, even the use of a two-wheeler scooter if I wanted!

All that remained to be done after that was to buy my tickets and get my visa. I travelled to India often enough, to see Mum and Dad—albeit only up to Delhi. Kerala was just a little further, I had thought then, not really anticipating how different a world it was going to be. I was to go and see Mum and Dad first in Delhi, taking my usual British Airways flight there. And then get an Indian Airlines connection down to Trivandrum. Perhaps I could persuade Mum and Dad to join me in Kerala for a while— if the house turned out to be the kind of place that they could live in too. Dad couldn't negotiate steps any more, spending increasing amounts of time in his wheelchair, despite Mum's best efforts to turf him out of it as often as she could.

After a week in Delhi, and unable to persuade Dad's doctor to allow him to make such a long journey without receiving the results of his various tests, I had finally arrived here, eager to get started on my new project. Arriving at Trivandrum airport in the heat of the midday sun, I had noticed the heat rise over the horizon, making the palm trees blur and melt, and wondered if I should have stayed around a little longer in Delhi, which had been a gentle twenty degrees—but was otherwise its usual polluted, crowded mess. But I had persisted, finding myself a cab, even enjoying the searing afternoon heat as the cab brought me to my new abode. I couldn't remember ever regretting any decision I had taken, however mad and impulsive. That was just the way I was. 'Cussed,' Anna used to say, hissing the word out between her teeth in those final few days, when she was seriously mad at me.

I knelt down next to my packing cases, pulled my penknife out of my pocket and started to cut away the plastic twine on the one that was holding my tabla-set. I hadn't played these in years, having bought myself an ancient, second-hand drum-kit within six months of arriving in England and falling in love with that straightaway. I peeled away the layers of newspaper with which Mum had helped me wrap my tablas in the days before leaving for England, and the two small drums emerged. I picked them up gently, feeling around them for any possible damage. They seemed to have weathered well, only needing a little tightening. I had first learnt to love the sound of drums on this small pair of tablas, enjoying the feel of the dhuk-dhuk travelling right through me, hitting against the walls of my chest. They had spent the last many years languishing in Mum's storeroom upstairs, and it seemed a good idea to bring them here with me, so I could practise playing them while picking up new mridangam skills. I hadn't bargained, however, for the proximity of the neighbouring houses here and would have to remember to keep the windows closed. On the left of my smallish house was a large, open, empty plot. That was good. But on the right was a much bigger house, with a neat little garden, way too close for enthusiastic drum practice. I looked at it out of the living-room window. It looked huge, covering most of the land area of the plot. Four bedrooms at least. Pristine white. Obviously, someone wealthy lived there.

'Saar, tea?' My new man Friday had taken off his shirt and seemed to have had a wash as well. His hair was slicked back and was dripping water on to his neck and shoulders.

'God, no! No tea when it's this hot! You have some, if you want. I'll just have some cold water.'

'Saar, no fridge, no cold water. But now I bring ice from next door.'

'You sure that's okay? Who lives next door?'

'My sister works for them next door. Cleaning house and cooking. 's no problem getting ice.' He grinned again, showing off a set of brilliantly white teeth. Pleasant sort of chap, I thought, and certainly acquainted with a good dentist.

'What's your name?' I asked.

'Kuttan,' he said. After a pause, he jutted his chin in my direction. 'Saar name?'

'Rahul,' I replied, 'and you don't have to saar me all the time. Too bloody tedious.'

'Ra-hul,' he said, struggling with the unfamiliar north Indian name, 'Rahulsaar.'

'Oh well,' I sighed, 'if that's the way you want to be.'

I rolled up the ancient and yellowing masking tape into a ball and threw it into the empty box. God, I couldn't even remember now when it was that I had packed these two tablas away . . . almost ten years ago, was it? When I first left for university in England, sometime in 1986. That was it, October '86. Jesus!

Kuttan materialized with a glass full of ice and water just as I finished pulling out the second of the two small drums. Standing up to take the glass from his hands and sipping at the deliciously cool water, I took a few steps back to admire my beautiful old tablas with a rush of pride. The feeling was almost like the frisson of meeting an old girlfriend again, still pretty, still just a tiny bit in love.

I threw my head back, draining the glass dry. 'That was great, Kuttan. Thanks,' I said, returning the empty glass to him. 'And thank your sister from me too!'

He grinned again and retreated to the kitchen once more. It didn't look like I had found either a conversationalist or a drumming enthusiast there. I spent the rest of the afternoon finishing my unpacking, setting up my tablas on a reed floor mat in the corner of the sparsely furnished living room. When that was done, I started on the clothes, shaking them out. Some of these tee-shirts hadn't been worn since summer last year and I hung them in the single steel cupboard that was occupying a corner of the roomy bedroom. The house was in a better state than I had expected. Mr Pannicker had written that it belonged to a friend of his who had moved to Dubai. He had left his furniture and gas stove and even a telephone behind and, while everything looked quite basic, it certainly seemed to have more than I needed. A large enough bed with an extra sheet and pillow cover at its foot, net curtains that were now battling to filter out the heat, an attached bathroom, with a bucket and mug, and even a tiny piece of red medicinal soap.

I wandered into the kitchen. Kuttan was sweeping the floor with an emaciated broom. He threw it in a corner before following me back into the living room.

'Saar, I go to market to buy some things?' he asked, deftly retying his dhoti.

'Do you want to write a list? Can you write?' I asked

'I am SSLC fail, saar,' he beamed proudly.

I wasn't sure what SSLC was, but failing anything was not generally deserving of such a magnificent smile. 'Does that mean you *can* write? English?'

'Little, little,' he said, showing me a tiny space between his fingers.

'That doesn't look like a lot,' I replied, 'but let's give it a shot, shall we?' I handed him a pad and pen from the side pocket of my computer case. 'What do we need?'

He put pen to paper, furrowing his brow, writing slowly and laboriously. 'Choolu,' he muttered, finishing his effort with a firm full stop before looking up and showing it to me.

I looked at his effort. 'Chlu', the writing on the paper said. 'What's that?' I asked, mystified.

'Choolu, saarey,' he replied, waving an arm, looking around to illustrate. Vanishing to the kitchen, he emerged a second later holding a broom. 'Choolu this.'

'Oh, broom!'

'Yes, saarey, vroom. Choolu is in Malayalam.'

'Well, there's not much point writing in English if what you're writing is Malayalam, is there?'

'You ask if I write English, I write English, saar,' he explained with impeccable logic.

'Yes, of course. But, tell you what, if I tell you what we need in English and then you write the Malayalam word for it on your list, I think we'll get somewhere.'

''s all right, saar,' he said, sighing patiently as he crossed out his earlier efforts and started again.

'So . . . broom. How do you say it? Chool?' He giggled and wrote, marginally quicker than before. 'What else?' I asked.

'Mmmm . . . eating things . . . veghitables . . .'

'Yes, we'll need all the vegetables and things. Potatoes, onions . . .'

'Potteto . . . oh-nion . . .' he muttered as he continued to write laboriously.

I wasn't sure which language he was writing in. I could only barely tell which language he was speaking in. The whole process seemed to be taking up an inordinate amount of time as well. Perhaps a list wasn't such a great idea. 'Look, why don't you just go and get a few things to start us off with. And then, we'll see about everything else later, shall we?'

''s okay, saar,' he replied obligingly, putting pad and pen down with some relief. 'Also soap powder, soap and all, saarey?'

'Yes, get all of that, Kuttan. I leave it to you. In your able hands!'

'Now?'

'Yes, you go now. You can show me where the shops are later, so I can nip out and do my own shopping, too, when I need anything.' I pulled out my wallet again and took out a hundred-rupee note. 'Enough?'

He tucked the note in a fold of his dhoti tied around the waist. He then went back into the kitchen and emerged again, pulling on a brightly coloured polyester shirt. I noticed his hair was now neatly combed and carefully piled on the top of his head in an oily black quiff. He was barefooted and I made a mental note to get him a pair of chappals when I went to the shops. 'Whaddaya know! Film star!' I exclaimed admiringly at his shirt. He giggled again and left the room hastily. A minute later, I heard the creaking of iron gates and the tinkle of a cycle bell as he closed the gates behind him before riding off.

I stepped out into the front veranda. The day had cooled slightly, but it was still hot and muggy. I could hear a film song play from one of the neighbouring houses. Through the sound of . . . rain? But it wasn't raining at all! At least, not over this house. I stepped down the few stairs that joined my veranda to the minuscule, overgrown garden. I could hear the rain more clearly now. And see it as well, as it rose from somewhere in the garden next door in a gleaming silver arc, falling deliciously over a row of long lilac flowers that seemed to be growing out of the top of the dividing wall. The flowers had grown heavy and drooped their heads, burdened by the profusion of gleaming jewels they had suddenly acquired on their leaves and petals. Amethysts on the petals and emeralds on the leaves. Then the source of the water appeared and I stepped back, aware that it could look like I was lurking. She had a hosepipe in her hands and was holding her thumb fiercely down over the end of the pipe, to make the water form a spray. From where she stood, beyond the wall, she looked as though she was wearing some of her lilac wall-blooms in her hair. She was extremely beautiful.

I pulled my gaze back, and surveyed my own little garden, embarrassed that I had been staring. When I looked up again, her eyes were on me. We looked at each other through a spray of water that was turning the world between us wet. For just a couple of seconds perhaps. Before the spray from her hosepipe crept unbidden over the wall, landing all over the dusty plants in front of me, completely soaking the ends of my jeans and my feet.

'Oh, sorry!' she cried, clapping her hand over her mouth, as I jumped back in surprise at this sudden attack. The hosepipe in her other hand jerked once again, and this time the water rose over her head, falling slowly back to the earth, showering her own slim figure before she could move out of the way.

'Oh, oh . . .' she said, shocked into pink, flustered, dripping mortification. I couldn't believe how attractive she was, even with stray water drops hanging off her chin and her nose.

'Oh no, *I'm sorry*,' I said, 'I didn't mean to frighten you like that, standing there . . . you know . . .'

'You're wet! I didn't mean to . . .' she said, wiping her face with the back of her hand.

'It doesn't matter,' I responded cheerfully, 'you're wet too!'

Her hand was still covering her mouth as she started to laugh.

'Oh no, please don't laugh,' I said, 'you might lose control of that hosepipe again, you know!'

But she was bending over, a long braid of hair slipping over her shoulder, still laughing, now aiming the hosepipe carefully somewhere at her feet.

'Do you always attack people unprovoked like that?' I asked. 'New neighbours, particularly?'

She stopped laughing and took a few breaths to calm herself down. 'You're the new neighbour,' she stated, now only smiling shyly.

'As of this morning . . . but I believe we're already related.' She looked puzzled. 'My domestic help says his sister works for you,' I explained.

'Oh yes, Kuttan was to start work today! *You're* the foreigner who needed ice?'

'Only as foreign as Delhi!' I protested.

'But Kuttan said a "sahippu" had come from London.'

'Oh well, confession time then. From England, yes, because that's where I live. But yesterday from Delhi because that's where my parents live.'

But she hadn't heard my last few words. She seemed to have stopped listening for some reason, and the smile had suddenly faded from her face. I followed her gaze out of the gate where a white Esteem was approaching the house from the road. 'My husband,' she whispered as she moved quickly away from the wall, taking the errant hosepipe with her. Something seemed to have closed shut on that pretty face as she stepped away. Even the hosepipe was temporarily tamed, obediently emptying its contents into the flower beds now. I watched her turn the tap off and hook the pipe over a tree trunk before turning to open the gates. The Esteem pulled into the concrete drive of the house, its darkly shuttered windows not giving anything away. The engine spluttered to a halt and then the front door clicked open. A large man got out of the driver's seat and looked straight at me. He didn't look particularly friendly, but I smiled and walked over to the wall.

'Hello,' I said, 'I was just introducing myself to your wife. I'm your new neighbour, Rahul Tiwari.'

He walked across to the wall and shook my hand briefly. Something about him indicated that he was in a hurry and wasn't intending to stand around and chat. 'Govind Warrier,' he said, flicking his eyes over my wet jeans. 'And you have come from?'

'England,' I said, 'via Delhi.'

'Holiday?'

'Well, an extended holiday, I suppose. I'm here to learn the mridangam actually.'

That bit of information usually evoked a smile or a response of some sort. But there wasn't a flicker of a smile.

'How long are you here?' he asked.

'About two months, maybe more . . .' I trailed off. He was looking across at his wife now, taking in her wet clothes. His eyes narrowed. He said something to her that I couldn't understand, in Malayalam. I saw her flinch and make for the front door. He nodded at me and turned to follow her indoors.

'Oh, I nearly forgot,' I called out after her, 'thank you for the ice.'

Both faces looked back at me sharply. Hers was without any smiles now—confused and alarmed. His face was in the shadows but I could see it wasn't smiling. I felt a sudden chill travel down my spine.

*

It was only later, much later at night that I became conscious of my mistake. I had spent the rest of my evening on the veranda, slapping away the mosquitoes as I read. Or *attempted* to read, still faintly distracted by my earlier encounter with the neighbours. The sun, beginning its majestic descent towards the line of darkening palm trees in the distance, was not making my task any easier and I finally put down my book in exasperation. Kuttan had finished making a potato curry with chapattis for my dinner and was covering the dishes on the dining table. He then called across the wall to his sister, who appeared at the back gate, a spitting image of Kuttan himself, her thin figure wrapped in a sari. I gave him instructions to arrive by eight in the morning and then watched him wobble off on his cycle, easily overtaking his sister who had already started walking briskly down the road. It was sometime after that, at about nine at night, that I first heard the voices from next door. Frozen on my chair, under a light far too weak to read by, I could hear him, and then her. They talked in Malayalam, but I could tell that he was angry, demanding explanations. She was explaining, pleading. It sounded like she might be crying. I wished I could understand the words. I thought I heard the word 'ice' a couple of times, but I could have been mistaken. Twice I got up from the chair, giving up pretending to read, tempted to go across and explain. But it might not have been anything to do with me or with the earlier episode. I went over all that had been said. Was it something to do with the ice? It couldn't be! Surely no one could be as unreasonable as that. I wished Kuttan had been here to translate. Without being sure of what was going on, I knew I couldn't intrude.

Then, in the midst of those angry voices, a baby's cry went up. Sleepy, annoyed, wanting to be fed. Merciful release, I thought, as the shouting stopped abruptly. Whose was the baby? I realized how little I knew about my new neighbours, or even about this place that I had arrived at. I picked up my book and went indoors, resolving to keep my head down as much as I possibly could.

I was familiar enough with life in small-town India to know better than to impose my semi-western, city-bred values on everything I saw around me. And I was truly sorry if my casual encounter with my pretty neighbour had landed her in trouble of any sort. She had seemed really nice, though, and her husband a complete wanker. But I had come here with a specific purpose in mind: mainly to get away from the dank grey of an English winter, to get away from Anna of course, and to enjoy myself as much as possible. Trouble with the neighbours was eminently avoidable.

three

I awoke the next morning with a strange feeling of unease in the pit of my stomach. I could feel it there, heavy and cold, before my eyes even opened. The false sensation of being afloat that had accompanied me as I left England and arrived in Delhi had dissipated away overnight, for some odd reason.

I got out of bed and staggered to the bathroom. Geckoes had dropped their small, nightly turds on the washbasin and I rinsed them down with a shudder before beginning to brush my teeth. My reflection in the small, cracked mirror was unflattering at this time of morning but, after I had washed my face and smoothed my thick hair down with some water, I could feel my spirits begin to rise slightly and grinned at myself conspiratorially in the mirror. 'Gosh, you handsome devil,' I muttered encouragingly.

There was no sign of Kuttan yet, but I wasn't expecting him before eight. I opened the door to the kitchen and clicked the kettle on. The kettle had been my one concession to western habits. Mum had let me borrow her old one ('Bring it back, *don't* give it away to anyone there,' she had warned sternly). Opening the back door, I breathed in the cool morning air. Stepping out, I sneaked a look out of the corner of my eye at the house next door. All was quiet. The big, white building held no sign of life, thankfully. What a bloody palaver, I thought to myself, still mystified at the night's events. I took in a deep breath, savouring the peace of the morning. Today I would go and meet Mr Pannicker, as agreed, and begin my lessons. If I made reasonable progress, I could even wind up things here and return to Delhi sooner than planned. Mum and Dad would love that.

'Unka!'

Had I imagined it or was that a tiny whisper? I looked around. The garden was empty and the dividing wall held only yesterday's lilac flowers.

'Unka!'

There it was again!

I moved closer to the wall, bending over on my side of it, looking for the source of the whisper. After a few seconds, a small black head materialized amongst the flowers, framing a cheeky round face on which mischief glittered. Just as she opened her mouth to whisper again, I stood up, startling her. Her smile vanished and I heard rustling and a small thud as she disappeared from view.

'Ammé . . .' her voice wailed as she raced back indoors.

'That is only Anjali mol.'

I turned to find Kuttan opening the gate. He was holding a packet of milk.

'Oh good, I'm glad you've brought the milk. The kettle must have boiled for the tea.' I followed him indoors. 'Who's Anjali mol?' I asked.

'Anjali mol,' he said again, cutting open the milk packet with a knife, pointing next door with his chin, 'Maya chechi's mol. Very naughty.'

'And who's Maya chechi?' I asked casually.

'Next-door chechi. Where my sister works. Very nice chechi. She gets me this job when Pannicker saar came looking.'

'Is she the one . . . about this tall . . .' I held my hand out about shoulder level. 'Long hair . . .?'

He nodded. 'Nice chechi,' he repeated.

'And who is she married to?'

'Govind saar,' Kuttan replied, busy stirring the milk on the fire now. I found his silence faintly annoying.

'And what does Govind saar do?' I asked finally.

'Business.'

'What business?'

'Oh, bump business,' he replied.

'Bump?'

'Bump, BUMPUH . . .' After a pause, he beckoned me to follow him to the door. 'Bump,' he said again, pointing this time to the water tank in the corner of the backyard.

'Oh, pumps!' I walked over to the tank to read the label on the pump that was attached to one side of it. Warrier Water Pumps, it said. Red letters glittering in the sun. Well, I was determined to steer clear of Mr Govind Warrier if I could help it. *However* impressive his pumps and however nice his chechi.

It was after I had eaten Kuttan's breakfast of 'Bombay toast', which turned out to be a very sweet version of French toast, served with thick, milky tea, that my next contact with my new neighbours took place. Avoiding the situation was proving to be more difficult than I thought.

'Saarey, see, a guest . . .' Kuttan was standing at the front door, carrying a small figure attached to the round face that had appeared over the wall this morning.

'Oh yes, hello!' I said, without too much enthusiasm.

She beamed and wriggled out of Kuttan's arms to land on the floor with a barefooted thump.

'Hello,' she said, pulling out the ends of her skirt with her two hands and dropping a little curtsey.

'And who may you be?' I asked.

'Eh?' she replied.

I tried another tack. 'What is your name?'

'*Mol de per entha*?' Kuttan translated helpfully.

'Anjali!' she said proudly, still holding her skirt and swaying from foot to foot.

'Oh, *nice* name,' I responded warmly.

'Poda,' she replied gingerly, stopping her swaying to watch me more carefully.

'What's that?' I asked, as Kuttan snorted.

'Poda,' she repeated more loudly, gaining confidence.

The conversation came to an abrupt halt as a voice called out from next door. 'Anjali!' We could hear her mother's voice call out again, more loudly and insistently. The little girl turned and ran out of the house with Kuttan in hot pursuit. I followed them out more slowly, unsure of what to expect. The woman from yesterday was standing in her garden. I looked around quickly. There seemed to be no sign of either her husband or his white Esteem in the car porch. She pulled Anjali into the gates and smacked her, saying something sharply in Malayalam. Although I could not see Anjali from where I was, I heard an indignant wail go up from the garden. Kuttan was saying something that sounded like he was taking the blame for Anjali's visit to us. 'Anjali' . . . 'sahippu' . . . I guessed he was saying that he had invited Anjali in to see the sahippu from England.

I decided to contribute a defence to the little girl who was still wailing piteously. I called out from where I was, 'No really, she wasn't troubling anyone at all.' The woman looked over at me.

'Please don't encourage her. She can be very naughty.' Her voice was sharp. There was none of yesterday's laughter bubbling up in it.

'She was lovely, no trouble at all. But I understand . . . I'll make sure Kuttan brings her back if she does ever wander over.'

Her face softened slightly. 'I'm sorry, I didn't mean to be rude . . .'

'That's okay, I understand,' I said, not really understanding at all, but alarmed now to see sudden tears spring up in her eyes.

As she quickly turned away, I called out, wanting to make things better, wanting to prolong the conversation now, foolishly. 'What does "poda" mean?' I asked.

Her eyes widened as Kuttan giggled again. 'Did Anjali—? Oh, that girl is so mischievous . . .' Then she smiled at me, her face resembling the one that had laughed so sweetly yesterday. 'It means "get lost",' she said solemnly.

Anjali had appeared among the flowers again. There must have been something she could stand on in that corner to be able to prop herself up so easily. I picked up a small pebble and hurled it at her in mock anger. 'Poda to you, too, matey,' I said. She chortled loudly, her earlier tears forgotten completely.

'Poda, poda, poda . . .' she chanted, mimicking my accent, making both her mother and Kuttan laugh. Kuttan was holding on to the gatepost, wheezing his nasal laughter like a hyena.

It wasn't *that* funny, I thought, but at least the atmosphere had cleared. I pretended, for Anjali's benefit, to be still angry. 'I'm going in now,' I said to her, 'to sulk! Come on Kuttan, we know where we're not wanted.'

'If you need more ice, send Kuttan over,' the woman said quickly. I looked at her face. I could see a stubbornness in those gentle features. A sudden willingness to flirt with danger.

'Yeah, sure. Thanks,' I replied, very certain—more on her behalf than mine—that I would not risk borrowing any ice again.

I went indoors and calm settled over the morning as I got ready for my first meeting with Mr Pannicker, my new mridangam tutor. I found myself whistling as I got ready, the bitter, dark feeling of the early part of the morning seeming to have dissolved in the heat of the day.

*

Mr Pannicker's house was a ten-minute walk away. He was small and bespectacled, not quite the rock-group drummer type. As

Jaishree Misra

he took me indoors and seated me on a reed mat in his music room, a woman materialized with a glass of orange squash on a plate. 'My wife,' he said. She smiled shyly at me and vanished indoors again. The music lesson turned out to be mainly a lecture about the theory of music.

'Couldn't we just play, Mr Pannicker?' I asked.

'But you must know about these things also, eh? Calculations of taal are very important in playing the mridangam,' Mr Pannicker said firmly. Finally, after a half-hour lecture, he took up position behind his instruments and started to play. He was good. I could see, and hear, the passion in his playing and felt my spirits rise along with the notes. I closed my eyes and allowed my thoughts to be carried along on the notes as they throbbed and floated around the room. As the tempo rose, beautiful pictures floated through my head, a melting orange globule of setting sun meeting the spiky darkness of distant palm trees, the puff of clouds through an aircraft window, a face . . . a face . . . pretty and tearful and stubborn . . . I knew I had to stop thinking about that face. I knew there could only be trouble ahead. I knew I had arrived, a foreigner, in a faraway place and already things were happening to spin me into a world I knew nothing about. I could feel myself spin and spin, a lonely top in an unfamiliar playground. Beware, beware, beware, the mrindangam notes were saying loudly and insistently as they finally drew to a stop.

'What beauty, eh?' Mr Pannicker breathed.

I nodded. 'You play wonderfully,' I said.

'Oh, it is nothing,' he said bashfully, suddenly losing his artistic pride. 'I can easily teach you, if you promise to be regular—regular with attendance and with practice.'

'That should be easy,' I said. 'I'm alone here, with no other job or anything else to distract me. Mr Pannicker, you're on,' I concluded with a grin.

'We'll start your proper lessons tomorrow then,' he said. 'Same time okay for you?'

'Yes, I can always fit in with you.'

'Is the servant boy doing okay?'

'Kuttan? Yes, thanks for finding him, he's a trooper,' I said. 'Very cheerful. Clean. His cooking's not bad too.'

'Goodgood. I've agreed six hundred rupees for the month, that is okay?'

'That's absolutely fine. And your own fees as agreed earlier?'

'Yesyes,' he beamed.

We shook hands and I began my walk back to the house. Kuttan was expecting me for lunch. I had tried to tell him that I only ever ate sandwiches for lunch, grabbing them from the Italian deli below my office back in London, but he was having none of that. 'You eat bread in morning and bread in lunch also! No, saarey, Kuttan makes rice and kootan,' he had said firmly. It was possible that he wouldn't be able to eat a proper meal if I didn't, and so I didn't argue. 'Whatever you say, mate,' I had agreed, saluting him and clicking my heels together, making him laugh his hyena laugh again.

I spotted a roadside vendor selling rubber chappals and walked over to get Kuttan a pair. I chose a bright blue pair, having already gathered that Kuttan was quite fondly disposed to bright colours. Wrapping them in old newspaper the vendor pointed to my feet, now steaming in my Nikes as the heat beat down on us. 'What a good idea,' I said, 'just not sure you'll have my size, that's all . . .' I pulled my shoes off and gave them to be wrapped along with Kuttan's chappals, balancing myself on one foot as he delved around in his pile looking for a large one. Emerging triumphantly with an enormous-looking pair tied together with string, he cut them separate with a knife and placed them at my feet. Grabbing him by the shoulder, I tried them on. 'Perfect!' I exclaimed as the man accepted the money for two pairs from me, tucking the notes away in a fold of his lungi.

At home, Kuttan's efforts to make a two-course meal were rewarded with the gift of the chappals. He grinned delightedly as I gave them to him. Then he smiled down at my feet and cried admiringly, 'Rahulsaar filmstar!'

'Cheeky bugger,' I muttered, pretending to cuff him around the ears.

Lunch was rice with sambar and a cabbage dish cooked with coconut. I noticed a glass of cold water, with ice in it, condensing next to my plate. As I pulled up my chair, Kuttan appeared with the pièce de résistance—a single piece of fried fish on an unfamiliar plate. A couple of rings of raw pink onion were garnishing it tastefully. 'Hey, did you do all of that? It looks terrific,' I exclaimed.

'I make sambaar and thoran, saarey,' he replied. 'The karimeen fish come from next door.'

'Who? Maya chechi . . . or your sister?' I asked hesitantly. I did not want *any* trouble with the man I had seen yesterday.

'Maya chechi sent it,' he said, 'also this.'

He handed me a note that was covered in oil stains from his hands. I opened it while he looked on. 'This is to say sorry for Anjali's "poda". Hope you enjoy the fish.' Another line had been added underneath, like a carefully considered afterthought: 'Please don't mention it in front of my husband.'

What was going *on* there? It was obviously an unhappy marriage or something. But *why*? She looked so pretty and she had that cute kid . . . for the tenth time I could hear that voice in my head reminding me that I wanted no part of it. No part of it at all.

'What is written, saar?' Kuttan asked.

'Oh, just sorry that Anjali said poda.'

'Anjali mol is verrry naughty,' he demurred, shaking his head.

'Oh, and Kuttan,' I called out as he returned to the kitchen, 'just make sure you never mention the ice and things in front of the next-door saar. He might not like it.'

Kuttan nodded before going back into the kitchen. Subtle sort of chap, I thought appreciatively. Whatever he knew from his sister, he wasn't about to tell me. I tried to quell the strange sense of curiosity that was welling up in me. I was *never* nosy about other people's business. That was one thing England had taught me well. I nodded at my neighbours, said hello, chatted briefly with the French guy across the road sometimes, if we were both washing our cars on a Saturday. But that was it. Other people's space was to be respected—and avoided. I knew India was different, but even here, in the cities, life was getting as impersonal as it was in the West. That was the best way for it to be. I would thank my pretty neighbour for her fish and then keep communication to a bare minimum. If the little girl turned up, I would send Kuttan to escort her back. I didn't even *like* kids that much anyway.

When I next met Maya, two days had passed since the gift of the fish. I had looked out for her, whenever there was no Esteem in the car porch, wanting to thank her for it. But things seemed to have gone very quiet. There was no sign of Anjali, either. Had they gone away somewhere? Kuttan's sister was still turning up to work next door every morning with him. I didn't want to ask.

Then, early in the evening on the third day, I heard the sound of a car pulling up. It didn't sound like an Esteem, I could hear the rough grind of a diesel engine. Looking up from the veranda, I saw a dark-brown Ambassador pull up in the car porch next door. As the doors opened, four people got out. One looked like a driver; he walked around the car and opened up the boot to pull a suitcase out. I saw Maya emerge from the back seat, carrying a sleeping Anjali over her shoulder. With her were an elderly couple, tall and spare. Parents? In-laws? Maya smiled at me over the wall. The elderly man who had got out of the other front seat, did not see me, but walked straight into the house. The older woman, however, caught the smile Maya had thrown at me and looked over the wall. Our eyes met for a fleeting moment and she nodded

Jaishree Misra

briefly before following Maya indoors. That was the first time I saw Maya's mother. And her father too. I was to meet Maya's mother again, some years later. It still sounds incredible, doesn't it, but I would meet her when Maya's death rites were to be performed for the third time. Three times over was an extraordinary thing under any circumstances, of course. It doesn't feel any less ordinary as I recall those events today, even though I might understand them better now.

*

For a day or two, the household next door sounded as though it was a busy place, full of laughter and voices. I could hear Anjali's high-pitched voice and occasionally Maya's infectious laugh. But I carried on with my business, making my trips to Mr Pannicker's house, starting my lessons, even buying myself a mridangam to practise at home. This I did as silently as I could, closing the doors and windows and trying not to get too carried away. I even practised the tablas occasionally, while playing music as loudly as I wanted on my CD Walkman, using the headphones. I was starting to feel as though my drumming was the only really important thing in my life again, reminding me rather of my early years in England, when my relationship with my neighbours was reawakened.

The brown Ambassador had gone, I could hear Anjali loudly bid it goodbye. 'Bye-bye Apoopa, bye-bye Ammumma,' she was hollering, hanging on to the gate. She was still yelling, long after the car had vanished around the corner. Somebody turn that kid off, I thought, trying to get back to my newspaper on the veranda. After a short, eerie silence, I could hear a rustling among the lilac flowers and saw, out of a corner of my eye, the small round head appear in its customary corner of the wall again.

'Unka,' the voice said, chattily.

I pretended not to hear and carried on reading.

'Unka!' Now the tone was peremptory and insistent.

'What's that? Who's that?' I said, pretending to be startled, dropping my papers to the floor.

I could hear her laughter and her mother's and looked up. Their faces, happy and smiling, were floating disembodied among the flowers.

'Hello,' I said, warily.

'Hello Unka!' Anjali shouted.

'Why does she keep calling me Unka?' I asked, getting up from my chair to see them better.

'Unka is uncle,' Maya explained. 'You know how it is in India—children call everyone older than them like that. Uncle and aunty. You're probably not used to it. In England it's not like that, is it?'

'No, first names all around. Very uncomplicated. But I do know about this uncle-aunty business, it's much the same in Delhi.'

'Of course,' she smiled, 'I keep forgetting that you're not really English.' She looked at me more carefully and added accusingly, 'You *look* English, somehow.'

I laughed. 'One of my grandparents was English, so something's obviously filtered through. But, really, I'm just a sort of eternal foreigner, I suppose, foreign looking when I'm here, foreign looking over there. No one ever mistakes me for being English in England!'

'I've never been to England, but I feel I know the place so well.'

'I know, I suppose it comes from all the books we read. And our education system here. I grew up reading English books in Delhi, and have to struggle to read even a newspaper in Hindi. Pity, isn't it?'

'And films too. I grew up in Bangalore and only ever wanted to see English films when I was young. I hated Hindi and Malayalam films then and only went when my mother forced me to go with her.' She laughed.

'Was that your mother? Visiting?'

She nodded. 'My parents still live in Bangalore, they visit sometimes. I'd gone with them to see my grandmother in

Jaishree Misra

Champakulam, in the old family home. My . . . husband is away, on a business tour, so they had come to keep me company.'

'Are you their only child?' I asked, feeling a lot more relaxed now that I knew her husband wasn't around.

'No, I have a little brother, but he's in a boarding school in Ooty . . . Anjali!'

Anjali, who had been busy delving about in the flower bed on top of the wall with a look of intense concentration on her face, had suddenly emerged, waving a flower stalk in her hand, bulb and all.

'My orchids! Put it back!'

Anjali obligingly shoved the bulb back into the soil and covered it liberally with thick black soil, patting the mound firmly down. She then lifted her two, small, muddy-black hands and waved them cheerily at me.

'That'll take at least half a bar of soap to wash off,' I said.

'Oh, mud everywhere, *silly* girl!' her mother said crossly. 'I have to take her in to wash her down,' she said to me, exasperatedly pushing back wisps of hair framing her face with the back of her own now muddy hand. She hoisted Anjali up, grabbing her by the armpits, struggling to walk while the little girl kicked out with her legs, giggling. 'I'll see you later,' she called out to me over her shoulder.

'Well, not if your husband's about to return today,' I muttered to myself as I wandered back to my wicker chair on the veranda.

Not an inauspicious thought because, as it happened, her husband was back by evening. While emerging from my bath sometime after sundown, I heard the sounds of the gates next door being pushed open and the Esteem pull up into the porch. As I towelled my wet hair, standing near the window, I could hear Anjali's shrill voice chatter excitedly. A man's voice responded, teasing and laughing. I stood rubbing my hands over my chest, allowing my bare body to dry under the hot air of the fan.

Remembering Anna, suddenly. Funny, I hadn't thought much about her since leaving England. The split had been too corrosive to allow for much reminiscing over the occasional good times we'd had. She had screamed all kinds of inanities at me as she had thrown her things into two large suitcases, that day just over a month ago. Things like 'Fuck you, Rahul! You're so bloody superior, you and your bloody music and your bloody India!' What had my music . . . and *India* . . . to do with it for Chrissake! In fact, if you asked me what exactly our problem had been, I would have difficulty trying to explain. Maybe I was bloody superior, or pretending to be bloody superior, because it was better than letting Anna think that, just because she was English, *she* was superior. It wasn't fair to accuse my music or India of having any part to play in it. They were both things I couldn't help. Merely parts of me, aspects of me. That had always seemed to bother her . . . that she herself could never become a part of me in the same way. And there was nothing I could say or do to let her know that it wasn't her fault necessarily. I was so sure then that no woman could ever be that important to me.

The days passed in a hot, hazy blur of drum practice, western and eastern. Mr Pannicker was a hard taskmaster and I found myself having to keep notes and memorize some of his theory lessons as well. Kuttan had proven himself to be a loyal and efficient cook, cleaner, valet, and butler, and I had more or less learnt to leave the running of the house to him. My first priority was still my music and a bit of sightseeing too. I had started to plan a few trips out, but had decided to make just short forays, keeping Trivandrum as my base. It made sense as I was paying the rent on this house and because of my mridangam classes. I had done Kovalam and Kanyakumari, those were near enough. Someone had mentioned a palace nearby . . . Padmanabha something.

There didn't seem to be too many opportunities to make friends in Trivandrum, unfortunately, even though I had made occasional visits to the British Council library and to the beach. English seemed to be a major problem here. I had heard about Kerala's high literacy rate and had imagined that everyone would be wandering around spouting high-quality English. But it hadn't turned out to be like that at all. People were pleasant enough, wherever I went, but seemed to shy away in a great hurry after helping me out in hesitant English. Efforts with Hindi had been even less successful. Anyway,

I hadn't come here with the intention of making friends, although that would have been a bonus. I hadn't seen much of my neighbours either and certainly hadn't attempted any contact as I was very aware of the white Esteem going up and down, past my gate, its windows telling me nothing about its occupant.

Then, about two weeks after our last conversation, I returned from Mr Pannicker's to find Anjali in the kitchen with Kuttan's sister. I had never seen Kuttan's sister so close before and noticed how painfully thin she was. She smiled shyly when she saw me and made as if to leave. Anjali gave me an exuberant welcome, rattling off a stream of what was probably a baby brand of Malayalam. None of which I could understand, of course.

'Whoa, whoa, whoa . . . English please!' I pleaded, putting my books down.

'Unka!' she said.

'Yes, I've heard that one before. Let's have something else this time.'

She looked up at Kuttan and said something urgently. He smiled at me and translated, 'She says, teach me English fast, Kuttanchetta, so that I can talk to this uncle.'

I squatted before her. 'Now let's see what we can teach you . . .' She waited expectantly. I furrowed my brow as though I was thinking very hard. In my best Hollywood accent, I twanged, 'Okay, how about this—Hi, I'm Anjali! Gawsh, I'm sure glad to meet you!'

Keeping her eyes on my face, she furrowed her small brow, mimicking my tone, accent and facial expression impeccably, but mashing the words up into a kind of incomprehensible 'Ameriyalam'.

'Very good!' I exclaimed, genuinely surprised at her smartness.

'Velly good!' she parroted back.

'No, no, one sentence a day is quite enough. Off with you now!'

'Off with you now!' she said easily.

'No! Don't repeat everything I say! I meant . . . really, off with *you*, Anjali. Go home. They'll be looking for you.'

'Off with *you*!' she said again, enjoying her new-found English, struggling to free herself of Kuttan's sister's grasp as she started pulling her away. 'Venda, venda!' she hollered and then loudly and perfectly accurately, she shouted, 'Off with you!' at her captor as she was picked up and carried away.

I wondered if she might use her new English skills on her father and hoped vaguely that I was not inadvertently about to cause trouble again. I certainly did not want that pretty mother of hers to have any trouble on my account. But, later that afternoon, it was her mother herself who turned up, catching me completely by surprise. I heard the gate creak open and, imagining Kuttan was returning from his trip to the shops, stayed sitting at my tablas, drumming softly, using the tips of my fingers. I didn't see her until she was inside the door, leaning on the wall with arms crossed, watching me smilingly. Spotting her only as I raised my eyes, I scrambled up, hurriedly buttoning my shirt.

'Oh, gosh, hi, I thought it was Kuttan,' I said somewhat stupidly.

'No, it's not Kuttan, it's me,' she replied, *also* somewhat stupidly, I thought with satisfaction.

She wandered over to my tablas, looking at them with curiosity. 'These are very similar to our mridangams, except you don't play two together here. I've seen these being played on TV, of course.'

'You can sit down there and try playing them, if you like,' I said, still feeling the uneasy throb of drums inside me somewhere.

She smiled and shook her head. 'No thanks.'

What was she *doing*, wandering around my living room all by herself, in the middle of the afternoon. Even Kuttan wasn't around! Or her daughter. I was sure this would look *very* bad to her husband if he returned suddenly.

'Where's Anjali?' I asked.

'Asleep,' she said. There was a certain dreamy quality to the way she was talking softly, wandering around my living room, looking at everything, my books and my furniture, as though she had imagined doing this many times over. Then, looking at me more directly she said, 'Don't worry, my husband's away. Touring again.' She said the last bit with an air of resignation.

What on earth was she getting at? I felt I had to say something. 'I'm not *worried* or anything . . .' Her smile stopped me. 'I mean, why would *I* be worried . . .' I asked, trailing off again.

'No, no reason,' she said and then, more to herself, she said softly, 'he's not a bad man, my husband, just not very friendly.' She bent over and stroked her fingers over the skin of my tablas, before straightening up and saying firmly, 'I have to go, Anjali might wake up and wonder where I am.'

I nodded. What a strange woman, I thought, and so bloody beautiful too! She was in a pale yellow sari that was trailing around as languidly as she was and I could see how slim her waist was. The wall, over which I had previously been able to see only her head, had contained all those lovely secrets from me. Of her grace in that sari, and the way in which it draped over her curves.

'Yes, perhaps it's best you go,' I said finally, 'I . . . I don't want you to get into any trouble.' I bit my tongue, having said this. How goddamned indiscreet! Especially as she'd just informed me of how nice a man her husband was.

'Yes, I thought you'd have heard the shouting that day . . .' This time I managed to hold my tongue and she carried on speaking, not looking at me. 'He can be odd like that sometimes . . . it was nothing to do with you, really . . . it's me that he . . .' She looked at me again and this time her eyes were shining, like hard dark jewels, impossible to penetrate. Her voice was suddenly hard as well as she said, 'Look, why don't you come over tomorrow . . . for dinner.'

Seeing the expression on my face, she added, smiling, 'Really!'

'No, I can't . . . I shouldn't . . .' I was pleading.

'Look, it's *my* house. *I'm* inviting you. As my neighbour. My husband's in Bombay for a week. I hate the loneliness in the evenings, especially. You must come. I insist.'

The drum beats were deafening in my ears, but I could hear the insistence in her voice . . . risky, defiant . . . what was she defying? What was it that made her seem so much like a caged bird, trapped and restless and now suddenly terrifyingly fearless.

I nodded. 'If you're sure it's okay . . . but I still . . .'

'*Of course*, it's okay. Come at eight.' She was running towards the gate now, opening it and then throwing me a brilliant smile over her shoulder before vanishing into her own house.

I walked back into my living room, all kinds of warnings screaming in my head. I couldn't deny feeling a kind of furtive pleasure, an illicit thrill in the unexpected invitation. But, on the other hand, it was crazy! It was obvious she was doing this behind her husband's back. However innocent the whole exercise, and however harmless my own intentions, I knew I ought not to be going there. I would say something to wriggle out of it tomorrow. That's what I would do—develop a sudden tummy ache or something and just not go. For *her* sake as well as mine. She's the one who would be in real trouble, not me. That was for sure.

But there was no sign of her all day. I could hear Anjali playing in the garden, but did not want to call out in case either Kuttan or his sister noticed. This was not good. Subterfuge was not something that sat easily with me. I was getting more and more uneasy, but by evening, after Kuttan had left for the day, I put his dish of chicken curry away into the fridge and went into the bath to get myself ready.

The day had been a scorcher and evening did not seem to be bringing much respite as it drew in now, still and heavy except for the nocturnal chorus of insects from the garden. By seven-thirty I was washed, shaved and nearly ready, pulling on the only pair of trousers I had brought with me from England. Earlier in the day,

I had ironed a shirt. I pulled it on now, feeling its crisp white cotton go limp at once against my humid body. I looked in the mirror—this was a far cry from the shorts and tee-shirts I usually wore to combat the daytime heat. I looked out of the window at the house next door, wondering at the nervous feeling inside, reminiscent—ridiculously—of schoolboy dates, I thought with a shudder. I wanted to laugh at the stupidity of the whole thing. Here I was, supposedly a man of the world, all of twenty-seven, well travelled, well heeled, 'foreign returned', behaving like a ruddy *schoolboy* getting ready for his first date, for heaven's sake! For the tenth time I reminded myself that it was probably only the secrecy—for long now a thing of the past as far as liaisons with the opposite sex were concerned—that was reminding me of such puerile, distant, forgotten things.

'Dinner . . . just *dinner* with a neighbour . . . there's *nothing* wrong with that,' I kept repeating in my head like a crazed mantra as I walked out of my garden and creaked open the gates next door. Before I could ring the bell, the door had opened and she was standing there, smiling.

'Sorry, I didn't want to startle you,' she whispered, 'but Anjali's asleep. I thought the doorbell might wake her up.' She stood aside to let me pass and I could smell fresh jasmines from somewhere.

The room was softly lit. There seemed to be a lot of shining, heavy brass and colourful cushions in the room. I looked around briefly, not really seeing anything properly, very aware of how lovely she looked as she closed the door and followed me in.

'You got dressed up!' She laughed.

'You look pretty nifty yourself,' I flashed back at her.

'Oh no, I'm just wearing my normal stuff, but I've never seen you in trousers before,' she protested, waving me to a sofa.

'Well, it isn't every day I get invited to dine at a smart Kerala residence, you know,' I said, sinking into a comfortable armchair.

For a moment a shadow crossed her face again as she retorted with, 'It certainly isn't every day *I* invite a friend home. I should have dressed up, too.'

I realized suddenly that I had never seen anyone else visit this house—just the husband, of course and, recently, the parents. I tried to make light of it. 'I . . . well, I haven't found it easy to make any friends in Trivandrum, if that's any consolation. That's if you don't count Kuttan and Mr Pannicker, my mridangam teacher.'

'Yes, but that's because you can't speak Malayalam,' she countered. 'That's a good reason, not a bad one.'

'And what's a bad reason?' I asked gently.

She looked at me ruefully for a moment, as if very tempted to tell me, and then asked instead, 'What can I get you to drink?'

'Er . . . a Limca or something should do fine . . .'

'There are some drinks and things . . . alcohol . . . in a cupboard upstairs, but I'm afraid I don't know the first thing about serving or mixing them.'

'No, that's okay, I don't drink the hard stuff anyway, just beer sometimes. No, more than sometimes . . . *often*,' I added more honestly.

She laughed. 'I'm sorry but that's the one drink we don't have here. My husband drinks that only when he's not drinking.'

I looked at her, nonplussed. '*Not* drinking?'

'You know, during the Sabarimala season, when you're not allowed alcohol, then he'll sometimes drink beer if he wants a drink, because he doesn't think of it as alcohol.'

That sounded like a terrific cop-out to me, but I held my tongue this time. She got up to fetch me a Limca from the kitchen and I watched her retreating back with its swaying braid of hair, wondering again about what strange sorrows this woman was hiding behind her graceful façade. Her house was lovely, clean and nicely decorated; her daughter was a cheeky monkey, but cute nonetheless; she herself was the only daughter of parents who seemed quite well off and caring . . . it was clear her husband wasn't a bundle of laughs, but was that such a big deal? She ought to be able to handle him . . .

She was back, with my drink that was fizzing and sparkling with the ice cubes with which she had generously filled the tall glass. 'Thanks—you're very generous with your ice,' I said, taking the glass off her tray. 'I have noticed the many times my lunchtime water has been too beautifully chilled to have come out of our corporation tap.'

'Oh, it's nothing. It's the least I can do to be a good neighbour,' she said, settling herself down on the sofa across from me. 'Tell me, don't you miss the luxuries of the West when you live here like this?'

I thought for a moment. 'Well, some things I do. Such as good newspapers, being able to drink milk straight from the carton, a mosquito-free atmosphere . . . big important things like that! But I'm fairly easy-going generally—I don't need very much.' There was a pause. 'Ice!' I added, raising my glass to her, 'a steady supply of it from a kindly neighbour—now *that* goes a long way in making life bearable though.'

But she was being serious now. 'But what about *people*? How can you manage to just set up home like this, so far from everyone that you know? Don't you ever feel lonely?'

'I'm not sure people are ever a guarantee against loneliness. Don't you think it's possible to get horribly lonely in the midst of a whole throng of people sometimes?'

'You're so right,' she said, looking pensive again, 'and maybe that's the worst kind of loneliness too. But then I've always been the opposite—sort of scared to think about being far away from the people I love. You'll think of that as silly . . . I suppose?'

'No, on the contrary! I'm quite envious of people who have such a strong sense of who they are and where they want to be. And who they want to be with!' Her face was filled with doubt and so I continued, 'My sort of existence can feel like a very selfish one sometimes. I just do what I want to do, go where I want to go . . . big, important things, like family ties and statehood and even nationhood seem to have passed me by completely.'

'How lovely to be so free!' she said softly. 'People like me just get so bogged down, thinking all the time about what other people want, what other people think . . .'

'No, I think that's sweet and generous—there must be a reward in that, somewhere. And, really there's not *that* much to be said for these western notions of individualism. Certainly, that's how it feels sometimes when you're there in the middle of it. *Especially* on miserable January nights, when there doesn't seem to be a soul in the world who cares that you're cold and wet as you return home from the tube-station after work.'

She laughed. 'Here, the whole town would want to know how you're feeling!'

'Which is essentially a good thing, isn't it?'

'Well, they'd want to know what's going on, but might not want to *help* necessarily. Is that a good thing?'

'Hmmm . . . I suppose people just have to make sure they have their own individual support systems in place, whatever those may be, and just try to ignore the rest.'

'What are yours?' she asked.

'My support systems?' I paused for a few seconds, disconcerted by the way her eyes were scanning my face. 'Music?' I offered, faintly embarrassed. She nodded. 'Friends,' I continued, 'not many, but a few old ones. Very old.' I smiled, imagining how annoyed Kevin would be if he heard me describe him as 'old' to a woman as pretty as this one.

'Family?' she asked.

'Yes, of course, family. My parents and my brother Anil. Although none of them are near me—my folks are in Delhi and my brother's in San Francisco. Although that's not a problem really, with telephones and the Internet and all that.'

'No girl? Wife?'

'Wife? Good God, no!' She looked amused at my emphatic response. 'I've had girlfriends, of course, but all those seem to have ended disastrously, for some reason. *Never* my fault, I can tell you,' I said, twinkling at her, fully aware of how untrue that was.

'I'm sure that's entirely true,' she said with mock seriousness. 'Dinner?' she asked after a short pause, looking at my empty glass.

'I'd love dinner,' I said, getting up with her. 'Mridangam seems to whet my appetite something horrid, I tell you.'

'I'll just need to warm up a few things, you keep sitting,' she said.

But I followed her into the kitchen. 'I can't sit there in style while you work,' I said. 'Let me help.'

She seemed momentarily flustered. 'I'm not used to having men in my kitchen,' she said, laughing, as I spotted an apron and wound it daintily around my waist. 'Oh don't spoil that lovely white shirt!'

'I can't see tonight being the start of a hectic round of dinner parties all around Trivandrum, somehow. I'm sure I won't be wearing this shirt again for a while, so please give me something to do.'

'Oh okay, stir this while I get the rice out,' she said, sounding more relaxed. I took up my station at the stove, stirring a chicken curry that was now breaking into brown bubbles. It looked delicious.

'Smells heavenly,' I said, sniffing appreciatively.

'Look, you must let me send food across occasionally. I'm sure that Kuttan's cooking is useless.'

'He's surprisingly good actually. We do manage well. And I certainly don't want to be causing any trouble for you.'

Her back was turned as she continued to scoop steaming rice into a bowl. She knew I meant trouble with her husband, but she was silent. Loyalty was a funny sort of thing, I thought, jabbing at the chicken with my ladle, extended to the least deserving of people sometimes.

Jaisbree Misra

We sat down to dinner together, as I refused to be served first. 'Let's just put everything on the table and help ourselves as we go along,' I insisted.

The food was far tastier than anything Kuttan had concocted for me so far and I was genuinely appreciative of the trouble she had obviously taken for me. There was fried fish, dark and golden, that flaked into pearly whiteness as my fingers touched the piece Maya placed on my plate. I watched as she poured yellow yoghurt broth over the mound of rice on her own plate, wrapping tiny finger-fulls of this around pieces of fish before putting it in her mouth. I attempted to copy her, my fingers far less able than hers to transfer food so delicately to my mouth.

The conversation was general. Maya was full of questions about life in England and it transpired that she had studied English Literature at college before she had dropped out in her second year to get married to Govind Warrier. She had spent most of her school days in Bangalore and had been sent to the Women's College Hostel in Trivandrum when she started her college education. It was while she was here that Govind had spotted her in the town one day. She had been shopping for hairclips with her friends in Spenser's department store. He had come in for something and had noticed her as she laughed and chatted with her friends. Later, he had made enquiries, without her knowledge, and a few days after this her family had been approached by a broker with a wedding proposal.

'He was very well off, my father had been very impressed that he had set up this business on his own and had done so well for himself. Then, of course, they were pleased that they would not be too far from me, so it was fixed,' she said simply.

'Didn't you have any concerns about marrying a stranger?' I asked, aware of how like a westerner I sounded.

She shrugged. 'I had no one else in mind. It seemed silly to object when there was nothing to object to.'

'Your education? Didn't you want to complete that?'

'I had thought I'd be able to, as I'd still be in Trivandrum. But Govind was not too keen.'

I was careful not to sound like a horrified westerner again as I knew how often a good marriage could take over the importance of everything else. I had heard my own mother accuse Dad on numerous occasions over the years of having whisked her away from a perfectly good education when she herself had been nineteen. But I still could not resist a final, 'You could have insisted.'

She looked at me squarely this time and, without flinching, replied firmly, 'Sometimes it's just not worth that much trouble.'

Dinner over, I helped Maya clear away, even though she protested long and hard that she could do it after I had gone. She still seemed both impressed as well as amused at my obvious ease in the kitchen, laughing at the deftness with which I arranged all her dishes to fit into the fridge.

'I believe you now when you say that you don't have a girlfriend. You've obviously been doing that for a very long time!'

'In England, Maya, it's when they *have* a girlfriend or a wife that men become expert at this kind of thing. Cooking, cleaning, clearing up after their women. The land of dragon-women, the whole of the western world,' I said with mock weariness, wiping my brow.

'To me, it sounds like heaven,' she laughed.

'Well, thank you for the fabulous dinner,' I said, wiping my hands on the towel she was holding out.

'No, thank *you* for the company, Rahul, I enjoyed every minute.'

'Anjali slept through it all, amazingly, didn't she?'

'Once she's asleep, earthquakes won't wake that child up. In fact, earthquakes would probably know better than to mess with that child, even when she is awake.' She laughed, her face going all soft and sweet with maternal pride.

'She's loads of fun, but I don't suppose we'd have had much sane conversation if she had been awake.'

'Too right, I made sure she was in bed and asleep before you came,' she replied, opening the door. Cool floral breezes drifted in from her garden.

'Good night, Maya,' I said, 'and thanks again. My stomach's purring!'

'Good night, Rahul,' she said gently, her face dark against the light. I turned and walked out of her garden, looking back at her door as I closed the gate, but she was gone. The door was shut and she was indoors, closed in with her secrets again.

five

Early the next morning, I collected my rubber-banded newspaper from the driveway near the gate. As I straightened up I saw her, at an upstairs window. She leaned her forehead against the window grill and waved an arm out to me.

'Sleep well?'

'Hmm, very! And you?'

'I slept beautifully!'

'Anjali still asleep?'

'Yes, thankfully. Listen, I was thinking, Rahul . . . when she wakes up, let's go somewhere with her. You haven't seen much of Trivandrum, have you?'

'Where? I have my classes.'

'After your classes then. In the evening, it'll be cooler too.'

'Where did you have in mind?'

'The beach, maybe? Kovalam?'

'Are you sure, Maya? I mean I'd like to go, but . . .'

'Okay, that's settled then.'

'What? Where . . .' But she was no longer at the window. Only the curtains were fluttering carelessly at me now. I could feel a faint sense of breathlessness again at the speed with which I seemed to be getting caught up in my neighbours' lives. Maya was gorgeous— I had found her warm and caring and intelligent last night. And terribly beautiful too, of course, just to complicate things. But she wasn't mine to have. I had to keep reminding myself of that, however hard it was, given what an utter prat her husband seemed to be. I wasn't even sure she was really attracted to me anyway. Again, her husband's foolishness was probably a contributory factor in what was obviously some sort of growing fondness for me. But the whole damn thing was dangerous. *Dangerous.* I was sure it wasn't an exaggeration to describe it as that. If . . . *when* her husband did discover our new-found friendship, there was surely going to be a heavy price to pay. I wasn't to know, of course, exactly how heavy that would be.

'I've asked Karthu, Kuttan's sister, to leave early today, after she's cleared away the lunch things. If you let Kuttan out by then, we can get an early start.' I had just returned from my morning classes and had found Maya waiting for me at the wall. She was talking to me with Anjali perched on her hip. The little girl was playing with her mother's hair, putting her own head under it and preening as though it was hers.

I had no words for the little girl today as I felt a sudden small tremor of fear and unease. 'Where are we going?'

'Padmanabhapuram Palace,' she said, 'it's beautiful there, you must see it.'

'How do we get there?'

'Oh, I've arranged a taxi,' she replied cheerfully, 'that was no trouble at all.'

'You've gone to a lot of trouble,' I said, 'I'm still not sure it's—'

'Would it make you feel better if I said I was doing it as much for Anjali and me as for you, Rahul? It'll be marvellous to get out of Trivandrum for a bit. *Really.*'

'Okay, what time?'

'Two o'clock?'

*

At two, after an unsuspecting Kuttan and his sister had left, Maya and Anjali walked in through my gate. Maya had a bag slung on her shoulder, Anjali was dragging a smaller one along in the dust. I put Maya's bag on my wicker chair. It seemed to be crammed full of food. I could see biscuit packets, crisp packets, bottles of water . . . Anjali refused to let go of the smaller bag she was carrying.

'She wanted to pack one of her own, God knows what's in it,' Maya laughed.

Anjali tugged at my hand, palpitating as she prattled on in excited high-pitched Malayalam. I could only discern the occasional 'Unka'.

'Won't she mention this to her father?' I asked Maya. 'Surely he won't be chuffed with a little outing like this?'

'Her language is not too clear yet—he can hardly understand what she's trying to say, although I can now make out most of it.'

She appeared to be ignoring my second question, but I insisted, 'But what about him, Maya? Govind. If he does find out?'

She looked away as she said, angrily, 'Well, he can't control me forever. He has to learn that.'

'What do you think he will do, though?'

'Kill me,' she said playfully, tossing her head.

'And me too, probably?' I asked, only half joking myself.

'Are you scared?' she asked.

Scared? Not many things scared me. 'I'll handle it if it comes,' I said confidently, pleased to see her eyes shining at me approvingly.

The taxi drew up and we climbed into the back seat, piling the bags on the seat next to the driver. To him we must have looked like any ordinary, happy family out on a day trip. Anjali clambered on her mother's lap to see better out of the window and Maya put her arms around her little daughter and gave her a tight squeeze. 'Anjalimolu's going out! In a taxi!' she said gaily, while her daughter laughed up at her, obviously delighted to see her mother in such a joyous mood.

It was hot in the car, and we rolled all the windows down to let the breeze flow through. Anjali's hair, straight, black and shiny, flew back from her face, exposing its chubby smiles to the world. The soft curling wisps that usually framed Maya's face were flying into her eyes and her mouth, and she pushed them aside impatiently with her free hand, smiling her exasperation at me. I breathed more easily, now that we had driven away from her house. The chance of us being spotted by anyone we knew were remote now and I could feel my shoulders start to un-stiffen.

'Unka joos?' Anjali was offering me the loan of her small juice bottle.

'No thanks, sunshine, you drink that.'

She flashed me a cheesy smile and stuck her bottle back in her mouth, leaning her head on her mother's chest. I looked up at Maya's face. Her eyes were closed and a tiny smile was playing at the corners of her mouth. What was she thinking? Did she feel any of the guilt that I did? What was inuring her from it? The love she did not seem to be able to get from Govind? The beginnings of feelings for me, perhaps . . . ? I knew she was fond of me, but how much of that sprang from her own loneliness, I wondered. There was no point pretending that I was not horribly attracted to her. I had taken a long time to get to sleep after returning from her house last night and had paced up and down my tiny veranda, willing my head to rid itself of its swirling, suffocating thoughts. Things would have been far less complicated if she hadn't been so maddeningly pretty.

Her eyes were still closed and I let my gaze travel down her neck in a way I had not been able to so far. It was long, with a nice shape, marked with a few stray moles. Her chest was rising and falling gently under the thin orange silk of her sari. The breeze from the window, playing with the pallav of her sari, were flattening and rippling the silk against her breasts. Anjali's head had made for itself a indentation on that pillow. I realized, with some shock, that the little girl's eyes were still fixed on my face as she watched me watch her mother. I smiled at her guiltily, but she continued to gaze at me solemnly, sucking on her bottle. That was the other thing, goddammit, you couldn't just go falling in love with some poor kid's *mother*, could you? Some things ought to be sacrosanct. Other people's lives, other men's wives, the trust of little children, most of all. They were sacrosanct, going by all the rules. I knew that. In fact, I was painfully conscious of that and had never had any trouble with it before. But now the rules appeared to have temporarily uprooted themselves and invaded me, demanding to be flouted. I could have tried harder to stop them, perhaps, but it felt as though these people's lives had opened up to draw me in, rather than the other way around. Or else how could I explain that another man's wife was sitting here, next to me, looking for all the world as though she were indeed mine. Worst of all, worst of bloody all, her small child was looking at me now, as though already aware that I was about to transgress that one final rule. And change the course of her world along with ours.

I looked out of the window as we sped past lush green countryside. Maya had opened her eyes and was rummaging in her bag, leaning over on to the front seat. She emerged with a bottle of water.

'Thanks,' I said, as she offered it to me, taking a long and relieved swig. I returned it to her and watched her put her mouth to it unhesitatingly and drink from it, her neck muscles moving as she gulped. She did not seem to mind the fact that I had just put my mouth to the bottle.

'How far are we from this palace?' I asked.

'Not far now,' she replied, 'we should be there by four.'

'It must be quite plush if it's a palace?' I asked.

'On the contrary, it's a tiny little palace, quite exquisite. The Travancore royal family never really believed in pomp and glory, unlike royal families elsewhere. And Keralites are quite proud of that—of their simplicity.'

She was right. The building I could see, as we drove into the compound fifteen minutes later, was plain and whitewashed and had an old tiled roof. But something did indeed make it seem exquisite. Perhaps it was the deep veranda framed by fat, gracefully curved pillars. There were not too many people about. Just one other car languished in the heat of the car park. We walked up to the building, Anjali running along ahead. A sleepy-looking man in the ticket office issued us entry tickets. In keeping with the general atmosphere of the place, he appeared to be in no hurry, slowly counting the notes one by one, putting them away carefully in a wooden drawer on his desk as though they were the only takings of the day. Anjali had already got past the security man as we walked up some stairs to the veranda. Maya called her back to pull her sandals off while we kicked off our shoes under a sign that said, 'No footwear please'. The floor shot our reflections back at us as we stepped on its smooth cool surface. I had expected it to be made of marble like the palaces I had seen in Ajmer and Jaisalmer, but this was a stunning deep black.

'How on earth do they keep it as shiny as this?' I asked, marvelling, as I squatted down, running my palm over the smooth blackness.

'It was made out of a strange mixture, into which, apparently thousands of egg shells went in at one stage.' Maya was running one bare foot over the black floor.

'Egg shells!'

'Egg—motta!' Anjali exclaimed.

Maya laughed and bent down to give her daughter a delighted hug. 'Clever molu! She's been wanting to learn English ever since you came along, so I've started to teach her a bit.'

'What else do you know then?' I asked Anjali, still kneeling on the floor.

'Mmmm . . .' she said, screwing up her nose and eyes in

concentration. Maya prompted her softly in Malayalam. Anjali's face brightened, she pointed to her chest and said, 'Tummy.'

'Very good,' I said admiringly, picking up her hand and moving it further down to rest on the right protuberance. 'That's more like it—*that's* your tummy. And a very nice tummy too, if I may say so.'

She grinned and tried another protuberance, more accurately this time. 'Nose!'

'Gosh, you are getting rather clever, aren't you? And so *terribly* English, they certainly won't bother asking you for a visa if you turned up there speaking like that!'

'That's it, though, the sum total of her English vocabulary at the moment,' Maya laughed. 'We'd better walk on, we might have to be out of here at six.'

'I'm glad we came to this place. It's like being in another world,' I said, looking around at the dim, quiet interior. 'A world of great gentleness or dignity or something.'

'I must teach you to say the name,' Maya said, 'It's not "this place". Be brave and try saying Padma-nabha-puram.'

I stumbled through it, while she watched my mouth.

'Not bad,' she laughed.

'Bloody awkward language, but no one can accuse me of not trying.'

'Would you like to learn Malayalam?' she asked. 'It is a very difficult language to teach, though. And I'm not too fluent in it myself because I grew up outside Kerala, too.'

'Also, language lessons for both Anjali and me will leave you with no time for anything else.'

'Oh I wouldn't mind that at all. I need to be much busier than I am at the moment.'

She was now looking at a large Ravi Varma painting on the wall. Of a woman brushing her long flowing mass of black hair in front of a large mirror.

'Well, I'm game for a quick language lesson, if you are. Let's start right now, shall we?'

'Okay, try saying this,' she said, turning to me. '*Ningal vallarey nallu manushyan aanu.*' Her brown eyes were dancing.

'It's something naughty, isn't it?' I asked suspiciously.

Brown eyes now widened indignantly. 'Would I do something as awful as that!' she cried.

'Oh, I don't know, tell me what it means first.'

'It was a compliment, silly,' she laughed, 'but you've missed it now. Never mind, try this . . . *endey peru Rahul aanu* . . .'

This I was already familiar with, the obligatory self-introductory sentence everyone starts a language lesson with. But I repeated it carefully, humouring her.

'You already knew that one, didn't you? Okay, here comes a tough one then . . . but very important, though, you'll never know when you need it . . . hmmm . . . *vallaathu vedana* . . .' She stretched the words out, her face going serious, brown eyes turning unexpectedly still and dark.

'What does that mean?' I asked, suddenly cautious.

She paused for a moment, still unsmiling, and said, 'It means, "I feel a terrible pain."'

The mood in the quiet dignified palace had shifted. I knew the language lesson was over and that we were now talking about something completely different. Maybe she had needed to come all the way out here, to this hushed, silent place, to be able to start voicing all her unspoken stuff.

'Where? Where does it pain?' I asked gently, in English and not in Malayalam, to indicate that I understood we had moved into another territory altogether.

She patted her hand on her chest, much like Anjali had done earlier, but instead of announcing her own body parts, she whispered, 'Here, Rahul, in this stupid heart of mine, I don't know how to explain it, but it hurts really badly.' I stood stock still, feeling her pain wash over me. Her hand had now travelled up to her throat. She curled her fingers around it, and in a voice now full of tears, she said, 'And here too . . . there's always this pain . . . all the time . . . every day . . .'

'Maya, I wish I could help. What can I do?'

'You can't, no one can. All I know is I can't hold on any more.'

'What is it, what do you want to do?'

'Just run away, I suppose,' she said bleakly, 'with Anjali. Somewhere, anywhere, far away.'

I took in a breath. 'Let's sit down there and talk, shall we? Where's Anjali? Anjali!' I called out. Anjali's head popped out from the adjoining room questioningly. 'Don't go wandering off, kiddo, we're sitting here.' Her head retreated obligingly and I turned to Maya again.

'What is it? Tell me exactly what it is.'

She was shaking her head, now wiping her nose with the end of her sari pallav. It was a good thing this place was as empty as it was, there wasn't a soul to witness this heartbreak.

'You've got to tell me. Is he . . . Govind . . . really nasty to you? Is that it?' I had put one hand on her back and tried to look at her face. She shook her bent head and mumbled something I couldn't hear. 'What's that?' I asked.

She looked up, her eyes wet and red, and said more clearly, 'He doesn't beat me or anything . . .'

Hallelujah, I was tempted to say, as it could only have been something pretty much on a par with beatings to make her as miserable as she was. 'What is it then, Maya?' I asked, trying not to threaten her by being too insistent.

There was a long pause before she said, 'He's just . . . just *suspicious* . . .' She whispered the word as though the very mention of it could conjure up the misery accompanying that ghastly burden.

'What's he suspicious of?'

'Me,' she said, 'all the time.'

'Is that why he didn't let you go to college?'

She nodded. 'Or the shops, or to make friends, anywhere . . . except to see my parents. And even then he prefers that they come here.'

'Have you told them? Your parents?'

She shook her head. 'They sort of know, they must know, maybe not the full extent of his possessiveness. But what they want to see is that I live in a nice house, have a nice car, a husband who gives me everything. They don't want to see the other side of that.' I nodded and she continued, 'Do you know, people think I'm so lucky. They think I have everything a woman can want.'

'In some ways you do really,' I said, watching Anjali cheerfully and unsuccessfully attempt hopping on one foot in the next room. 'But I can imagine how all that can seem utterly meaningless when you have to deal with this thing every day. Suspicion.' A wry thought floated into my head.

She looked up at me. 'What are you smiling at?' she asked in consternation.

I removed my arm from her shoulder and rubbed my face down with my hands. 'It's not funny, I know, but my problem was the exact opposite. My ex-girlfriend left after a huge row because she thought I wasn't possessive *enough*. She thought I just wasn't bothered about her. Arrogant, she called it, or rather, superior!'

I looked at Maya. She had wiped her eyes now and was looking less miserable, attempting a dismal little smile at me. I caught her gently by the chin and looked into her eyes, framed now by wet, pointy lashes. 'I don't wish to make light of it. It must be sheer hell to live with. Might it . . . do you think it *might* get better somehow over the years?'

'I did think that at first. I thought a child would make a difference.'

'Didn't it?'

'Oh, he's okay with her. He's quite nice to her, that's when he is around, which isn't a whole lot. In some ways, that is the problem, you see. Because he has the sort of business that takes him away on so many tours, he gets suspicious thinking of all the things I might get up to in his absence.'

'Does he have a family? Couldn't they help?'

'His parents live near Cochin. With their two younger daughters. They're not too well off. His father is a retired schoolteacher and his mother has never worked. It's hard to explain, but they are quite in . . . in *awe* of him, that's the only way I can put it. You see, he started this business and made all the money on his own. And now he sends them money every month, so that his sisters can be married off into good families. I don't mind any of that but, because they are so dependent on him for everything, they will never, ever say anything against him. It's almost as if they have to make sure they always please him.'

'Do you see them often?'

'Not really. Govind likes to keep a bit of distance. Sometimes he says they will be here all the time if he lets them come and he doesn't want to encourage that. Anyway, I don't think his family likes me that much or anything. I sometimes think they worry that I'll take their precious son away from them. Or somehow make him stop him sending them money . . .'

'It's funny that he's so dutiful when it comes to sending them money, though?'

'Yes, but that's something to do with how good it all looks to other people. Same reason for which he married me, too . . .' She laughed and intoned sarcastically, 'Good-looking girl, good family, convent educated . . . but once he got me, he didn't know what on earth to do with me!'

'So he puts you safely away into a little cage . . .'

'You must admit it's a *nice* cage, though. Three bedrooms, three attached bathrooms, stainless steel sink in a fully tiled

Jaishree Misra

kitchen . . .' Her sing-song tone was half mocking and half sorrowful again.

'Maya, I don't need to tell you, it's a cruel world out there when you *don't* have all those things.'

'I know! But, *having* had all those things, I know how little it can all mean if you don't have the really important things in life, Rahul. Can't you understand that?'

'Oh, I can understand. To someone like me, that kind of loss of freedom would be sheer torture.'

'Please help me,' she whispered.

'What can I do, Maya? How can I help?'

'Please help me to get a job—in Delhi or somewhere. Any job, please!'

'But you haven't even got a degree, Maya,' I reminded her gently. 'And you have little Anjali.'

'I could work in a nursery or something. Keep Anjali with me. I could study part-time—I used to be a good student.'

'You'll earn a pittance, work your fingers to the bone, and then feel really bad that you've had to put Anjali through all that too . . . you don't really want any of that, do you? Rents in Delhi aren't cheap, you won't even get a decent place to live. I don't need to tell you any of this, Maya.' I was pleading with her now.

'You won't help me,' she said flatly, as though I had been her last resort.

'I'm trying to help you. By showing you that you might not be any better off by flying out of the cage you're in at the moment, Maya.'

'You—who are so free yourself. How can you even begin to tell me how to enjoy my imprisonment.' She was fighting back tears again, spitting her words out in a choked voice.

How could I make her see that by helping her escape I would only be creating another kind of captivity for her? I wasn't even sure a suspicious husband could create so much despair. These were things I had never had to think about before. Perhaps it was just that she was a free spirit stifled by the confines of marriage. And I had turned up rather conveniently as a potential escape route. 'Maya, I'm trying to speak like a friend . . .' I started before trailing off. I didn't feel like much of a friend, telling her in a hundred different ways that I really wasn't going to help.

We were silent as the evening drew in around us. Anjali, tired of her solitary games, ran out of the inner room and flopped down on her mother's back, wrapping her arms around her neck. Maya pulled her on to her lap and buried her face in the little girl's hair. Then, looking at me over her daughter's shiny black mop, she said in a voice full of sadness, 'You're right, Rahul. You've been kind enough not to take advantage of me in my situation, promising me this and that . . . not everybody would have done that. Thank you.'

'Oh no, don't thank me. I feel rotten that I can't do more to help . . .'

'Please don't feel bad. Just being able to talk about it has been a help. Really. Let's go and see the rest of the palace now, shall we?'

We got up, and Anjali let out a delighted whoop that we were on the move again. But the joy of the evening had dimmed as we walked around the slowly darkening interior of the palace. Maya pointed out a few things, telling me a little about the history that had unfolded within these walls down the years. I could tell what a big effort she was making to be cheerful and felt my heart go out to her. But we spoke no more about the earlier conversation. Not even in the car on the way back. It was as though it was best to go back to the footing we had been on before setting out on our day trip here. Neighbours and new friends, but only up to a point. To transgress that limit was too frightening for me to contemplate at the moment.

Things were very quiet the following day. I went for my classes as usual, looking out at the house next door as I came and went, but there was little sign of life in the garden and at the windows. I still didn't know if I had let Maya down or done the decent thing, as she had seemed to suggest. But it was obvious she was now staying out of my way. Another day passed and just when I was contemplating calling out to ask her if she was okay, I noticed that the Esteem had returned, sometime in the night, taking its place in the car porch once again.

I strained to listen for sounds of their conversation, worried that Govind might somehow have found out about either the dinner or the trip out of Trivandrum. The consequences did not bear thinking about and I marvelled again, both at Maya's boldness and the ease with which it was possible for situations to grow and develop into something completely out of control. Except for Anjali's occasional babble, things were quiet. Eerily quiet. Ice continued to appear at my lunchtime meal, but I did not ask Kuttan if it was his sister or Maya who was sending it. If it was Maya, I knew that that discovery alone could send her husband flying into a fury, but I had no way to tell her to stop sending it.

I missed her too, that was the other thing. Perhaps it was my own loneliness, but that was unlikely as I was usually a fairly self-contained sort. Not given to depending on anyone for anything. Not ice, certainly not friendship and companionship and all that stuff. So it was odd—and most disconcerting—that I thought about Maya as often as I did. Not just of how beautiful she looked when she threw back her head and laughed. Or how gracefully she walked in a sari. But also less flattering things—her pain, her vulnerability, her capacity to deceive. It was surprising that those things were not as distasteful in her as they would normally have seemed to me.

Of course it's clear, looking back now, that I was already falling in love. I was starting to want to help her escape her cage, not just for her, but for what I would get too. The thing is, I could probably have held on to those feelings silently and then merely left Trivandrum sooner than planned. I could have coped with that, I'm fairly sure. Returned to England at some point and let the memory of a pretty neighbour framed by the flowers in her wall slowly fade away. And moved on to other things, other concerns, other people . . . as I had managed to do all my life so far.

But a ceaseless nagging seemed to have taken up inside me. Voices raging in my head. Telling me things, urging me to take risks, to feel free, to do the unthinkable. And that was how, one afternoon, after I had returned from a trip to the shops, I did it. I walked, not up to my own gate, but to Maya's. Up her drive, through the empty car porch and to the front door. The bell shrieked somewhere deep inside the house. In her fully tiled kitchen, with the stainless steel sink, I thought sardonically. She opened the door, her eyes widening slightly in alarm at seeing me.

'Rahul! What is it?'

'No, maybe I ought to be asking you that? Why have you gone all silent on me? Your husband isn't around all the time, is he? You haven't looked over the wall even once. Was it because of our conversation at the palace?'

'Well, yes I suppose . . .'

'You were angry that I wouldn't help?'

'No, not angry. I thought you were right. And decent. And kind. And I didn't want to burden you any more.'

'So you were trying to let me off the hook?'

'I'm not sure I'd put it that way . . . I thought you'd been as kind as you possibly could. What was the point in risking your happiness after that?'

'And risking your safety with your husband?'

'You know I'm not that bothered about that any more.'

'No?'

'No,' she replied firmly.

'Have you decided what you're going to do?'

'I thought you were right in what you said. Trying to get out now would just bring misery on everyone. Anjali especially. I'm going to enrol on a course, whether Govind likes it or not. Study interior design. When I'm in a position to support myself and Anjali, I'll go.'

It sounded like an eminently sensible plan to me, but I heard myself say, without even knowing where the words were coming from, 'I've thought about things too. I could take you to Delhi with me. My parents could be persuaded to help—they'd do it for me. I'll support you until you find your feet, maybe even try to get you a visa to England . . . maybe . . .'

Maya smiled ruefully. She was silent for a few moments before she said, 'Do you know, Rahul, when I talked to you at Padmanabhapuram Palace, that's what I was hoping you would say—'

'Well I'm sorry I didn't say it then. I'm saying it now.' I didn't want to hear the 'but' that was hovering at the end of her sentence, but she carried on speaking, her eyes not looking into my face any more.

'Rahul, it's so sweet of you. But you were right. I'd just be exchanging one kind of captivity for another, wouldn't I?'

'But you'd be able to get away from Govind, you said you couldn't bear his suspicion any more.'

'Yes, that's true. But then I'd become dependent on you. Both me and Anjali.'

'I like Anjali, she'd be no trouble. If you were working in Delhi, you'd be able to hire help to look after her.'

Her eyes were closed now, as though she needed to shut everything out because it was too confusing, too tormenting, too tempting.

'Rahul, please go back. Govind will be here for lunch. Please, I don't want you to get into any trouble.'

'Yes, but will you think about what I said. I mean it, really. I really do want to help.'

She was starting to close her door now. 'You're confused, Rahul. I'm so sorry I confused you. You don't want to be burdened with me and Anjali. You think you do, but you were more right back there at the palace.'

'I've changed my mind, Maya. I've thought things through . . .'

Her eyes were now full of alarm and fear as she tried to close her door. 'Rahul, *go*! Only I can help myself. No one else can and no one else should . . . so please go now.'

Her door slammed shut. I stood for a few moments, blindly watching a bee dance through the sunlit plants, and then slowly walked back down the drive and out of the gate. A few minutes later, I heard the Esteem come down the road.

I called Mr Pannicker and told him I did not feel up to classes today. Must have been something I ate, I said. You really should be careful of the water here, he said, I hope you will be better tomorrow. Yes, I'm sure I'll be better tomorrow, I'll see you then, I replied before hanging up. I lay on my bed, watching the ceiling fan do its metronomic thing, seeing myself spreadeagled in its steel plates. She was right, I ought not to have given in to impulse like that. Not when it affected other people in such a serious way.

I ought to pack my bags and leave Trivandrum. Make some explanation when I got back to Delhi earlier than expected. Mum and Dad were used to my strange ways, and would not ask too many questions hopefully. They would be quite pleased to see me anyway. And I could look back on my attempted mridangam schooling as a bit of a joke afterwards. And my brief liaison with Maya as one of life's odd encounters. Odd and unusual and hopefully forgettable. Luckily, the situation had never got completely out of hand. Luckily!

I got up from the bed. It was still too hot to go out. I needed to step out for an energetic run or something. Kuttan wandered in, asking why I hadn't eaten lunch. I gave him the same story I had given Mr Pannicker and asked him to finish his lunch and leave when he was done. I walked into the living room, deciding to play something on my tablas to cheer myself up. That usually worked. I found my CD walkman and the track I wanted to accompany. Fitting my headphones to my ears, I started to play. Kuttan came in a few minutes later to indicate he had finished his lunch and had left mine covered on the table. I nodded and signalled that he close the doors and windows before he left, so I could use the full force of my hands. Today I didn't feel especially concerned about the well-being of my neighbours. Then I started to play.

It was a long track and I could feel the muscles in my arms start to ache after a few minutes. On and on and on I played, hardly noticing that the track had played itself out after a while. My arms became the automated limbs of some poor crazed robot, lifting and beating and crashing down, thrashing out the feelings that surged within me, wanting to beat them into submission, wanting to stamp them out, kill them off, deaden and quieten them forever.

My door came crashing open. Maya. She had caught me like this once before, on an afternoon less crazed, on an afternoon full of mysterious and languid grace.

I stopped my drumming and pulled off my headphones,

alarmed at the expression on her face. Her face was red, her eyes wore the same wild expression that mine must have done.

'Maya, what's wrong!' I cried, jumping off my seat and going up to her.

She fell into my arms, sobbing, her words coming tumbling out, between raging sobs, 'He . . . saw . . . he saw you . . . coming out of the gate . . . he was furious . . .'

I held her by the shoulders. 'What did he do, where is he . . .'

She could barely speak now for her sobbing. 'He . . . he waited for Karthu to leave and . . . then . . . he hit me, Rahul . . .'

'What! The bast—why didn't you call . . . where is he . . .'

'I don't know . . . he hit me . . . pulled my hair . . . shouting things . . . Anjali was screaming . . .'

'Where is she?'

'In the back garden . . . she's okay now . . .'

'Why didn't you call me?' Even as I asked the question, I realized that I would not have heard her over the crashing of my own drums.

'I was crying . . . you didn't hear . . .'

'Where did he hit you?'

She did not answer me, her eyes still mirroring the shock of her recent experience. It was a pretty pointless thing to ask in the circumstances anyway.

'He threatened me . . .' she said, her voice breaking up again.

'What did he say?' I asked, gripping her by the shoulders and giving her a little shake as the words seemed to stick in her throat.

'My face . . .' she sobbed.

I put my hands on her face, cupping her cheeks. 'What about your face?'

'He said he would . . . destroy my face . . . that that was what was causing all the problems . . .'

'Christ! *Jesus Christ*! Is the man mad?'

'That's what he looked like . . . like he'd gone mad . . .' She was sobbing uncontrollably now.

Jaishree Misra

'Where is he now?' I asked, feeling my own heart start to throb in terror.

'I don't know . . . he rushed out after that . . . he'll be back . . . I have to go.'

'No! Don't go back!'

'I have to. Anjali.'

My mind was whirling, but I knew I had to think fast. 'Okay, go now. Get Anjali. Pack something. You have to get out of here.'

She looked at me, clutching the rolled-up end of her sari to her mouth, her eyes wide with fear and full of tears. She was shaking her head.

'Go *quickly*!' I said again, the urgency making my voice crack. 'You don't know when he'll be back. You don't know what he'll do when he gets back. He might take you somewhere else. From where you won't be able to get out. Hurry!'

She turned and ran out of the house. I pulled the telephone directory out of the shelf and scanned the pages for the Indian Airlines telephone number. I knew she wouldn't be safe anywhere in Trivandrum. We had to get to Delhi, I could take her there. He would never find us there. Could he call the police? Claim abduction or something? I would get Maya to write a note. She could address it to her parents, leave it here in this house, or post it from Delhi. They would need to know that she had left of her own volition. Kuttan! I would have to leave a note for him as well— make some explanation, to him and to Mr Pannicker. Poor people who had been nothing but kindness to me. Fucking hell! What a bloody mess!

The woman on the phone said tickets were available on the Delhi flight, if we flew via Bombay. The flight was at five, we had less than two hours. I gave her my credit card number and told her I would collect the tickets in under an hour.

I pulled my suitcase out from under the bed and started to throw my clothes into it. I would have to leave my tablas behind, and my books. Perhaps I could have them sent for afterwards. Kuttan could forward them to me. On the other hand, I did not want anyone to have my address in Delhi, not even Kuttan. Mr Pannicker! Did he have the address? I remembered, with relief, that all he had was my email address in England.

Closing my suitcase shut, I wrote a hasty note to Kuttan, trying to keep the letters clear and large, so that he could read them without too much trouble. Unforeseen circumstances. He would know, everybody would know it was something to do with the pretty woman next door. What would they say? How many people, even those who had liked Maya, would be generous enough to suggest it might have been something she had to do? How many people would believe that we were not lovers?

I called a cab company whose number I found in the book. Money! Good grief, I would have to leave money for all the people to whom I owed various amounts. I found three envelopes and stuffed some notes into each of them. One for Mr Pannicker, with his fees, one for the rent on the house and the last one for Kuttan, with a big tip that I hoped would tell him how much I had appreciated his talents as cook, valet and butler, all rolled into one. I took the keys to the house and left them next to the kettle, where Kuttan would hopefully find them when he came in tomorrow morning and prepared to make my tea. I stepped out into the veranda and looked over the wall. The door was closed and there was no sign of the Esteem in the porch. 'Christ, Maya, hurry!' I thought, wondering if I ought to go across and get her.

She emerged, just as the taxi drew up at the door. I ran out to help her with her suitcase and shoved it hastily into the boot of the car. Anjali, who was being dragged unceremoniously along by her elbow, greeted me with a gleeful 'Unka!'. This was no time for pleasantries, unfortunately, and so I bundled her into the back seat of the car before leaving Maya to get in next to her. I then ran back into my house and picked up my suitcase. I looked again at

Jaishree Misra

my tablas, gleaming softly in the afternoon light that was filtering through the windows. It was silly to be behaving as though I was leaving an old friend behind. I remembered vaguely some hasty promise I had made to Mum that I wouldn't leave anything behind or give anything away. Slamming the door behind me, I raced back to the taxi and got hurriedly into the front seat, next to the driver.

'Airport. Domestic,' I said, taking a deep breath as he started up the car. It started in one go, fortunately, and I slowly let my breath out as we began to move down the road.

There was no sign of the Esteem and, as we left the city behind us, I heaved a sigh of relief before turning back to look at Maya. She still seemed to be in a state of shock, her eyes wide open and red, her face tense and unsmiling. I smiled at her, hoping to reassure her of my support. I knew we couldn't talk much in front of the driver.

'Anjali!' I said, looking at the little girl, trying to break the tension.

'Unka!' she replied cheerfully.

'Where are you off to now?'

'Ammumma house!' she replied confidently.

Maya's eyes started to well up again. She put her arm around the small figure sitting next to her holding on to a doll.

'Don't worry, it'll be okay,' I whispered at her. She nodded and tried to smile as Anjali echoed my last word.

'Okay, okay, okay . . .' she babbled as we drove on to Trivandrum airport to catch the Bombay flight.

*

And so it came to pass that Maya left Kerala with Anjali and with me. It wasn't quite an elopement, but that was certainly how it was seen by everyone else. Trivandrum would have reeled from the shock of it for days after that. But we were not to know what was being said. It wasn't hard to guess, though, and I certainly didn't want to make things worse for Maya by speculating about it.

We arrived in Delhi and my parents took Maya and her daughter in, not entirely without reluctance or suspicion, I have to admit. But I managed to persuade them without even saying very much. They knew, I suppose, that I was the kind of chap who would merely have moved out of their place and found somewhere else in the city to live if they had been too vociferous in their objections.

Maya and Anjali were given my old room next to Mum and Dad's, while I used the new guest bedroom upstairs. Maya was subdued, saying very little and eating frugally, even though Dad tried quite hard to joke around at the dining table to put her at ease. Anjali, on the other hand, bounced around perfectly happy to have found surrogate grandparents to replace the old ones who were hardly mentioned after the first few days. Dad was the first to be conquered and, within days, she had him eating out of the palm of her hand, ordering him to do this and that in some brand-new Hindi. Grandfatherly tasks he seemed delighted to finally be getting a chance to do. It was clear that Mum too was finding it hard to remain frosty around that chubby, smiling presence. I knew the ice had been broken when, a few days after our arrival, they took Anjali with them to visit the neighbours, introducing her as the granddaughter of an old friend. Maya seemed to relax a little as her daughter made herself completely at home, but I noticed she was still trying too hard to make herself useful around the house, even though the cook and the maid made sure there wasn't that much for her to do. I fended off Mum's questions as best as I could, without being too short with her. I could see her confusion, particularly given Maya's obvious devotion to her daughter. But, after a couple of months, even Mum's initial suspicions, having circled around Maya, sniffing to find something unseemly, something to really dislike, finally settled down with a disappointed thump.

I got on with trying to find a way for Maya to travel to England. It was clear that Delhi wasn't the right sort of place for someone like her, particularly as I certainly had to get back to England and my job at some point. I could imagine Delhi swallowing her up in my absence with its easy, thoughtless, hard-edged materialism. England, I was sure, would have better opportunities for her and for her child. At least she would have a friend in me.

I wasn't sure early on why I was doing all this for Maya. Did I feel responsible for having helped her to leave Kerala and doubly responsible when it became clear that there could be no going back? Had my earlier attraction for her already become something else? But, in a few months' time I was, as my mother had glumly predicted, completely in love with Maya. I was keen not to have her think I was taking advantage of her vulnerability. But she seemed to respond to my attentions with a kind of relief. I wouldn't be able to say if she loved me too. Or was merely grateful for not having pushed her into anything with which she might have been uncomfortable. I convinced myself that she had not used me as a means out of her marriage, and events had sort of spiralled out of control somewhere along the way. It wasn't something I really wanted to think too hard about. As far as I was concerned, Maya's and my love grew in those months out of our circumstances, without haste and without embarrassment. We couldn't get married of course, but that didn't matter, certainly not to me. An old schoolmate of mine who worked at the British High Commission helped us with the visas eventually. And, after some months, both Maya and Anjali followed me here, to England.

In the first week of our arrival in Delhi, Maya had attempted to call her mother. But her father had answered the telephone and had slammed it down the minute he heard her voice. 'My mother will talk to me, I know,' she had said and tried again. But, on that occasion, all she got was silence before the phone went dead again. She did not know, of course, that they had made the same assumptions about her hasty departure as everyone else had. It was only sometime afterwards that we would find out how, overwhelmed by their own sorrow, Maya's parents conducted her death rites. As is sometimes done when a person has brought great shame and dishonour on the name of an old and noble family. Red rice and gingili seeds are placed on banana leaves as incantations for death are chanted. When it's done for the dead, it is meant to bring peace to the soul. But when it's done for the living, it is to do the very opposite I believe.

I cannot say Maya had no peace at all after that. The laughter did return to her eyes, and I was glad to have been partially responsible for that. Anjali was obviously her most constant source of happiness and what kept her busiest when she most needed to be that. But England was a new and exciting place, too. Where no one knew our history, and our life was free to grow and develop, which it did. I don't believe I would be lying if I said that, in the three years that we had together, I did my very best to make it all up to her. And I'm fairly sure she had loved me deeply for that. If anyone asked, I would certainly describe that time as a very happy one. But, in an odd sort of way, it's precisely the happiness of those years that make them so difficult to describe in any detail now. I don't think I even want to try. Maybe I will be able to recount every little detail of that as well someday. Sometimes I rather like imagining such a day, when Anjali might actually be seated in front of me and I would find myself looking in her face for traces of the woman we both lost.

But I suppose I ought to explain how I came to lose not just Maya but Anjali as well. I started the first part of my story a few hours before I first met Maya, in 1996. Perhaps it's best then that this next one should begin, nearly three years later, a few hours after she died.

Part II

1999

The beer was cold, frosting the glass into murky gold. I lifted it to my lips, waiting for my change, looking out at the street through the glass. London's bustling Chinatown turned to gold as in a childhood fairy tale. Shimmering, beaded restaurant fronts beckoned temptingly, offering a golden warm world that I knew for sure didn't exist. The only warning being dead roast ducks in restaurant windows, hanging forlornly upside down.

'Two pounds sixty change, sir.'

'Thanks.'

She was pretty. Normally, that would have been reason enough to exchange a few pleasantries. If for nothing else than to see Maya glower at me when I returned to the table with the drinks. Not that she really minded, and not that I really ever seriously flirted anyway, it was just one of those things we always did. I pretended to flirt and she pretended to glower. Silly, I suppose, thinking about it now. But most people who have been together for a while will recognize the business of tired old jokes becoming a part of the relationship, of life itself after a while. Funny, how the endless repetition of the same old jokes and games, instead of palling and becoming irritating, actually become a part of the intimacy between two people. A bit like the sex, same and unchanging, and yet comforting in its very sameness.

Two years, nine months and a day. Exactly. Not that I sit and count all the time. That's the kind of thing she would have done, probably. I did it this afternoon for the first time, but that was only because someone asked me how long we had been married. Married or together? We hadn't really been married, of course, but that was something we didn't talk about very much because there was nothing we could have done about it. A lot of our English acquaintances always wanted to know: had ours been an *arranged* marriage? Trying not to look embarrassed, wanting to look blithe about the fact that they could accommodate our cultural differences. We would exchange a look that said, couldn't have been *less* arranged, eh? Smiling at each other in memory of that time and the terror with which we had fled. Smiling, because there wasn't anything we could have done to change those things or make them better. Although we had tried.

Anyway, it's all a bit meaningless now, isn't it? These calculations, these finer points. Three years or thirty? Does it matter any more? It would have, if there was more to come, I suppose. We could have added year upon year, tallied up the days, argued over the correct starting point. But it isn't much fun now, is it? Now that all we have is this static, unchanging, mercilessly final end point. Where was our ever after, I wanted to shout. Wasn't every story meant to have an afterwards? Even if it were imaginary and never actually written, merely offering the *suggestion* of hope? Here there was no room for argument even, no hope, no future. That, for me, was the strange thing. The very finality of it. For someone like me, confident always in my ability to change events, it was about the most frightening thing that had ever happened.

Why did you have to go and spoil it all, Maya? Just when we were cruising along nicely. What a goddamned stupid, idiotic, half-arsed thing to do! I wouldn't have done it to *you*, you know! I would have stopped to consider what it would be like for you if I went off and had an accident. I would have looked around at that blasted traffic light to check that there wasn't some half-witted learner driver speeding along in his mother's beat-up jalopy, concentrating on his scratchy Nirvana tape rather than on the fact that the lights had changed. The lights had changed, you bastard, you had a red. A RED! And you didn't bloody stop! Instead, you went and ploughed into the side of Maya's car. Splintering the glass, smashing the metal, sending cruel shards of both into her lovely body. Her warm soft body that smelt of lavender talc as I held it every night before drifting off to sleep. I wonder, oh *God*, I wonder, did it hurt her? Did she know of the metal that plunged into her waist and did she know that her head had crashed right through the glass? They said she had probably died instantaneously. What did that mean? Did that mean she knew nothing, no pain at all? Did that mean she could not have had the time to let her last thoughts fly to me and to her poor little daughter. Did that mean that she genuinely did not know what had happened, that some fucking bastard had just taken her life? My life, our life.

'You all right, love?'

I looked up at two women who had stopped at my table. Fucking hell, my whole face was wet, what a blubbering drunken idiot I must seem. I wiped my face hastily with my palms, mumbling something. I never carried handkerchiefs, Maya always had that kind of thing in her bag. Tissues, paracetamol, sweeties . . . I was always amazed at how she managed to produce life-saving objects at moments of crisis, even if all she was carrying was the tiny shoulder purse she used for our trips to central London. The older of the two women had pulled a packet of tissues from her purse and was offering it to me with a gentle, motherly air. She looked like the sort who was capable of putting that bit of tissue firmly to my nose, grabbing me by the back of my head to say firmly, go on love, blow hard, believe me you'll feel *much* better.

'Thanks,' I said, taking her tissue, 'and . . . sorry . . . I-I don't usually do this.'

The older woman nodded sympathetically. She did not believe me, but still wanted to help. The younger girl (her daughter, a niece?) was hanging back. She had obviously tried to prevent the older woman from approaching me and was both suspicious and annoyed. She was the Londoner, trained by custom and common sense to stay away from strangers. Especially the sort who blubbered into their beer in public places. Oh *Christ*, how mortifying!

'I'm really sorry,' I said again. 'I . . . I'm not . . . I've just had a bit of a crisis.'

If I told them, I would seem a lot less ridiculous. But, if I did, they would either not believe me or scuttle away in fright—allowing the Soho crowds to swallow up their embarrassed and flustered selves. I couldn't very well say it, could I? ('Thanks for the tissue, it's awfully kind of you. I should have anticipated needing one today, but I usually leave things like that to my girlfriend . . . Sounds crazy, but I forgot, temporarily, that she'd just died and that a pack of tissues would probably come in handy sometime in the course of the day . . . When? Oh, just this afternoon . . . Yes, it was rather sudden actually. Most unexpected.')

'You *quite* sure you're all right, love?'

She had a lovely Irish lilt in her soft voice and eyes that were asking a genuine question.

'My girlfriend's just died,' I said, hardly believing my own temerity.

Her eyes widened. Did she dare believe me? Her niece (or daughter) had only half heard this and was edging closer, ready to grab her aunt's elbow and do a runner if I babbled on in similar vein. Mad, the city's full of them, she would have panted exasperatedly to her aunt, dragging her along. It's that bloody Community Care Act thing—let all those loonies out on the streets, it did.

Jaishree Misra

The older woman pulled up the chair in front of me and sat down heavily. 'Oh, sweet Jesus, you poor thing . . .'

Having lived in London for nearly seven years now, I had a circle of friends and acquaintances. I did not need to open my heart to a stranger, even a woman with a such a kind face, old enough to be my mum. I was certainly not *deserving* of the stricken look she was giving me. I was as much a Londoner as the younger woman, never offering kindness to strangers in this vast maelstrom of a city. I was one of those men in smart suits who strode past young women begging at tube stations with grubby children in their laps. I sent a cheque to the NSPCC once a year and considered that my annual assuagement of guilt. These people don't need to be begging, I had said to a horrified Maya who felt poverty here was much worse than it was in India. At least, it's *warm* there, she would say, opening her purse, despite my peevishness. Kindness was something that embarrassed me, unless it was offered to or came from people who mattered very much. I certainly did not expect it from strangers. So why was I crying again, wanting this strange woman to say something, *anything* to make me feel better?

'How . . . oh dear Lord! How did she die, my dear?' She looked horrified, rather than sympathetic. The younger woman was still hovering, now very uncertain of what to do next. Despite her superior, street-smart London-ness, she was confused enough to let the wisdom of the other woman's years take over the situation.

How did she die? I thought of how, in the screeching and crunching of rubber and metal, Maya would have gone. The smell of scorched tyres filling her nostrils, the millions of tiny glass pieces embedding themselves in her beautiful face. I could not describe that to them. I shook my head, looking down.

'You shouldn't be out here by yourself, love. Have you . . . haven't you got any family here . . .' She said this tentatively, as though worried that the question would open another can of worms. I shook my head. Mum and Dad in Delhi, Dad swelling up by the day on cortisone, completely confined now to his wheelchair. Anil, my brother, in San Francisco. He was trying to get leave from the bank, he had said on the telephone earlier today. 'I should be there by next weekend, hang on in there, Rahul,' he had said. I had *friends*, of course I had friends. People at work I went for a drink with every Friday . . . people who laughed loudly and laughed a lot, whose personal lives I knew nothing about. They didn't know yet, unless somebody—my boss David Watts maybe—had broken the news to them today. I didn't know how much leave I would get before I would have to go back and face them all. Nobody would want to spend the weekend with someone who had just lost his girlfriend, for Chrissake! I had other friends too. The old rock band, now scattered all over England. Kevin. I had called Kevin immediately, he was coming down tomorrow. I hoped he wasn't bringing that noisy new girlfriend of his, the one whose name I kept mixing up with the previous one, much to Maya's annoyance. And then there was Sandra from next door, a friend of sorts. She was more Maya's friend, of course, but she had been a comforting presence today, bustling around, making tea, clearing away some of Maya's things when she thought I wasn't looking: her slippers from under the bed, her soft white cotton night-shirt hanging behind the bathroom door . . . Oh God, I had to stop thinking of these things, especially out here, in public. In the middle of this pub in China Bloody Town. I sat up in my chair, rubbing my hands over my face again and tried to sound firm.

'Look, I'm so sorry, I don't wish to ruin your evening. I'm . . . I'll be all right . . . really.'

'I just can't believe what I've just heard,' the older woman replied, 'and I feel you need to be somewhere else, not here . . . by yourself, I mean—'

'No really, I'll be all right. I'm just going to finish this and then get myself something to eat.'

She looked relieved. The mention of food made things seem

more normal. That's the kind of thing people came to Chinatown for, not to try and forget dark unspeakable sorrows. I needed to convince her I wasn't going to top myself so that she could go away in peace.

'We used to . . . I mean, I used to come here often with her. I just sort of got drawn back here today. I'm . . . I mean, I will be all right once I get home. Really.'

We got up together with a scraping of chairs. She still looked doubtful, holding on tightly to the strap of her handbag. How goddamned stupid of me to throw her into such confusion. And on her day out in London. I took her other hand, it felt papery and dry in my hot grasp. 'I'm really so terribly sorry you got dragged into this . . .'

'No, no, love, *I* stopped at your table, remember? I couldn't very well have walked past seeing you like that.'

'That's so kind. People aren't usually so kind in a city like this . . .' I looked across at the younger woman to signal that I hadn't really minded her reluctance to help.

She shuffled her feet in embarrassment and nodded. 'Yes, we do tend to be suspicious of everybody, don't we,' she mumbled.

The older woman was feeling better now. 'Well, all I can say is, I'm glad we're not like that in Waterford. None of these hard city ways among us, thank the Lord.'

We all smiled, the kind of smiles that didn't quite reach the eyes. The conversation was over. I didn't want to say any more in case they thought I was trying to prolong it, to hang on to them. There was an awkward pause. A group of youths wearing loose shirts and cropped, gelled hairstyles came up with their drinks.

'You goin', mate?'

'Yes, yes . . . it's all yours,' I said as we moved away from the table. I nodded again at the two women, giving them a very definite signal now. It's okay, ladies, drama's over, the lights are coming on and velvet curtains are descending. I watched while the girl took her companion's arm and guided her firmly out of the pub. In a couple of seconds the greedy, manic crowd had swallowed them up. 'What a terribly sad man,' the older woman would have exclaimed. 'Yes, well, it's hard to know what to believe and what not to believe these days,' the younger woman would have replied. Would they talk about me later as they went into another pub to finally have a drink in peace? Would they tell their friends and families about their strange encounter when they got home? How odd to think that they were among the first few people to know of Maya's death. Apart from the policemen at the scene of the accident who had called me . . . and the people in the hospital . . . and my folks in India over a humming telephone line. Surely there were plenty of other people I could have chosen from my phone book, or Maya's, if I needed to break down at all.

I still had my glass full of beer. From where I stood, the sign in the window of the pub read, sllieN'O, as if acknowledging that things were not the way they were meant to be at all. Outside, all those lucky people (on the right side of the glass) milled about, unconcerned, in the soft evening sunshine. Some reading restaurant menus in glass cases. Some smiling and laughing at a silver man standing on one foot. He moved only when someone threw a coin into his cap. His clothes, shoes, face and shiny bald pate were all painted silver. I had seen him before and had dragged Maya away, warning her that his accomplice would be around asking for money if we stopped for even a moment. Like the yellow man who stood on a yellow box further up Gerrard Street, they were all a part of the city's tourist attractions now. In places as far away as Karachi and Osaka, ex-tourists now asked each other if they had seen Big Ben and the Tower of London and the silver man of Soho.

I needed another drink, the other one had gone warm. This time, I found myself a very quiet corner and promised myself I would not blubber any more. I felt no anger, just surprise, that life around me was able to go on as normal. The group that had commandeered my old table was in rapidly escalating spirits. They looked like they had been drinking much before coming into O'Neills, their faces red and sweating, laughing, expletives and glottal stops piercing the air around them . . . fuckin' this, fuckin' tha' . . . . A courting couple were huddled together at the far table; an older couple were sitting nearer me, up from Gravesend or Orpington for a show, followed by a Chinese; two men were at the next table, gay maybe. Had Maya and I ever been looked at enviously by someone as alone as I was tonight? While *we* talked and laughed heedlessly? Oh God, I needed the loo.

I stumbled down the dark stairs and pulled open the door in a hurry. I wasn't sure which would come bursting forth first—beer-induced pee or another bloody bout of tears. Which should I go for first—face or flies? I burst into the dank toilet, shivering with the effort of holding on. The silver man was standing at one of the urinals. I took up my station next to him and we peed in companionable silence—he, no doubt appreciating my refraining from making any cheesy comment over his appearance, I appreciating his not mentioning my tears, rolling as rapidly out of me as my pee. We nodded at each other solemnly as we zipped up, acknowledging silently that the world wasn't always what it promised to be. I would have liked to tell Maya about this. She would have loved it—a silver man with golden pee. We would have laughed about it all the way home on the Northern Line.

I waited for the silver man to leave the toilet, which he did after a quick look at himself in the mirror to make sure his silvery get-up hadn't worn off anywhere. He didn't wash his hands, of course. I did, and my face, and blew my nose very loudly. It was over now. I was going to spend the rest of the evening without worrying about unexpected tears. Get myself something to eat. There wasn't a damn thing in the fridge at home. Just some cheese and milk. Sandra must have got rid of the leftovers from the meal

Maya cooked last night—aloo-mattar and daal, it had been. I had helped her with the rotis, standing next to her, buttering them, as she baled them out and cooked them, telling me about the Italian family she had visited in the morning. 'Social Services are going to take care orders out on the children,' she had said. 'That poor mother can't bear the thought of them going into foster care.' I found it hard sometimes when she talked about her work, all those abusive parents and desperate kids—it was a world too far removed from my own. I just wanted assurance that she wasn't putting herself at risk, going into all those people's houses. She was so good at what she did, as though she had found her calling in life, helping vulnerable women and children. Even though it was only voluntary work. She didn't have permission to work here because we had not been able to get married without her producing a divorce certificate.

She was agitated, talking all through dinner about how sad it would be to tear those kids away from their parents and how she hated to be a part of the whole messy business. 'Can't stand the idea of foster care,' she had said, 'leaving kids in sole charge of people whose motives you can never be too sure of . . . if you ask me, residential care is much better—at least there's safety in numbers.' I had attempted arguing the point that foster carers were screened and that her prejudices stemmed from the fact that it was a system unknown in India, but her views had seemed trenchant. That had been our last proper conversation. In the morning, we had rushed around as we always did, getting ready for work, shovelling breakfast down our throats . . . not knowing, not *knowing* . . .

Maya never liked to throw food away. 'I'll eat it for lunch tomorrow,' she had said, as we put leftovers from dinner into the fridge. 'Should be able to come home after the Capriano visit.' Was that what she had been doing? Racing to get home during lunch hour? To eat those goddamned leftovers? Driving too fast to notice that idiot coming at her through the red lights. Why couldn't something, anything, *anyone* have stopped her? The policeman had asked, 'Where do you think she might have been going, sir?' Does it matter, officer? I wanted to say. But I had stayed silent and he hadn't pressed me, of course. I wonder whether he had kicked himself later for asking such a stupid question. Everybody was trying to be kind, but it didn't seem to be working. I *could* have said, she was probably rushing home to eat last night's leftover daal and rotis, officer, because, even after three years in England, she still hated the thought of sandwiches for lunch and would go to any lengths to avoid them. Would he have written all that down in his little book? Crazy, isn't it? *If* she had just bought herself a sandwich from the shop down the road from the Women's Refuge, she might still be here. Here, with me, in this Soho pub. Sandra must have cleared all the leftovers out of the fridge. It must have been her, because I certainly hadn't and they were all gone when I got the milk out this evening.

My drink was finished and I walked down Gerrard Street, hands in my pockets, desperately missing the feel of Maya's arm in the crook of mine. A summer breeze was dispersing the heat of the day, I bent down and picked up a bit of newspaper that was getting entangled between my feet. I had never seen a Chinese newspaper before. Carrying news of muggings and robberies in Shanghai, no doubt, and the obituary of a bearded patriarch whose only trip to London was destined to happen in so ignominious a manner. He looked cross as I let go of the paper and watched it blow and drift down the street aimlessly. He and I could be twin souls, I thought, brought, by design or accident, to this country. Me, to get an English education many years ago; him, wrapping pak choi and Chinese greens in their crates. We were both equally incongruous among these happy faces. And equally dead, at the moment.

The old Chinese pan-pipe guy was at his usual corner, playing the theme from *Titanic* again. I was sure he knew no other tune. It couldn't be coincidence that every time I walked by, he happened to be playing the same one. Tonight it didn't sound too bad, surprisingly. He was playing it with feeling for some reason today, probably hoping that the group of Americans clustered around him, talking in loud voices, were in generous mood. I let the plaintive notes swirl around me as I stopped outside one of Chinatown's new places—big inviting windows showing off modern interiors and white (cloth, not paper) tablecloths—and read its menu. This was what Dad called 'time-pass'. The mindless occupation of time spent in useless endeavours. 'Indians,' Dad liked to say, mysteriously excluding himself from that group, 'are past masters at time-pass,' as he gazed irritatedly out of the car window at the hundreds of office workers lounging around playing card at two p.m. on the lawns around Connaught Place in Delhi. 'No wonder our country is in the deplorable state it is'. Poor Dad, now condemned to endless time-pass himself, stuck in his wheelchair, dying a slow, mysterious death. Five years and they didn't even know what it *was* yet . . . and so they continued to pump him full of steroids, making his wait for the end both agonizing and somehow hopeful.

He had worked far too hard all his life, though, wanting little for himself and a lot for us, his two sons. Foreign educations, flashy jobs. He must have been pleased, one son in the US, the other in England. 'Both earning *very* well, thank the good lord,' he liked to say. I hadn't quite inherited Dad's passion for hard work, grumbling as loudly as my workmates about our long hours. But tonight—tonight I'm *entitled* to some time-pass too, Dad. If I didn't allow my time to be spent mindlessly, if I didn't just keep walking somewhere, anywhere, I would go stark staring mad. True, I wasn't really interested in the menu of the brand-new and gleaming Mr Wong's; I was going to end up at Hoo Fung's as usual, with such excellent grub that it was difficult to mind the surly service. We had heard that people sometimes ate there just to check out if the waiters were really as rude as reputed. They are. They are as rude as hell, we would want to assure them as they queued up outside, wide-eyed and shivering in anticipation. Although we had only once spotted the waiters in real action—yelling high-pitched Chinese abuse at a group of Englishmen in suits with their ties askew who wisely got up and filed out, red-faced and silent. What had they *done*? we had wondered. Had they taken too long placing their order, had they underpaid, could they have asked, God forbid, for a dish to be *returned*? Didn't the poor sods *know* that everyone who entered these portals sensibly left all western notions of customer service out in the street before coming in? This was Hoo Fung's, for Chrissake, where you went in, obediently occupied the table you were ordered to, often huddled together with other nervous diners, barked your order, ate double-quick, paid up and left, sans pleasantries. If all you wanted was the best food (and the cheapest) Chinatown had to offer, that was what you did. That was what Maya and I had done, every Saturday, for three years now. Leaving Anjali at the babysitter's, our four hours alone together every week.

'HOW MANY?'

I was used to this abrupt greeting at the door. Not so used, however, to saying 'One' instead of the usual 'Two'.

'One,' I mumbled.

'WAN! WAN or THOO?'

Maybe, incredibly, he remembered me from previous visits! You never got a flicker of recognition out of them, though. But he was shouting, as if I might have got it wrong, just to mess his seating system up. Now, would I have got it wrong? *Would* I? Tonight? So soon after? I might, of course, on some distant night. But *tonight*, when I couldn't wipe it out of my mind, hard as I was trying, was I likely to make such an idiotic mistake?

'One,' I said again, very slowly and very calmly, pursing my lips, narrowing my eyes, hoping to signal my displeasure calmly.

'UPSTAIR,' he shouted, clattering a lot of dirty plates together.

I wended my way past the diners on the ground floor, guzzling and sweating among the steaming large vats of boiled noodles. Upside-down (marinated and roasted) ducks hung their heads sadly as I went past. At the first floor, I was waved peremptorily on again. No room. Upstair! The second floor was marginally more welcoming, although I was asked the same weary question again, 'How many?' All he had to do was *look*, the idiot, what did he mean, one or two, couldn't he see for himself! One, I said, coldly. This time it seemed to be less of a problem. One was easier to tuck in than two. One was so small and so insignificant, you could do anything with it, almost not notice it—squeeze it into that corner there, or compress it between these people here.

I was waved to a large round table with its odd assortment of eaters. Three girls were already tucking into large bowls of soup, I could catch the odd approving Spanish exclamation. Two young pimply fellows were watching the girls, slavering over either their choice of soup or their brown Latin American breasts bursting out of tee-shirts, I couldn't tell. A young English couple were ordering their food quickly and confidently. They must have been here before, they knew the rules. I slid unobtrusively into my seat, promising these happy diners silently that I would eat up and go home without ruining any of their evenings out. This was usually the point at which Maya and I shifted into Hindi, to be able to openly discuss our fellow diners and their food. Her Hindi wasn't too fluent, but she would have understood if I had said, '*Ya khaa ley, ya mammo pe ghoor le*', and gone into fits of giggles, no doubt. It was true, the young fellow's attention was certainly not on the noodles he was slurping; his eyes were firmly fixed on a boob bobbing pertly before his tortured gaze.

I turned my attention to the well-thumbed menu card. Must have Singapore noodles, we always have that. And roast duck and pork rice, Maya eating the duck, me the pork. Would that be too much for me on my own? Who would eat the duck? I was hungry and remembered suddenly that I hadn't eaten anything since that awful moment the phone rang at work just as I was returning from lunch with a half-eaten sandwich. 'There's been an accident, sir. We believe one of the persons involved might be your partner. Maya Warrier? She's in a serious condition at the A&E department at Kings in South London . . . do you know where that is, sir . . .?' Did they always use the words 'in a serious condition' when they really meant 'dead'?

'Ready?'

I looked uncomprehendingly at the waiter who had materialized at my elbow, pen poised over pad. Ready? Oh God, of course, I needed to place my order.

'Er . . . no, one minute please . . .' I fumbled over the menu card again. The waiter clicked his tongue in irritation and put his pad back in his pocket, muttering something in Chinese to his mate clearing the plates at the next table. I was normally the picture of efficiency here, ordering, eating and clearing out—Maya keeping up gamely—in under thirty minutes. I was certainly not used to being called a nincompoop in Chinese.

'Yes, yes, I have my order now . . .' I attempted calling him back.

'Wait,' he said brusquely. He was going to get someone else's order now, wreaking his little revenge on me for having upset his routine. I waited while he took an order at the next table, deposited the slip of paper on the restaurant counter, before making his way back to me, still looking at his pad. Look at me, you bastard, I thought to myself, I'm your customer, I'm paying for this, not asking you for a *favour* goddammit. But, to him I merely said, 'One Singapore noodles, one kung bao prawn and one plain boiled rice.' He scribbled in his pad, the surly expression on his face remaining unchanged. Did he have a woman at home who loved him?

The chatter around me was rising and waning in waves that rocked me, occasionally engulfing me. I looked around. There were some lone diners like me, thankfully. Who were all these people— I had never noticed them before. What made lonely people seek out places filled with the chatter of happy souls who looked like they had never experienced a lonely day even once in their lives? And where did lonely people fix their gazes if they had no one to look at or talk to? How many times was it permissible to look nonchalantly around a room? The windows were too far away to look out of. If I didn't look around the room, I would have to look at the faces of the people sitting around my table. They wouldn't want that, especially as they struggled with their chopsticks and noodles. I sympathized suddenly with the pimply youth's gaze at the Latin American boobs—at least he was gazing honestly at his chosen subject. I turned my attention to the sauces on the table, an odd assortment of bottles and vials and a glass tumbler with chilli oil, its sediment of dried chillies at the bottom. There was a bottle of Kikkoman's soya, just like the one at home—we had taken to buying that brand ever since we noticed it at Hoo Fung's. If anyone knew their soya sauces, it had to be these guys, we had decided. Our attempts at Chinese cooking had all been unmitigated disasters, though my efforts turned out marginally better than Maya's. I'm going to stick to cooking my Kerala food, she had declared, and Hoo Fung's is just a tube ride away whenever we fancy Chinese food. Which had been roughly once a week, Saturday evenings, sometimes going to the cinema or into Haagen Dazs before returning home. Coffee for me, cakey chocolatey things for her.

I had finished examining the sauces now, what next? I could ask for the chilli sauce to be topped up. There was only a tiny bit of the dried chillies under the hot red oil. That was the bit I liked over my rice, although I figured it was the oil that the Chinese use to lace their soups with. A plate was clattered in front of me.

The Singapore noodles always came first, steaming into my face deliciously.

'Could I have some more chilli sauce, please?' I asked while he cleared the soup bowls away.

'Finish that first,' he said, jabbing his chin at the glass tumbler.

I was always prepared for rudeness here, but sometimes their irascibility was astounding. I repeated my request as calmly as I could. I was feeling reckless. Very slowly, I said, 'I'd like some more chilli in that sauce please, I don't mean the oil.'

For the first time I had eye contact. His mate was saying something to him in Chinese that I couldn't understand but it sounded as if he might be telling him to tell me where to get off. I held his inscrutable gaze for a few moments, sensing a ripple go around the table. Spanish eyes were looking on wide-eyed; the pimply youth had finally taken his eyes off the bursting boobs; hardened, old Hoo Fung customers breathlessly waited to see what would happen next.

'No,' he barked, 'no more chilli sauce, plenty in there.'

'There isn't bloody plenty in there, can't you see?' I said loudly, lifting the tumbler and jerking it under his face. He took a step back, anticipating a stream of chilli oil across his shirt and in his eyes. The soup bowls clattered against his chest. His eyes went a hard black, like small bits of jet gleaming angrily in his face. It was his turn to shout now.

'GET OUU' . . .' he screeched, eyes vanishing into his puckered face.

'Oh, with pleasure,' I said, jumping up. 'I don't know what the *hell* I'm doing here anyway. The next time I'm looking to punish myself, I'll be sure to be back. For now, just stick this where it hurts most, will you.' I thumped the tumbler of chilli oil upside down on the table and watched it spread its oily tentacles across the paper tablecloth. Now both waiters were screaming incoherently at me. They couldn't have rushed at me even if they wanted, weighed down with dirty plates as they were. I thought I caught the words 'pig' and 'animal'. Fellow diners were all looking up, noodles hanging limply out of gaping mouths. I stalked out of the room and down the stairs, Chinese abuse ringing in my ears. I was half expecting a kitchen knife to come zinging through the air to land with a bone-crunching thump between my shoulder blades, but it didn't. At this point in time, that possibility was hardly likely to either worry or frighten me.

I stepped out into the darkening Soho night, feeling strangely uplifted. A thin drizzle had broken out and I lifted my face to its freshness. Neon signs were flashing wondrous promises at me. Girls-girls-girls, said one. A girl—no, woman (forty something, maybe even fifty)—stood smoking a cigarette in the doorway, shivering in a latex miniskirt and fishnet stockings. I walked on, past her and past video parlours and restaurants, in the direction of the tube station. I could feel a semblance of control return to my life. I didn't have to take every bit of shit that came my way. Some shit couldn't be helped, but some could and it was good to know I hadn't forgotten how to deal with the latter sort.

I quickened my steps and ducked into the warmth of Leicester Square tube station as the drizzle hardened into a patter. Girls in miniskirts were tottering up the stairs, squealing like piglets. On their way to be slaughtered, I would have said wryly to Maya. She liked silly puns, especially ever since she became familiar with Britspeak. A bedraggled man sat on the wet floor, staring blankly in front of him. Homeless, said a small explanatory piece of cardboard at his feet. I reached into my pocket and threw the coin he would almost certainly have received from Maya into his upturned cap. At least I had a home and a bed to go back to. And a television on which *something* would be showing. My stomach rumbled angrily at me as I pushed through the turnstiles. And there was also that Chinese takeaway on the way home from the tube station. That would do for tonight.

eight

I woke up sweating, screaming car tyres resounding in my ears. What time was it? God, three a.m.! I got out of bed and staggered to the loo. The small red light on our telephone answering machine was flashing insistently in the darkness of the study. I must have forgotten to check it last night. It could wait. I had a vague sense, through my sleep-addled brain, that all the important things had happened anyway. Whatever was left could definitely wait. I staggered to the bathroom and relieved myself noisily. Feeling my bladder return to painless repose, I returned to my room and threw myself down on my bed again.

An hour later, I was still awake, gazing at dark shapes on the ceiling, very conscious of the emptiness of the bed next to me. There was no point fighting my inability to sleep. I pulled myself up and padded to the telephone.

'You have three new messages,' it intoned nasally. I jabbed blearily at it again in the half-darkness. Aha, a human voice. 'Hi Rahul, it's Kevin. Just checking on you, mate. Give us a call when you get back. Bye.' I jabbed again. A quavery voice came on. I melted at the maternal, caring tone, wanting to reach out in the darkness to touch her. 'Beta Rahul, it's Mummy. Are you okay, darling?' She was speaking slowly, searching for the words. 'Where are you . . . call me up as soon as you can, beta, your dad and I were worrying about you . . . we just felt like speaking to you again . . .' I leaned my head against the metal frame of the shelf on which the phone sat. It felt cool against my hot skin. Poor Mum and Dad, they could have done without this. So far away. And Dad now so weak and in so much physical pain himself. I pressed the button again. 'Oh, hello? Mr Tiwari? This is Elizabeth Hawke, the social worker who visited you earlier, calling from the Faunce Way Children's Home. I was just calling to ask if Anjali had any particular night-time routine before going to bed. We're trying to make things as normal as possible for her, of course. Do call me as soon as you're able to. Thank you.'

Yes, of course, Anjali had a night-time routine. A much-loved night-time routine filled with squeals and giggles. Starting with her and her mother closing me out of the bathroom, making a big thing of Boys-Not-Allowed. Maya said we had to teach her early on about modesty and what was appropriate and so on. Sometimes, if I was bored, I would stand outside the bathroom door, banging on it, pretending I wanted to be let in, just to wind Anjali up and hear her scream her indignation. Then, after I had been properly shooed off, Maya gave Anjali her bath and helped her into her pyjamas. She still needed help with things like hooks and buttons at the back. Next came the nightly exchange of great big cuddles and noisy nuzzles for which I was called to join in, with the imperious yell of 'Papa' floating up the staircase. Then, as her mother made numerous attempts to leave the room, she used one excuse after another to keep her back. 'Hair hurting,' she would say, tugging at her minuscule ponytail, or 'Ear itching', something, anything, to bring her mother back into the bedroom before relinquishing her to me. That was the thing she didn't care for much. That I was still allowed to be up, chatting and laughing with her mum. Why can't *he* be put to bed too, she must have been thinking in that funny little head of hers. Might that be what she was imagining now, poor kid? That we had sent her off so we could be alone together. Like we did whenever we had our weekly babysitting arrangement. God, I couldn't bear to imagine what she was thinking about all this. Why didn't I think of calling the children's home about her bedtime routine before I went out? I was only thinking about myself and how awful I felt. How could I have forgotten about Anjali for Chrissake—Maya would never forgive me for that.

She had seemed okay earlier today, waving happily as the social worker held her in the frame of the window when I left her at the children's home. She helped me pack a small bag before we left the house, racing to her chest of drawers to fetch pants and vests, excited at the thought of an unexpected holiday. 'Where's Mum?' she asked a couple of times, after she was brought back from the nursery by her teacher and the social worker, not seeming too bothered at my vague, mumbled replies. Well, she was certainly used to being separated from Maya with her occasional trips to the babysitter's or to Sandra's. How long would it be before it would dawn on her that she had never stayed away from her mum for more than one night before. Would she notice, as day turned into night and then into day again that something was different this time. That her mother had not called for her. Did kids, kids of four, have a really good concept of time and things like that? Who was going to tell her and what words would they use to explain that her mum had gone and would never be back? Were social workers trained in telling children that their mothers had just *died*, for God's sake?

They had certainly seemed to know their stuff today, when the world first fell apart and I just sat there, unable to even think coherently. Sandra had called them to explain, and one of them had brought Anjali home from school. I had never seen this woman, Elizabeth Hawke, before. She looked very young, but with a stern face, lots of frizzy hair and dangly earrings. I wished I could remember if Maya had ever mentioned having met her whenever her work took her to the department of children's services. It somehow felt very important to know if Maya had liked her as she seemed to be the person making the decisions about Anjali now.

'Mr Tiwari, I'm aware that you are not Anjali's biological father and I need to ask you whether you have parental responsibility for Anjali?' she had said, sitting on the edge of our sofa, looking awkward with her knees pressed tightly together, sandalled feet splayed apart.

'Yes, of course, I've felt very responsible for her since she became a part of my life. I am her other parent, I suppose.'

'Of course,' she replied more gently, 'I should have explained better. Parental responsibility would have been granted by a court of law if you had applied for it. Have you any recollection of having done that?'

'No, I don't think so. What does that mean?'

A worried look came across her face. 'Well, what it means at the moment is that you cannot give us authorization on decisions to be made on Anjali's behalf.'

I stared blankly at her. 'But I've helped . . . Maya, you know, my . . . my partner . . . with Anjali's care for about three or four years now. Surely that should count for something.'

'Of course, of course,' she said, a placatory note in her voice, 'it must have sounded awful. Of *course* your wishes for Anjali will be taken into consideration as well. Unfortunately, legally we will need someone else's permission for decisions on Anjali's future.'

'Someone else's? Whose? There is no one else in England.'

'I know, I have been told, by Sandra your neighbour, that you have no family in this country.'

'So who's responsible for her now? Are you saying I can have nothing to do with her?'

'Oh, of course not, Mr Tiwari. Do you think you *will* be able

Jaishree Misra

to care for Anjali, though? I mean, this is all very difficult for you too, isn't it?'

'Yes it is.' I knew I was being unnecessarily short with this poor young woman, but I couldn't seem to help myself. 'But I see no reason why I shouldn't be able to manage things with Anjali. This is terrible for her and she needs as much of my support as possible.'

'Of *course*, we all agree on that. For now, perhaps it's best we focus on the situation immediately at hand. What do you think we should do with Anjali tonight? Can I suggest a couple of options?'

I looked at her, unable to think of more arguments, even though I was itching, illogically, for a disagreement.

'What options?'

'Well, she could either stay here, with you, and we could arrange for a peripatetic social worker to come in and help with her care. I don't know how you feel about that. I have to say that could only be a temporary arrangement anyway.'

I had forgotten about bath and all the things Maya had always done for Anjali. In my anger at this woman and at the world, I hadn't wanted to think of all that.

She was still speaking, sounding more sure of herself now, 'Or, we could arrange for Faunce Way to provide emergency cover, seeing that they're already familiar with her . . . she stayed with them recently when her mother had a miscarriage, I believe. The third option, of course, would be foster care.'

'No, not foster care,' I said quickly. I was sure Maya would not want that. She had not wanted it even on that ghastly night when she was rushed into hospital, bleeding, miscarrying our child. Our child—now there never would be one, of course. Strange how my losses seemed to be accruing gradually in my mind, as though someone knew I wouldn't have been able to cope had they been presented to me all at once.

'I could try to have Anjali stay on here with you, if we sent a social worker in for a few hours perhaps?' She sounded as though she was thinking aloud. 'Although she'll probably have to go to Faunce Way at some point as it's difficult to get the same peripatetic worker in all the time. We don't really want a succession of carers, do we?'

I sat staring vacantly at the social worker. Yes, of course, I wanted Anjali here with me, I was used to having her buzz around the house. For that matter, I wanted Maya here with me too. Now, try and solve that little problem, I wanted to say. Let's think of what kind of orders needed to be revoked for that one. Parental responsibility could pale into beautiful insignificance against the ghastly rules that governed who died, and when and why. Why, in God's name, *why*? What was I *doing*, sitting with a social worker, talking about how Anjali would cope without Maya? How was *I* going to cope? This was some sort of mad dream. It had to be. Things like this happened in the movies, not to ordinary people like us! What the hell was parental responsibility anyway? I had been Anjali's parent for . . . what was it—two and a half years? Nearly three years of her four . . . I had taken my responsibility seriously. I loved that crazy kid, however maddening she was sometimes. Why were we jumping through all these goddamned hoops now, on this crazy unreal, unending day? Why couldn't I reach out to that clock ticking cheerfully on the wall and turn it back, to yesterday, when everything was fine, when Maya was here, sitting with her feet tucked under her, on that sofa, reading something after Anjali had been put to bed. She had looked up when I asked if she wanted a coffee. (Do you want me to do it? . . . No, I'll get it . . .) At which she had smiled, turning her attention back to her book, the light from the pedestal lamp turning her hair into black gold. In fact, there it was! Her book, half-read and waiting to be finished, open and upside down, on top of the CD rack. I was looking at it in surprise, as if it should have known better than to be waiting there so foolishly to be picked up again.

'Mr Tiwari?'

I looked at the social worker. A great indissoluble lump seemed to have lodged squarely in my throat.

'Mr Tiwari, you're upset, I can see. I want to be able to help you. If you don't mind my suggesting it, it will probably be best for Anjali to go into foster care for a few days. We might not be able to find an Asian family at such notice, but I'm sure we could find someone good.'

'Please, not foster care,' I said again. This I could clearly remember Maya saying. That there was safety in numbers when a child was in a group home as opposed to being in a foster home. An idea she had probably picked up from one of her cases at the Refuge. There must be good foster carers around, she had said, but I seem to keep meeting the ones who are clearly in it only for the money. 'I'm sure Maya would not have wanted foster care for Anjali,' I said more resolutely. 'We don't have such a system in India and she could never cope with it. Please.'

'I respect that,' Elizabeth Hawke replied, 'we must respect that. But I could arrange for an emergency place for Anjali at Faunce Way for a few days. I'll make sure she's kept busy and happy there. I do think you need some space to yourself to grieve too, don't you?'

Her face suddenly looked yellow under the lights. Long lines had appeared on her forehead with the effort of concentrating on choosing words carefully. 'Mr Tiwari, do you think you could help me put a few things together for Anjali? Just some emergency things. We will, of course, be popping in to collect more things as and when necessary, if you don't mind. And you'll be able to visit her at the home too, of course . . .' She trailed off as I got up and made my way silently to Anjali's room. Up the stairs, past our bedroom, the bed neatly made, she had done it this morning . . .

Anjali was sitting cross-legged on the floor in her room, cross-eyed in intense concentration, cutting a piece of paper into tiny shreds. She was bent over double with the effort of doing so, her hair falling all over her face.

'Don't hold that paper so close to your face or you'll end up cutting your nose off,' I said absently. Wasn't force of habit a wonderful thing, perhaps the very thing that secretly held the world together.

'Where's Mum?' she asked without looking up, ignoring my admonition completely.

She was very good at those. Those one-line stumpers. Language had, for a while, been her biggest problem in adjusting to life in England. Malayalam and English had at first congealed into one big inseparable mess, before she went through a silent phase, preferring not to say very much at all. We consulted a language specialist at the time, at a local speech therapy centre, who suggested she just be given time to adjust to all the changes in her life. It wasn't too long before she had learnt to tackle English, but still had a very un-English manner of zooming right into the crux of whatever matter was at hand, invariably cutting through the crap with a masterful economy of words. Just a sentence or two, that was all she ever thought was necessary to make herself understood, but somehow she made it seem enough.

'Where's Mum!' she demanded more stridently. Silence was rubbish as a reply.

I squatted on the floor next to her, picking up some shredded paper in my hand, allowing it to drift through my fingers like snow. Watching it fall, careful not to make eye contact, I said, 'Mum's gone away. She wants you to go with that nice lady to that children's home. You know, that Faunce Way home. You liked going there that time, didn't you?'

'I don't want the lady. I want Mum.' She had on her 'I'm-taking-no-nonsense' look.

'Mum couldn't stay, sweetie, to take you there. That's why the lady's come. She's a nice lady, *pretty* too. Big dangly earrings. Great, big Ford Fiesta car to take you out in. Look, you can see it parked outside the window.'

Anjali stuck her lower lip out. I could see her mentally cutting through the crap. What pretty lady? Mum's much prettier. Far more desirable company on an outing in a car. I could feel myself agreeing with everything Anjali was thinking.

'Outing?' I asked, nevertheless, in a wheedling tone. 'The lady wants to take you out. You love outings. Maybe she'll take you somewhere nice.'

'Papa, come too,' she said.

I wasn't Mum, but I came a close second. Now wasn't that what parental responsibility ought to be about? Didn't common sense come into social work at all? How I hated all those social worker types, with their dangly earrings and pale sandalled feet, spouting silly social worker rules.

'Yeah, Papa too,' I said, lifting the little girl in my arms. Perhaps not so little any more, I thought, staggering a little as I stood up and then tottered exaggeratedly as she started to giggle. 'Why do I keep forgetting that you're growing at the speed of knots,' I puffed.

'No-o-o! Falling!' she screamed, clinging to my neck.

'Aaaargh . . . falling! Can't carry this sack of potatoes who's just pretending to be a girl called Anjali,' I said, attempting to swing her around. 'When did it get so big—aaaaargh!'

She was now screaming and laughing hysterically, little arms wrapped tight around my neck, as I staggered around her room, pretending to bump into chairs and tables. 'FALLING,' I yelled again, this time meaning it as I felt my foot get caught in Anjali's beanbag. Always, it was *always* in the wrong place, that goddamned beanbag, just waiting to trip me up. Still holding Anjali, I felt myself keel slowly over. The room turned ass over tit just as the bewildered social worker appeared at the door. Her mouth, which was now where her feet were meant to be, was a perfect round 'O' as we landed—me first, a screaming Anjali on top—in a splintering crash on Anjali's blue wooden bed.

Strange noises and voices were swirling around me as the world came to a slow, spinning stop. 'Mr Tiwari! Heavens *above*, the child! Get up, Anjali, are you okay? Come on, take my hand now, child. Mr Tiwari, what on *earth* were you doing!' Her voice was all high-pitched and indignant now, ringing horribly through fuzzy sounds in my ears. I pushed at Anjali who was wriggling on top of me, trying to get herself up. She was still giggling, having bounced quite firmly on top of me in our fall on to the bed. I, on the other hand, was sure that a few of my lower vertebrae had dislodged themselves in my sudden journey downwards. The bed— I would have to check the bed later—I was sure it was broken. The social worker had hauled Anjali off me and was examining her head and body while Anjali brushed her hands off in irritation. Gingerly feeling my back with one hand, I used the other to push myself into a sitting position. Anjali and her social worker were both standing in front of me now, the social worker glaring at me with baffled disapproval, Anjali bouncing up and down pleading hopefully, 'More, more!'

'I thought you came upstairs to pack some clothes for Anjali,' the woman said accusingly. I was sure I had no explanation that would sound adequate for the scene she had just witnessed and decided silence was less likely to incur further annoyance. Feeling thoroughly chastened at my puerile behaviour, I muttered an apology and ducked my head under the bed, pulling out a small overnighter from under it. Fat chance they would now ever consider me parentally responsible, I thought, suddenly very depressed again. I unzipped the bag in silence and removed a ball of dirty fluff that had gathered at the bottom. Still unsure about being able to get up, I reached out for the top drawer of Anjali's chest of drawers. I knew Maya kept all of Anjali's underwear in the top

Jaishree Misra

drawer. There they were, all washed and folded, vests, pants and socks. I was pleased the social worker could see how neat and organized everything was. At least she would know Maya was a responsible parent, even though my own credentials were severely in doubt.

Feeling my heart settle firmly into the region of my feet, I started to put small items of clothing into the bag. Three vests, three pants, three pairs of socks, tartan pyjamas, tee-shirts, two pairs of jeans, a sundress. I got up slowly, testing my limbs, and went into the bathroom—bottles and tubes gleamed darkly at me. I picked out a few—toothbrush, deodorant, talc, bubble-bath—dropping them into a carrier bag I found in the cupboard under the sink. Will she need a towel? Will that do for the weekend? What will happen *after* the weekend, ma'am? Do you think you might be able to get another legal order that would return things to normal again? Just so that our little family can be together again? Just for a day or two . . . please ma'am . . .

I returned to Anjali's bedroom with the toiletries. She was helping the social worker stuff a few books into the side pocket of her bag. Now she was excited, this was all vaguely reminiscent of holidays and weekends away. 'Waydio?' she asked me, picking up her tape recorder. I nodded. 'Telly?' I shook my head. 'Papa come?' she asked, unhappy with the expression on my face. I nodded again, not trusting myself to speak.

Zipped and ready, the bag waited ominously on the bed, while I combed Anjali's hair down, securing it with a clip. I didn't usually have to do things like that, but I knew the routine, thankfully, and only fumbled slightly with the tiny plastic butterfly hair-grip as the social worker looked on. I wondered whether she was noticing how trustingly Anjali was allowing me to hold her chin and comb her hair down, only going 'ouch' once, and that too for effect, as I slid the plastic butterfly in. The social worker said nothing, but nodded approvingly as I looked at her to signal our readiness.

Silently, we filed down the stairs, the social worker leading the way, Anjali leaping down in happy, careless double-step jumps, me clutching the bag and holding on tightly to the banisters. Bloody hell, I was feeling almost nauseous now, although that could have been due to the fall.

Outside, the birds were singing raucously in the trees. It was going to be a beautiful clear night. 'It would probably be best if you came, too, Mr Tiwari, just to settle her in.' I nodded. Had I swallowed my tongue in that fall?

'Do you have a car?' she asked carefully. She was thinking, I knew, about the other one that had been towed away this afternoon, a mangled heap. I nodded again. She looked relieved. 'Could you follow me, perhaps in your car? So that I can stay on there with Anjali to settle her in after you've gone.'

I went back into the house to get my keys. I turned a few lights on, a habit I had acquired from Maya who didn't like returning to a dark house. Everything seemed so silent, so wrong. As I walked back to the car, I could see Anjali already perched on a booster seat in the Ford Fiesta next to the social worker. She was waving a boisterous farewell to Sandra who had materialized at the gate next door. Sandra's face was white and her mouth was working silently, although her arm was waving enthusiastically back at Anjali. I nodded at her, although what I really wanted to do was thank her for her silent help earlier in the afternoon. I knew I couldn't talk to her today and hoped she would understand.

Getting into my car, I followed the Fiesta as it slowly made its way down the quiet road towards the crowded main road. Rush-hour traffic in London—how often had I warned Maya of how careful she had to be. I could see Anjali's head bobbing excitedly in the car in front as I tailed it through the evening traffic. Every so often, I could see her head swivel around, making sure I was still there.

In less than five minutes we were pulling up outside the Faunce

Way Home. I had been here once before, on that terrifying and frantic night when Maya had to be rushed to hospital as she started to miscarry. Unfamiliar faces were now opening the door and letting us in, shaking our hands, offering us tea and chatting to Anjali. Had any of these people ever met Maya? They all seemed so eager to be kind, no one was putting a foot wrong. They were all wearing uniformly calm expressions, exuding that peculiarly British combination of briskness and kindliness. God, I needed some Indian breast-beating and wailing at this point in time. Some goddamn release from that tight knot that seemed to be taking over my insides.

Anjali seemed to remember some of the staff members, smiling at them in shy recognition. She followed a pleasant-looking young girl into the kitchen to examine the contents of a fridge. Where were all the other kids? I could hear distant chatter and laughter, but it looked like they had all been mindfully tucked away to make way for us. I knew I ought to feel grateful, for the care and the attention we were being given, but I couldn't wait to get out. Anjali had vanished into the bowels of the home anyway, there was nothing more for me to do here. I got up and asked to leave, trying not to sound impolite, ungrateful. The kindly faces were all nodding in sympathy and agreement. Someone called for Anjali to come out and say goodbye. I wasn't sure I wanted that, but it turned out to be easier than expected. She came back into the room, still tailed by one of the residential workers, swaggering now and showing off to me her familiarity with this place. 'Bye bye, Papa,' she yelled exuberantly, making everyone laugh. I reached down and gave her a quick hug. 'See you tomorrow, baby,' I whispered and left. As quickly as I could.

She was at the window, with the social worker holding her, as I reversed out of the car park. She looked happy, waving energetically. Well, she seemed sorted for the moment, maybe there was something to be said for the social services department in this country after all. I had never been sure they played any really useful role. How come we've always managed without them in India, I had argued with Maya once. My theory being that they only served to make families *less* responsible. But she hadn't agreed with me, very impressed with all the things we could never hope to have in India. And now, perhaps she was vindicated.

I drove on autopilot, aimlessly traversing familiar roads, not making an effort to get back home. I couldn't go back there, I thought in sudden panic. Not without Maya or Anjali around to lift the silence, to fill spaces up with their noisy warmth. I swung under a sign for Waterloo Bridge, ignoring the angry toot I received for doing that. The rush-hour traffic had reduced considerably and I drove slowly across the bridge, looking at the sky turn pink behind the Houses of Parliament. Maya loved the view from here— 'the best in London' she used to say. I needed to be somewhere busy, somewhere thronging with people. Soho. I turned left at the Strand. I would park somewhere, walk to a tube station, drown myself in the Chinatown crowds, get myself something to eat . . . that was how I landed up at Hoo Fung's. I didn't really want a meal out. In fact, I eventually got through the night without eating anything at all. The thing was—what do you *do* with yourself when something like this happens? At home in India, I suppose I would have been surrounded by family and we would have been kept fairly busy, receiving other members of our family as they arrived from distant places. We probably would have all sat around in a kind of communal tut-tutting with some occasional wailing from the room where the women sat. But I came from one of those modern dispersed families that people like Dad took immense pride in. 'One in San Francisco, one in London,' he liked to boast to anyone who would listen.

We had loved our life here, Maya and I. London, we both knew, had given us the space without which our relationship might not have grown and survived. But now, in this big, crazy, coveted city,

I didn't have a clue where to take my grief. Do I ring up friends, acquaintances and workmates and *tell* them? Slip it gently into the conversation, perhaps . . . er . . . you'll never believe this . . . Maya's just died! But . . . you don't call people in their warm, snug homes with bad news. You called them if you wanted to arrange to meet them for a game of squash two weeks from now. You called them if you planned to meet at a restaurant in central London the following Saturday—and then keyed it in your digital diary. It didn't fit in with the rules of this very busy, very important, swinging, cool place, to go and become needy, for heaven's sake. People only wanted to know you if you didn't *need* to know them— that was how it worked.

I remember having always managed within the solitude of this big city before. I was the sort who was perfectly content with his own company. But that was before Maya. Before she came along, with little Anjali, to fill up the life that, without my realizing so, had been a pretty empty one until then. Now I knew that if you didn't have your home and your family to return home to, you were no better than those poor sods huddled with their mangy curs under cardboard boxes.

———————

I knew it was a sunny day well before opening my eyes. The insides of my eyelids were glowing red embers. I kept them closed for a while, watching the fires swirl into different patterns. Just before opening my eyes, it came to me. Like a sharp electric shock jabbing out from the sleep that had briefly engulfed me. She's gone. She's dead, it said.

I opened my eyes, wondering why I was bothering to. Despite having slept, I felt no less tired. Same room—painting of Indian dancer on one wall, Rajasthani mirror-work piece on the other, some sort of flowering plant on the window sill, bursting inanely with cheerful violet blooms. How often would the damn thing need watering? The phone started to ring with a piercing insistence. I stumbled out of bed and jabbed at its speaker button as I raced into the adjoining toilet. A cheery voice floated behind me into the toilet.

'Rahul, hi, it's me—Kevin.'

'Kev, hi,' I responded, emptying my bladder.

'Rahul? Where are you, what's that sound?'

'It's bloody me trying to take a leak in peace, do you mind?'

'Oh, sorry,' he sounded relieved, 'you sounded like you were drowning in the bathtub. Do you normally answer the phone while performing in the john?'

'Hang on,' I shouted, washing my hands and face before walking back to the phone. 'Yeah, hi Kev, sorry about that.'

'Never mind, I just called to find out how you were. I'd called last night and left a message.'

'I know. I'd gone out for something to eat.'

'Are you all right, Rahul?'

Good question. Was I all right? I hadn't got around to analysing my feelings this morning yet. It felt like a dangerous thing to do. 'Yeah, I think so. As much as can be expected at this point in time, I suppose.'

'I'm calling from work, so I can't talk for long. I just wanted to check that you're still on for me to come down to see you tonight.'

From *work*. Christ, it was as if I had forgotten that the world existed at all. 'Yeah, yeah. Tonight's still good. Is . . . is . . . hmm . . . will you be alone?'

'I was going to ask you, will it be okay if Carol came too?'

Oh damn! 'Yeah, sure, that'll be fine.'

'We'll stay till Sunday morning. Would that be okay?'

'Yeah, yeah, of course.'

'Is there anything you'd like us to bring? Some food or shopping or anything?'

'No, nothing . . . perhaps we can do some shopping while you're here.'

'Yeah, all right.'

There were a few seconds of silence. Even conversations with old friends needed to be considered carefully and then recast, the way things were. Wasn't anything ever going to be normal again?

'Is Anjali okay in that place?' he asked.

'She is, by all accounts, Kev. I don't think she quite knows what's going on yet.'

'I know nothing about kids' psychology, of course. I guess those social workers know what they're doing.'

'Yeah . . .' I trailed off. Those very thoughts were excruciating,

I could hardly bear to formulate them into words. 'Right then,' I said, trying to sound brisk, 'I'll see you and Carol this evening. What sort of time will it be?' As if it mattered in the slightest what time they were to arrive in the midst of the very un-busy schedule I had stretching ahead of me.

'It'll take us a couple of hours, I suppose. But I'm trying to get away early. Sevenish?'

'Okay, fine, I'll see you then,' I said before hanging up. I looked at my watch. It was nearly half past ten, which left about eight hours for me to think of something to do before Kevin and his girlfriend arrived. Shave, I told myself. The five 'shs'—they always made me feel better, whatever the crisis at hand. Shave, shit, shampoo, shag and shower. And, if I took as long as I could getting myself ready, the routine could take up the next two hours easily. I made my way back to the bathroom.

It was when my face was covered in lather that the phone rang again. Could be Mum and Dad, I thought, washing my hands hurriedly.

'Hello?'

'Ah, hello Mr Tiwari, I hope I didn't disturb you. It's Elizabeth Hawke again, the social worker.'

'Yes, hi, no you didn't disturb me. I was meaning to call you. How's Anjali?'

'She's been fine, actually. Asked for you . . . and for her mum . . . a couple of times, but in a very natural sort of way. There didn't seem to be any trauma there . . .' she trailed off.

'Would it be possible for me to see her, take her out perhaps?'

Did I sense a moment's hesitation before she said quickly, 'Yes, of course. When would you like to do that? You see, the children's home needs prior information of visits as they tend to plan their day quite early on themselves.'

'Sure. Later this morning perhaps. Around twelve? I could buy her lunch and take her to the zoo or park or something.'

Jaishree Misra

'Yes, I'm sure she'll enjoy that.'

Of course, she'll bloody enjoy that, I thought, feeling yesterday's rush of blood to my brain again. I think I know my little girl just a little better than you do, Ms Hawke. I have been, alternately, her Unka (she still reverted to that sometimes, depending on how fondly she was feeling towards me), and Papa (for the times I called her Nicole in a phoney French accent, copying the man in the Peugeot ad) for, let's see now, *three* good years. I don't bloody need a social worker's suggestions now on what Anjali would want to do. For years, Maya and I had decided and shared out our elaborate Keeping-Anjali-Entertained-Timetable on weekends. Taking it in turns, trawling through the children's section of Hot Tickets to find things Anjali would be interested in. I had always tried not to mind that I got so little time with Maya alone, although she sometimes felt a little guilty, I think. I had taken her on with Anjali in tow and the little girl had always been as much a part of my life as Maya herself was. Now that the world had turned upside down, what was the bloody problem with Social Services? I could feel myself slipping into adversarial mode again but was outwardly silent.

'Well, I'll inform Faunce Way that you wish to see Anjali at around noon today, shall I?'

'Yes, to take her out,' I said firmly.

There was another moment's hesitation before she said, 'Yes, of course.'

'All right then . . .'

I was about to hang up but she cut in quickly, 'Actually, Mr Tiwari, I was calling for something else. Would it be possible . . . you haven't by any chance got Anjali's *father's* address and telephone number on you, have you?'

'Ms Hawke, I think I've already told you, as far as Anjali knows, I am her father.'

'Yes, of course, I have no intention of denigrating the importance of your role in Anjali's life, Mr Tiwari, but—'

I cut in, letting her feel the cold jagged anger of my words, 'If, by "father" you're referring to Maya's ex-husband, I think you ought to be aware that he lives in Kerala, halfway around the world. You also need to know that he was of pitifully little help to Maya when Anjali was a baby. He was, in fact, one of the main reasons why Maya fled from there. With Anjali. All those years ago.'

Ms Hawke sounded rattled by the tone of my voice, but ploughed on, 'Well, we do need to inform him of . . . of . . .'

I wasn't going to help her. Let her say those words herself, I thought, knowing the kind thing to do was to allow them to remain unsaid by cutting in quickly with something else.

She waited a moment, expecting, like any decent person would, that I was about to let her off the hook, say something, anything, to stop those terrible words from being said. Come on, say them, I thought sneering inwardly. You think it's difficult for you? Try, just for a moment, try getting into *my* head, Ms Hawke. Even over the telephone her struggle was apparent.

'Mr Tiwari, you're not suggesting that we do not inform him at all of . . . of Mrs Warrier's accident, are you?'

There, she had said them. Mrs Warrier's Accident. As if it were some sort of annual event, or a brand-new comedy showing now on the London fringe scene. Starring Art Malik and Madhur Jaffrey, a rollicking new production by Asianarts. Unmissable. *Mrs Warrier's Accident.*

'Accident!' I exploded. Imagine coming up with an euphemism at a moment of extreme crisis! 'An *accident*, for Christ's sake? She's dead, Ms Hawke, dead! All that's left is that poor little kid in a children's home who doesn't even know it yet. Who will probably not understand what's going on when somebody does tell her. I don't think any of you are really aware of what she needs at this time. Like it or not, I'm bringing her back here. Today!'

'Mr Tiwari, I know this is so terrible for you, but, as a childcare social worker, it is my duty to see that Anjali is looked after as best as possible at this terrible time.'

'Has it occurred to you that that might be precisely what I aim for myself?'

'I believe I explained to you yesterday, Mr Tiwari, that there is a genuine problem in your not having parental responsibility for Anjali. We do need to be acting on such a person's permission, while keeping Anjali's future welfare in mind. Unfortunately, legally speaking—'

'Ms Hawke, at this point in time, it matters very little to me what my legal responsibilities are. What I do know is that Maya's gone, leaving me to sort out something half-decent for her daughter. What that is, I'm not sure yet, but I'm working on it, I tell you, legally, emotionally and financially—whether you like it or not.'

'We have no problem with that, Mr Tiwari. In fact, we would like very much for you to be involved as well in the plans we make for Anjali.'

We? Why did she keep calling herself, 'We'? Was she trying to *frighten* me by suggesting there was a whole brigade out there not just watching, but sanctioning my every move?

She wasn't giving up. 'In the meantime, I do need to ask you again, Mr Tiwari, for the telephone number of Anjali's biological father in India.'

'It might surprise you to know, Ms Hawke, that we were not exactly on a friendly footing, his perception being that I took his wife away from him three years ago. We are not in the habit of having long-distance chats just to say hello. If you need to find his number, I suggest you get yourself an Indian telephone directory.'

She was starting to say something further, trying to sound quietly assertive, but at that point I hung up. Sitting down heavily on my armchair, I buried my face in my hands, feeling the shaving foam squeeze gloopily through my fingers. Damn, damn, damn, damn, damn!

The telephone was ringing again. Was it going to be like this all day? If it was that social worker again, I was going to give her such a bollocking, she would never ever bother me in the future. I sprang out of my chair and jabbed a foamy forefinger at the speaker button with the fierceness of a playground bully poking someone in the eye.

'Beta, Rahul?'

'Mum . . .' I whispered, and started to cry.

'Beta, can you hear me?'

'Yes, yes, Mum,' I said, trying not to let her hear the tears.

'Oh, beta, where were you last night? We were so worried about you . . .'

'I know, Mum, I had to go out for some food.'

'Are you eating?'

She had never been a terribly good listener, dear Mum. Always asking questions which had already been answered. I skipped her question.

'How's Dad?'

'Not good, beta. He couldn't sleep all night, worrying about you.'

I could hear a scuffling at the end of the phone line before Dad's voice came gruffly down the line, 'Rahul, my son, what can I say to you . . . what can I say?'

I could tell he was crying. There was more scuffling, Mum was trying to get the phone back from him. She was worried about either him or me . . . or both of us, probably. I raised my voice, hoping she would hear me.

'Mum, it's okay, let him speak.'

Despite being in a wheelchair, Dad was obviously still stronger of the two. His voice reappeared on the line. I could hear him snap angrily at Mum, 'Yes, I know, I *know* how he feels . . .' and then, more gently, to me, 'Sorry son, tell me, how are you coping?'

'Okay, Dad, okay,' I said, lying through my teeth, glad that they couldn't see me now, clad only in a towel, in this room strewn carelessly with my clothes from last night, tears mingling messily with the shaving foam still on my cheeks. 'Are you all right, Dad? Mum said you haven't been sleeping well.'

'As well as can be expected, son . . . how can a father cope with such terrible news, eh?' There was more scuffling, this was exactly the kind of conversation Mum had wanted to avoid.

'Anil's arriving next weekend,' I said, trying to sound as if that would end our collective grief. I was fond enough of my younger brother, but couldn't think exactly what his arrival would achieve.

'Yes, I know, he called us last night to tell us. I wish I were in a position to travel. Your mother is stuck here with me, or she'd have come at least.'

Mum was back on the line. 'Beta, why don't you just take some leave and come here. That might help you forget things.'

'I might later, Mum, but not right away.'

'Why not?'

'There's things that need to be sorted out here . . .'

'What things?'

'Well, Anjali, for one . . .'

'Oh, bechari, what can the poor child think of all this. Where is she at the moment?'

'The Social Services people have taken her away for a couple of days. She's okay, I think. I don't suppose she really understands anything at the moment.'

'Hai ram, bechari,' Mum repeated, her voice oozing sympathy for Anjali's plight, but I could guess what she would start worrying about next. 'But, surely, beta, they must be making some arrangements for her on a permanent basis. They can't be expecting you to care for her?'

'No, I don't think they are, Mum.' I wanted to hang up now. I didn't know what I wanted for Anjali at the moment and it certainly wasn't the right time to be starting a discussion on what I *didn't* know. Not with Mum, anyway. Her early fears about my taking Maya and Anjali on, all those years ago, had always stayed with her, although of late she no longer spoke about it. When she first found out that Maya had run away from her husband and parents, she was genuinely horrified, asking me how much I knew about her, suspicious whether she had cast some sort of spell on me. Gradually, having observed how quiet and sorrowful Maya had seemed and how genuinely keen to make it up to them for taking her into their house, Mum finally stopped nagging me, with a grudging, 'You're an adult. I can't tell you what to do, can I?' Although she was clearly very tempted at times. But, over the years, she gathered from our letters and phone calls that Maya was as caring a woman as she would have wanted for me and that we were happy in our life with Anjali, which was when she finally went silent on the subject. I also knew that she sometimes thought, although she fortunately always refrained from saying it out loud, 'Well, at least she's an Indian girl and not a firangee—could never stand the sound of that Anna he went out with till she jilted him, thank *God*!'

'Mum, I've got to go. I'll call you later tonight, about ten o'clock your time.'

'What are you doing today, beta? Please eat and look after yourself.'

'I will, I will, Mum. I've got Kevin coming around tonight, he'll probably stay over the weekend.'

'Oh, thank God for that! He's a good boy—Kevin—give him my love . . .'

'I will, kisses to both of you . . . and . . . don't worry about me if you can help it.'

I hung up, feeling that wretched knot settle itself firmly in my stomach again. I went back into the bathroom and started to lather my face once more. Just carry on doing all the normal everyday things, I told myself. The world's still spinning on its axis, the sun came up in the east as usual a few hours ago. Everything is, amazingly, just as it used to be. I'm not special, I'm just another of the world's many billion inhabitants. Other people suffer too—worse things sometimes. I tried to think of all those things worse than losing a lovely woman to a meaningless accident. It wasn't easy. I could think of some, but none of them were making me feel any better. Focus on *Anjali*, I thought, she's here, she's real . . . and, by God, she has real needs now that her mum's gone.

I wondered which might be more traumatic for her—all this or her hasty departure from Kerala nearly three years ago. She had spent her first few months in Delhi in a state of some bewilderment, asking occasionally for her father and more often for 'Kathoo', Maya's maid, Kuttan's sister. Being the sort of child she was, she gradually inveigled her way into my parents' hearts and they were quite sorry to let her go when she left, with her mother, for England a few months later. I had already left for England a couple of weeks before they arrived, to help with their immigration at this end and had turned up at Heathrow to pick them up. Bemused with yet more changes in her life, and not having particularly enjoyed the flight, she did not come rushing into my arms, despite the big teddy bear I was carrying. All I was able to see of her was a pudgy pair of hands, clutching her mother's knees from behind.

'Now might that be Miss Anjali behind there,' I had asked, kneeling down after I had given Maya a kiss. A muffled mumble greeted me.

'What's that? Well, the Anjali I knew used to have a face and a voice.'

At that, her round face framed in black hair and bangs appeared from behind Maya's knees. 'Poda,' she had said crossly, indicating her dissatisfaction with the whole business of long haul flights.

'She still uses that stupid word,' I said to Maya, straightening up to smile at her again.

'I'm sure she doesn't mean she wants *you* to get lost. Even if she does, know that *I'm* really happy to see you again, Rahul.' Her eyes were full of love as she smiled.

I had missed her terribly, even though it had been just two weeks. Who would have ever thought that I was capable of that kind of soppy stuff. I kissed her again, very tenderly, on her lips, in a way that you never could in India in public. 'I never *ever* want to be separated from you again,' I said, much to my own surprise actually meaning it. I bent over again to try and woo Anjali one more time. 'Well, there's a brand-new car seat (blue and red) in a bright white car, waiting to whisk a nice girl down a big, exciting motorway. But only if she smiles at me,' I said loudly.

That was rewarded with a loud artificial giggle and the reappearance of the face, this time with both grimy hands extended for the teddy bear. It wasn't quite a propitious arrival in England, I suppose, but it set the tone for the relationship we were to develop over the years. Maya was Mum, meant for the drudge stuff—baths, meals, trips to shops and nursery. I was, alternately, Unka or Papa, meant for messing about and having fun with. Good for being turned upside down by, and that kind of thing. I was sure there were occasions when she thought of me as a darned nuisance, whenever I butted in to help Maya sort her out, for instance. There were times, certainly, when she made it plain that she absolutely hated me for having to share her mum with me. And, if I were honest, that feeling could sometimes be mutual although I tried to never let Maya know. I knew she would be hurt. In any case, most of the time I really rather liked having Anjali around. All of which made it too knotty to try and elucidate.

It was more a matter of ambivalence rather than annoyance, to be perfectly accurate. I had never been a broody, kiddy type. Just sort of liked them when they were the well brought up, polite sort of kids that some of my acquaintances seemed to have. Who came in to say hello and then had the good grace to bugger off to their rooms and keep themselves amused. Only once was I really impressed by a kid—when Helen, in the accounts department at work, brought her eleven-year-old to office on a Bring-Your-Child-to-Work Day. He turned out to be a bit of a tennis prodigy, picked to play for the Surrey County under-14 team. Now *that* really impressed me. Kids like him really were a treat to talk to.

Admittedly, Anjali never demonstrated that sort of promise. Not very polite at the best of times, with a predilection for rude Malayalam words that Maya had to translate for me. Worse, showing no sign of talent at any sport. I took her with me a few times to my local tennis club but she always seemed terrified that the ball would hit her face, ducking it whenever it came her way rather than trying to swat it with her racquet. Maya, too, had never been much help on those occasions, hanging around the edges of the court, looking every bit as nervous as Anjali. But, that was the thing. Perhaps it was because I loved Maya, and because I never knew her *minus* Anjali, that I never really tried to separate them in my mind. They were just indisputable parts of each other. And I never, in my happiness at finding love with someone like Maya, ever thought with any seriousness of Anjali being a presence we could have done without. That's the truth. Although I never got sentimental about it and preferred to take the jokey stance, joshing with Maya that getting her with Anjali was a bit like the 'buy one get one free' offers in supermarkets, where a tiny bottle would be strapped on to a larger one, to add to the irresistibility of the product.

And it's hard to think back to exactly when and how a kid, a *step-kid* for God's sake, starts to belong, starts to worm her way under the skin in a nice, natural sort of way—without any sudden rushes of realization, without any formal dates to later note as anniversaries. But, gradually, Anjali and I started to belong to each other. It was complex, but we had it all worked out, and certainly didn't need any social workers to come in now and order us to start defining things, pinpointing and nailing them down to legal details.

I had finished shaving and wiped my face with a towel. I was now feeling much better, I decided, and was quite looking forward to a day out with Anjali. It would make everything (or most things) seem normal again and I wanted to make it really special for her. It was a warm morning, perfect for a traipse around Primrose Hill—she loved the playground there. And then we could perhaps wander across to the cafés on Regents Park Road. I could have a coffee and buy her a swish meal, followed by a giant slab of cake. I smiled in anticipation of her two large front teeth appearing ecstatically in the huge grin I would be rewarded with for that. I pulled on a pair of jeans and chose a decent shirt. I certainly didn't want the people at that children's home to eye me askance if I went to pick her up looking scruffy. Surveying myself one last time in the mirror, I grabbed the car keys and made for the door.

Jaishree Misra

Sun-washed walls were making even the old 1960s building that was the children's home look warm and welcoming. I rang the bell and strained to hear Anjali's voice in the distant clamour. Was that her—that manic cackle? Footsteps came running to the door and a pleasant face with ruddy cheeks appeared as it opened.

'Hi?'

'Oh hello, I'm Anjali's dad . . .'

'Oh yes, *hi*!' Her effusive greeting and twanging Aussie 'yis' surprised me. I had half expected to have to wage battles again today.

'Did the social worker . . . Elizabeth Hawke . . . let you know I was coming?' I asked as I followed her in.

'Yes, yes she did. You're a little earlier than we'd expected though.'

'Sorry, but I didn't want to hang around once I was ready. How is she? Was she all right last night?'

'Oh, she's been fabulous. Chirping away to everybody here. I don't think she really knows what's happened, though . . .' she trailed off, suddenly awkward and embarrassed.

'Has anyone tried to explain to her?'

'I'm not sure. I think Elizabeth Hawke did last night. But, although she seems to know the meaning of the word "forever", it's hard to say if she really understands it in this context.'

I wasn't sure I trusted words like 'forever' myself any more, but I nodded mutely. We were now in a lounge. A television was blaring some kid stuff and toys and tattered books were strewn everywhere.

'If you'll wait here one moment I'll go and fetch her for you. They're all out in the garden.'

I sat on a sofa, noticing that it had been slashed on one arm. Dirty white stuffing was starting to peep out of the hole. Won't be long before that becomes a very unstuffed arm, I thought, if the other kids in this place are anything like Anjali. The carpet beneath my feet was worn through, its once flowery pattern barely discernible. I felt sorry for the kids who had to spend long periods of time in places like this—council-run houses which were always short of funds and having to make do with whatever they could lay their hands on. Poor Anjali, this was a far cry from her smart little bedroom at home, with its own TV and the biggest collection of beanie animals this side of the Atlantic. I felt a sudden impatience again at the thought that I hadn't seen her cheery face for nearly a whole day now. Suddenly, I was very eager to wrap her in my arms and give her the tightest hug she had ever had. I got up at the sound of running footsteps and a happy stream of unintelligible chatter in the hall. I knew that voice. Anjali came bursting into the room, face wreathed in smiles.

'Papa!' she shouted, taking a flying leap into my outstretched arms. I could feel sudden tears run down my face as I buried it in her plump shoulder, taking in deep breaths of her lovely familiar smell.

'Hello, baby,' I mumbled. I tried to hold on to her for a while longer, but she was already starting to wriggle out of my arms.

'Papa, have you come in the car?' she asked, looking for my keys, always eager to move on to the next thing.

'Yes, I've brought the car,' I said, wiping my face on my sleeve.

'Go out?' she asked, putting on her beseeching voice, pulling her face into what she imagined was a winsome, charming expression.

'You don't have to plead, of course we're going out,' I said. 'That's why I've come.'

Anjali clapped her hands and fell over into the sofa, attempting to execute a merry pirouette. She was wearing her sundress today, with some yellow clips in her hair and looked like a small, cheerful bunch of flowers. I felt a sudden sharp pain in my chest again at the thought of how pleased Maya would have been to see her looking so pretty.

'Where's Mum?' she asked. It was only a casual question, she still wasn't worried or suspicious, but the Australian girl and I were both silent for a few horrible minutes. Then we both spoke together.

'Elizabeth told you yesterday, didn't she, Anjali . . .' she was saying.

'Mum's . . . not here any more, sweetie . . .' I was trying to say.

But Anjali didn't seem too bothered. She had already moved on to the next thing. 'Come *on*, Papa. Let's go *out*!' she was saying, tugging at my arm.

'Yes, yes, go out,' I said, jangling my car keys loudly. I shot a quick look at the Australian girl, who was looking paler and less happy than before. Can't be easy for her either, I thought. 'Is that okay, then? I can take her out now, can't I?'

'Yes, of course,' she said, nodding vigorously. It had obviously all been discussed and finalized before I got here.

'Come on, babe,' I said to Anjali. She dug into her pocket and pulled out a pair of plastic sunglasses—red with white frames and the words 'Virgin Airlines' barely discernible along the side. It was part of the goody bag she was given when we took her to Orlando last year—no, two years ago now. When the photographs were developed she was wearing those damn shades in every one of them—even on the day we went to Epcot and it started to pour—

looking ridiculously cheesy and pleased with herself. Maya thought of having a few copies made, carefully weeding out those that had me in them to send to Govind and her parents. Earlier on, I know she sometimes wondered if she ought to try including them in Anjali's affairs, but I gradually talked her out of it—worried that Govind would find out where we lived and perhaps cause trouble. After a few months she stopped talking about it, agreeing with me once that it might actually be cruel to inadvertently unleash old emotions on Govind. 'He'd been fond enough of Anjali and it might be worse for him to see her pictures without knowing where she is, or how she is,' she had said. That settled it, although occasionally we talked about him, wondering whether he might have got married again. Her parents we talked about a lot less, that being a subject I was keener to avoid, not least because I knew how much it still hurt Maya to imagine the ease with which they had seemed able to forget her. Once she even said, jokingly of course, 'What if something happens to me, Anjali will probably have to go back to them, you know.' We should have discussed it. *Of course* we should have discussed it. Did other people discuss each other's deaths and wills and other similar things? Sensible and adult-like?

The Australian girl had opened the door, letting us out into the leafy, bright morning. 'I'm going out!' Anjali announced to a bemused couple who were getting into their car outside the home.

'Do you know them?' I asked her, starting up the car.

She shook her head, looking unconcerned.

'Well, you don't talk to people you don't know, do you?'

She was ignoring me, waving to the Aussie girl, bouncing on the seat, making cooing noises. Her happy noises, we called them. My happy fat pigeon, Maya said sometimes as a preamble to a huge cuddle. I leaned over her to belt her in and was rewarded with a wet kiss on my cheek.

'Your chin's not poky,' she said conversationally, appreciating my smooth shave.

'Shaved myself silly this morning, I did, because I was coming out to that home of yours,' I said, knowing she wouldn't really get it. 'Do you like your home? Your Faunce Way home? Are they all nice there?'

She shrugged.

'Don't you like it then? Okay, here, do it this way,' I said, holding out two fingers. Waggling one I repeated, 'Like it,' and then, waggling the other, 'Don't like it.' I had seen Maya do it often, in the days Anjali was still struggling between her three languages, preferring to speak none for a few worrying months. 'Cheese burger/chicken burger', 'Lydia/Mary', 'painting/crayoning'—for all those things for which Anjali had no words then. She always grabbed one finger obediently; she knew it was about choices, but I was always convinced that the actual choices she made were purely at random. 'Haven't you noticed, she always goes for the latter one,' I had said to Maya. 'Why don't you just decide what's best for her. It's not as if, at this age, any of her choices are going to be particularly informed ones, is it? Who are we all trying to kid here?' But she only smiled and insisted on getting Anjali's 'choice' out of her, even though Anjali herself seemed bored out of her tree with the whole business sometimes. And even though she never got any *real* choices, as I pointed out. 'Why don't I ever hear you ask her whether she'd like . . . chocolates instead of vegetables, for instance . . . or . . . going out and not going to bed? Now those would be real choices to offer a kid. Isn't it just a bit unfair that you merely offer her the choice between two things *you* want her to do.' That annoyed her. 'Why don't you leave her parenting to me,' she snapped. We ended up having quite a tiff that day. Not that we fought often or anything. Very rarely, in fact. But I wished I hadn't remembered that today.

I waggled my fingers again. Anjali grabbed my middle finger.

Don't like it. But she always went for the latter option, remember? I told myself crossly. It was a stupid system anyway. Now that she had words, all I needed to do was ask her.

'Come on, Anjali, what do you think of this Faunce Way place then?'

She looked out of the window and said, 'Look, a giwaffe, on the side of that bus!'

'Giraffe,' I corrected her absently. It seemed very important to know what she really felt about Faunce Way. I tried it again, driving along with one hand, offering her the choice of my two fingers again, 'Here, you haven't played my game *don't like the children's home/like the children's home very much*, come on, which one is it.' She grabbed my forefinger this time. It was still 'don't like it', *and* she hadn't gone for the latter choice as I thought she always did. Damn. That was the problem with real choices, wasn't it? What was the bloody point? How often did you actually get what you wanted anyway? We were all just going around making-do all the bloody time, weren't we, pretending to be in charge, in control of everything around us. Making *real* choices, like fuck!

I tooted the horn at a woman in a red Polo who was trying to cut me up from the bus lane. Anjali jumped and then giggled. 'More,' she said.

'Yes more, and more loudly too, if that woman tries edging in again,' I growled, adding hastily, 'no, *don't* stare out of the window at her like that!' Anjali had raised herself from the seat to peer encouragingly at the red Polo driver.

I turned into Regents Park Road, slowing down, looking for an empty parking meter. It was a weekday. I was banking on the fact that most people would be in their offices and not be planning on pleasure outings to the park. Which reminded me: I hadn't checked how many days I was to have off before being expected to return to work. Ah, I was right—plenty of parking. And the park looked beautifully empty for this time of year too. I only ever saw it on weekends when it was heaving with Londoners. There had to be some perks to compassionate leave, I thought as I pulled easily into a slot right next to the Primrose Hill entrance.

Letting Anjali out on the pavement, I locked the door and then followed her small colourful figure as it skipped towards the swings. She first learned of the attractions of parks after Maya and she arrived in England. The swings and the slides were unfamiliar treats to her at first and it had taken a lot of coaxing initially. The dogs were what she really loved. And Maya and I had talked, after her miscarriage in May, of getting Anjali a pet. A big Labrador, I had suggested, a little spaniel, she had said.

We got to the swings and Anjali managed to clamber on, swinging her legs madly, wondering why the swing was buffeting about without moving forward as anticipated.

'Kick with your legs, Anjali . . . no, not in the air, against the ground . . . here, let me show you.'

She chuckled as I stuffed my tall frame into the swing next to hers. With two or three kicks, I was airborne, feeling the wind blow through my hair. Anjali looked at me resentfully—your legs are *twice* as long as mine, her expression said.

'Here, watch me, you can do it too. Just watch how I do it and then try copying me,' I said, trying to do the whole thing again in slow motion.

'Papa, push me,' she said, whining.

'You try this first,' I repeated encouragingly. But she scowled at me and wriggled off her perch. Now she was cross, silly girl. I wasn't especially perturbed as her bad moods never lasted longer than about a tenth of a second. Catching up with her at the slide, I asked, 'Do you want to go up there?'

'Papa, put me there,' she said.

'What! You want me to go up there with you?' I looked

dubiously at the small steel structure. 'No, sweetie, I think I'm too big for that. The park policeman will come and get me. Lemme see if I can hoist you up there, though.'

She raised her arms and I lifted her on to the frame with a grunt. She flailed her legs about, giggling madly before finally hooking herself on to the top and hauling herself up. Lifting up her dress and wrapping it around the waist, she whooped with delight as she came down the slide in a flurry of flowered dress and panties, landing in a heap on the sand.

'More,' she demanded as she got up, dusting herself down.

'Oh all right, once more and then you do it yourself, okay? I'm sure you can negotiate those steps on your own.'

We repeated the earlier process with the same round of grunts and giggles.

'More, more, more,' she was saying. I took her around to the steps and said, firmly, 'Come on, it's much more fun this way because it doesn't finish so fast.' She looked doubtful, but I could already feel my back start to twinge with the strain. It was probably still sore from that toss I had taken on to Anjali's bed yesterday. I held her as she clambered clumsily up the stairs, her toes scrunched up anxiously in their sandals, and then clapped loudly as she made it to the summit. 'Good girl! See, it's easy, isn't it? Now you do that a few times while I sit here watching you.'

I walked over to a nearby bench and let out a sigh, stretching myself out. The sun was washing pleasantly over me and I closed my eyes for a few seconds, allowing the rays to pierce through my lids and flow into me. How beautiful the park looked when it was empty like this. Vast green spaces that I never knew existed had materialized and now lay basking, mellow and gold. A man was walking up the hill, with about six dogs on leashes. Professional dog-walker, probably—I had read about them somewhere, but had never actually seen one before. He looked contented and the dogs even more so, trotting along in silent, panting camaraderie. They were a funny bunch, six different shapes and sizes, but couldn't have looked more like they had always belonged together. A young mother was walking towards the park with two small children in brightly coloured jackets tumbling along ahead of her.

'Papa . . . Unka! . . . HELLO-O!'

'Anjali! Sorry babe, I wasn't listening . . . what's up?'

She had finished with the slide and was now sitting next to me, pulling urgently on my arm.

'Toilet,' she announced.

'Toilet? Oh hell! Are you sure?'

She nodded.

'I'm not sure I know where they are. How badly do you need to go? Can you wait until we get to a café or something?'

She screwed her face up to indicate pain and clutched at her groin dramatically.

'Well, if it's as bad as that, you should have asked to go at the home *before* we left, shouldn't you?' I said crossly, getting up from my bench. 'Let's see now, there must be one somewhere here . . .'

We started to walk, Anjali looking genuinely unhappy now, hobbling along with her fist still clutched in a ball between her legs. As I stopped to read a nearby map of the park, she started to hop up and down, making little hissing noises. I looked at her in alarm. Now she had crossed her legs, hopping all the while.

'Hang on, hang on, baby, I'll find you a toilet soon,' I said, trying to keep the panic out of my voice. 'Oh, excuse me please,' I accosted the young mother with her two children, 'you wouldn't happen to know if there are toilets near here, would you?'

She smiled at the desperate tone of my voice and pointed to a small brick building on the other side of the playground. 'There,' she said, adding in the voice of a person with vast amounts of experience in this matter, 'it's quickest to go that way, through the hole in the hedge over there.'

I appreciated her masterful economy of expression and

shouted out a hasty thanks. 'Come on Anjali, quick!' I pulled her along and then scooped her up by the armpits, careful not to squeeze her stomach thereby inducing unfortunate leakages. 'Through the hole in the hedge,' I said, pushing Anjali and myself through a hole carved out by numerous desperate mothers and their kids over the years. Much too small for the likes of me, I thought, as we scraped our way to the other side. 'Bloody hell! I think I've left a part of my ear behind in that hedge somewhere! Okay then, here we are, "Ladies" on this side, off with you.'

I put Anjali down, but she stood there, looking helplessly at me. 'What?' I asked her. 'Go on and do your thing—quickly . . .'

But she wouldn't budge. 'Papa, come with me,' she said.

'Don't be silly, I can't come in there with you! You can manage on your own—go on!'

'Papa,' she repeated. Her lower lip had extended and her eyes were filling up with tears. I knew Maya always went in with her, but I wasn't sure exactly what it was that she did in there, and whether I was allowed to do it. For one wild moment, I thought of going back out to the helpful mother but something told me she would not be too taken with such a reappearance. I had to make a decision quickly.

'Well, I can't come in there, but let's try this, shall we?' I scooped Anjali up again and raced around to the other side of the building in search of the Gents'. We dived in without checking to see if it was already occupied. Luckily, it wasn't, and I set Anjali down. I wasn't even sure if this was legal. 'Look, sweetie, here's the toilet, now go in there and do your wee wee. Papa will wait here for you. *Quick* before someone else comes in!'

She rushed for the single toilet, bunching up her dress as she went.

'Remember to take your panties off!' I called after her.

She left the door wide open, and I hoped again that no one else would come in while she was in there. Her relieved hissing seemed to go on forever and I heaved a sigh of relief as she emerged, pulling up her panties, a huge smile on her face.

'Good girl,' I said. 'Now wash your hands.' She walked across to one of the urinals, stopping in puzzlement at the fact that it didn't look anything like the washbasins in the Ladies'.

'Tap?' she asked, before spotting the real washbasin on the other wall. We chortled together at this. I lifted her up and she washed her hands as we pulled funny faces at each other in the cracked yellow mirror above the sink.

'Now out, quick,' I said, 'before someone thinks I'm molesting you in here.'

She giggled again, not having any idea what I was talking about, but sensing the relief in my voice. We emerged from the toilets and I took a few deep breaths of the fresh park air.

'Come on, sweetie,' I said as I took Anjali's hand, 'what do you say to a spot of lunch, old sport?'

She looked up at me. 'Yay, lunch!' she said, beaming her buck-toothed smile, as we started to walk jauntily away from the toilets. Lunch was a favourite word with her, I knew, and always generated a brilliant, hundred-watt radiance on her face. I nodded a 'thank you' to the young mother who had directed us to the hole in the hedge as we walked past the park to the gates. Anjali was holding my hand, skipping along, chanting something unfamiliar.

The café was perched on the edge of Regents Park Road, alongside many other clones of itself, all spilling out from dark Italian interiors on to the sun-washed pavement with a flurry of tin chairs and fluttering umbrellas.

'Outside?' I asked Anjali, aware that I was doing the very thing I had accused Maya of by offering Anjali the option of doing what I wanted us to do.

She nodded enthusiastically. 'Yes please!' She just wanted lunch, really.

I pushed the table closer to Anjali after she had perched herself on a chair, swinging her feet, and handed her a menu card. Maya usually chose her food and was, for a while now, trying to control her diet I remembered. Oh, let her eat what she wants today, I thought. Pulling the card out of Anjali's grasp and returning it to her, right side up, we read our menus for a few minutes in companionable silence. Anjali was moving her lips, mouthing the words she was pretending to read so seriously.

'So what'll it be?' I asked her.

She jabbed with her finger on the menu and I leaned across the table to look at what she was pointing at. Tiramisu.

'Not that, that's a pudding. You need some lunch.'

'Pudding,' she said firmly.

'Pudding after lunch,' I said more firmly.

With her uncanny knack for spotting a bargain, Anjali nodded and put her card away. 'Shall I order for you then?' She nodded her approval again. Words were failing her in her excitement. The waitress took our order—a chicken burger for Anjali and a tuna baguette for me, with a bowl of green salad to share and two diet cokes.

'Pudding,' Anjali reminded me.

'Yes, you'll get pudding, but do I have to order it now? Oh, all right, can I order her pudding now please,' I asked the girl. She smiled and waited patiently with her pad while Anjali took up her menu again and pointed with uncanny precision to the Tiramisu again.

'I'm not sure you'll like that, sweetie,' I said. 'It's got alcohol in it. Bitter, bleah,' I added to elucidate my point.

'Rum,' the waitress added inaccurately, trying to help.

'Yeah, rum. You can't have that.'

But Anjali was adamant and jabbed firmly on the T of the Tiramisu.

'There's no law against children having . . . er . . . alcoholic puddings, is there?' I asked the waitress, very unsure of what I might be getting into now.

'Naw, I don't think so, not if the parent allows it,' she drawled, not understanding my concern at all. I had to prove my parental credentials and was suddenly aware of how little I knew.

'There'll be no *smell* of alcohol about her, will there?'

The girl only smiled politely in response; she thought I was joking. I thought for a minute of the repercussions if I returned Anjali to the children's home reeking of alcohol. I never ate puddings myself but had a vague idea that some sort of liqueur was used in making Tiramisu. I had no idea at all what the thing would taste like, nor of how smelly it was likely to make Anjali's breath. But I wanted to do everything Anjali's way today.

'Tiramisu,' I said to the waitress.

'Two?' she asked.

'God, no, one's more than enough, thanks,' I replied as she closed her pad. Anjali rewarded the woman with another one of her ingratiating, buck-toothed smiles.

'Why *are* you such a perverse child?' I asked Anjali after the waitress had left. 'Other kids eat strawberry ice-cream and banana boats. You want Tiramisu when you don't have a clue what it is. If it upsets your tummy or something, *you'll* have to explain to the Faunce Way people, okay?'

She smiled at me affectionately. I could call her what I liked today, she was feeling too fondly towards me to care. I reached out and ruffled her hair. 'Silly killy,' I said, using one of Maya's endearments for her. Silly little bird, that meant in their mother tongue. I had never learnt to speak Malayalam myself, but I was pleased that I knew as much as Anjali did. She's a better tutor than you are, I often accused Maya jokingly.

'Where's Mum?' Anjali asked, looking genuinely puzzled this time.

'Mum . . .' I took a deep breath before carrying on, 'Mum's gone, darling. She's not coming back.'

It still felt incredible, saying it, thinking it. She's *gone*. She isn't at the newsagents over there, buying a paper, about to come running back over the road to rejoin us at this table in a minute. Gone, just like that. And forever. NOT COMING BACK, get it? Get it, Rahul? Get it, Anjali? But Anjali hadn't got it.

'I want to go to Mum,' she said firmly, then threw in a last-minute proviso. 'After lunch.'

'I know, I'd like to too, but we can't.'

She looked even more baffled, so I added, as gently as I could, 'Mum's gone *very* far away. We can't get there. Too far away, Anjali.'

'Indya?' she asked. She knew about far away. Far away was in India, a place you went to by plane, rather than by car or tube. Where her Appuppa and her Ammumma lived, about whom Maya told her sometimes, explaining that it was much too far away to get to. That was about the farthest place she knew.

'Farther away,' I said, '*more* far away than India. So far that there are no tickets, no aeroplanes going there.'

I could hardly bring myself to say it, but this wasn't exactly the time to try and assert my sporadic atheism. 'She's gone to heaven, Anjali,' I said, hoping desperately that the word 'heaven' would help explain it more concisely and, let's face it, more honestly too. Had Maya ever talked to her about heaven? And about life and death for heaven's sake? It wasn't a favoured subject between us anyway, given the events of three years ago. And I had only ever been good at the rough-and-tumble-stuff side of parenting anyway. All the rest was always left to Maya.

Anjali looked at me open-mouthed. What was going on in her head? Was the truth beginning to dawn on her? Please, please, make it easy for her, I thought, feeling a physical stab of pain in my gut. She looked away across the road. I couldn't tell what she was thinking, whether she was thinking of anything at all. She was now looking at a little dog on a leash.

'Papa, look, a puppy-dog,' she said, sitting up again in her chair.

'Yes, Anjali, puppy-dog,' I replied, feeling the words throttle me. If she could deal with it, shouldn't I too? Was she dealing with it? Did she know? She must know *something's* wrong by now, shouldn't she? Which of us was the more unfortunate—me, for knowing my grief, or her, for probably not knowing it existed at all?

We sat in silence until the food arrived—Anjali looking on in interest at the endless passage of life on the street; I, completely unable to understand life's temerity in being able to carry on regardless. My thoughts were swirling and threatening to engulf me again on this beautiful, warm morning. I rubbed my hands vigorously over my face, feeling the blood return to it. For Anjali's sake, I had to carry on as normal.

'Chicken burger over there,' I said to the waitress as she appeared with the plates.

'Ketcha,' Anjali said.

'Yes, could we have some ketchup please?' I said.

As the waitress went off, we started to eat. 'Don't gobble, Anjali,' I said, watching her fall upon her burger. I bit into my own tuna baguette that tasted of cardboard. 'Is it good?'

She nodded enthusiastically, lettuce bits hanging out of her mouth. Conversation, never Anjali's strong point, would have to be forsaken completely until she had finished her food. We ate in silence, as cars rolled past and people wandered around our table. Some of them smiled at Anjali, seeing only a chubby, pretty girl tucking obediently into her food. When she had eaten her burger, she gestured to the half baguette I had left behind on my plate, offering to finish it for me. I declined her offer.

'Pudding's on its way, remember? And we can't have you

bursting like a balloon just as we arrive back at the children's home, can we?'

She grinned again, not particularly upset at being refused the baguette. It was always worth a try. When the pudding arrived, she stuck into it straightaway, putting a large drippy spoonful of it into her mouth. Tasting the bitterness of the liqueur, she widened her eyes in surprise and then wrinkled her nose into a disapproving button.

'Bleah!' she said.

'Well, I did try to warn you . . . don't eat it if you don't want it . . .' I added as she went gamely for a second spoonful.

'I want it,' she muttered as she swallowed again, grimacing more openly this time.

'Oh, just return it, Anjali,' I snapped. 'I'll order you something else, ice-cream or something . . .'

But Anjali was determined not to forsake her pudding in hand and continued gulping spoonfuls of the Tiramisu down, wincing with each swallow. I watched her helplessly while she finished it, feeling amused, annoyed and deeply, deeply sad all at once. I was willing to do anything at this point in time to stave off the grief waiting so evilly to grab her any minute now. Surely it was only a matter of time before it would get her too? What could I do to save her from it, postpone it, *anything*? Here was this kid, just four for heaven's sake, her life turning completely and utterly and inexorably inside out and she did not even know it yet. Was that cruel, was that kind, wasn't that just too soul destroying to even bear thinking about? I could hardly handle my own chaos, what on earth was I to do with hers?

I put a twenty-pound note down on the bill that had been brought by the waitress and got up from the table, wiping Anjali's face with a paper serviette. 'Come on, sunshine,' I said as gently as I could, 'where would you like to go now?'

She got up and put her hand in mine. It felt sticky and hot. I

Jaishree Misra

attempted wiping her hands with the serviette, but they looked like they needed a good scrub with a bar of soap.

'Shall we go into the toilets here to wash them, do you think?' I asked.

'Can we go home?' she said in a small voice.

'Yes, I'm sure we can, sweetie, or do you want to go back to Faunce Way? You've got other kids to play with there, haven't you? That might be better.'

'My tummy hurts,' she said, sounding genuinely wobbly.

I knelt next to her on the pavement. 'Do you want to throw up or something?' I asked, feeling panic rise within me again.

She shook her head and said again, 'Wanna go home.'

'It'll have to be Faunce Way, darling. They'll know what to do about your tummy there. Give you some medicine, maybe.' I knew there was a vast collection of colourful medicine bottles in our bathroom cabinet back in the house but Maya always handled things like that. She even took care of my headaches and hangovers, leave alone Anjali's sniffles and stuff. We were back at the car by now and I strapped a very green-faced Anjali into her seat.

'Hang on, sweetie, we'll be back at Faunce Way before you know it. That nice girl there will then give you some yummy medicine and rub your tummy for you to make you feel better. How about that? And, when you're better, I'll take you back home so you can play with your toys again, yes?'

She made no reply to this. I felt like a complete heel. I didn't know whether she minded or not and I didn't dare ask. Would she think *I* didn't want her to come home? And could I make a go of it if I did take her home? Could I persuade Social Services that I really could arrange my life around Anjali's and care for her with some help? Could I? *Could I*? Is *that* what Maya would have wanted?

We drove back to the children's home in silence. Anjali was unusually quiet too, either still suffering that blasted Tiramisu revolting in her stomach or possibly reacting to my inability to carry on the pretence of a happy day out any more.

At the children's home, we were met at the door by a staff member who had been introduced as the senior officer on my last visit. I knew she would probably suggest that we discuss things with Elizabeth Hawke, but I took the plunge anyway.

'Look . . . I need to talk to you. I was wondering if it might be possible for me to take Anjali home . . . on a permanent basis, that is . . .'

She looked down at Anjali who was looking hopefully up at us. 'Anjali, sweetheart, do you want to go in while your papa and I have a chat?' she said, and called out to somebody. The Australian girl of the morning appeared to take Anjali indoors. I watched Anjali take her hand and trot obediently through another set of doors with her. I was then ushered into a small office and seated at a desk that was covered in files. On a notice board behind the desk were various cards and notes. One hand-made card proclaimed THANK YOU in childish, pink letters—the enormous letters were obviously in direct proportion to the gratitude expressed.

As the woman took the seat in front of the desk, I cleared my throat and spoke swiftly, 'I'm not sure this is working . . . Anjali, I think . . . needs to be at home. In fact, I'm sure that's what would be best.' I tried to sound convinced.

Her face and her voice were kindly. 'It's so hard, isn't it?' she said softly. 'She does seem to be less happy here now than she was yesterday and is probably missing home. The thing is, when she asks to go home, it's the home she *had* that she's asking for . . . the home in which she still had her mum and dad and everything was normal . . .' She stopped and looked at me, her eyes sad and serious. 'We can't provide that for her, can we?'

'Well, at the moment it feels as if she and I only have each other left. I don't want to let go of that . . . for her and for me. Can you understand that?'

'Oh I can, I most certainly can. You must understand that I do, I *do* really feel for you, Mr Tiwari. But, in your situation, you can't really be expected to provide the cheerful atmosphere that the poor child needs at the moment. Here, she has the company of the other children and she does seem to be enjoying that. And all the staff members who are making such a fuss over her too—'

'Her room, her toys . . . all that must count for a lot too.' I was floundering, drowning.

'They certainly do. But, at the moment, without her mum, all that might seem very strange to her, Mr Tiwari. I'm *so* sorry.' I was silent while she looked sympathetically at me.

I stood up. 'You're right,' I said, not sure at all of what was right. I just knew I had to get out. Soon. Before I cracked up completely. 'Please could I use your toilet before I go?' I seemed to have lost my voice as well. That hoarse whisper didn't sound like it had anything to do with me.

I was shown to a toilet down the corridor, where I held on tightly to the sink for a few minutes, composing myself. A shelf above the bathtub held seven different bottles of bath gel—one for each child here, probably. The linoleum under my feet was worn and scuffed. There was a peculiar smell of impersonality in the small bathroom. Very unlike a bathroom in a house, which seemed to take on the smells of a family—their favourite brands of shampoo and talc. Ours, for some reason, always smelt of lavender, and always had a potted plant of some description on the window-sill. All Maya's doing, of course, not mine. I had allowed Anjali to come to this, this bleak little place. It was just an institution, wasn't it—a ghastly, state-run institution masquerading as a fun place for a child to be. Oh *God*, what would Maya be thinking?

As I emerged from the toilet, Anjali came running into the lobby again, clutching a large rag doll to her chest. We hugged a three-way hug, Anjali, her doll and I, while the Australian girl and the senior officer looked on. Anjali had reverted to her cheerful self again. 'Bye-bye-see-you, I'll wave to you from the window,' she said, before running back in. By the time I was out of the doors, she had taken up her station in the window of the home, doll and all. I waved at her, trying to make it look like a jaunty, happy wave, as I walked back into the car park. They waved as I drove away, Anjali maternally holding her doll's arm to make sure she waved too. I kept my eyes on her in the rear-view mirror, even as I turned the corner in my car.

On reaching home, I went over to Maya's bureau and opened up her tattered, old address book. A wad of cards and bits of paper fell fluttering out—various names and addresses collected over the years, intended for copying into the book on some quiet afternoon, probably. Ignoring them, I turned over to the page marked G, until I finally found what I was looking for. Govind Warrier, Managing Partner, Warrier Water Pumps, Kovil Road, Thampanoor, Trivandrum. I copied it on a piece of paper, noting down the telephone number as well. I couldn't see how I could ask him for permission to look after Anjali after all these years. Going upstairs for the telephone, I tried to remember where I had written Elizabeth Hawke's telephone number. It was probably on the pad on the bookshelf. The time was four o'clock. If I called right now, I would probably get her before the office closed for the weekend.

eleven

Sleep that knits up the ravelled sleeve of care . . . I couldn't remember who had said that. The gentle but insistent bonging of the doorbell gradually pierced my consciousness. I lay awake for a few seconds, wondering why I had crashed out fully clothed on my bed and why the morning sunshine was not pouring into my room as usual. Because it's evening, you idiot, I thought, and that's bloody Kevin at the door! I leaped out of bed and raced down the stairs, taking them two at a time.

Kevin was leaning on the doorbell, his new girlfriend fluttering anxiously behind him when I opened the door.

'Stop ringing the damn thing, I'm not deaf—although there's the strong chance I will be now.'

Kevin looked unmistakably relieved to see me at the door and gave me a long hug as he came in. We didn't normally hug each other when we met, even if weeks had passed since our last meeting. This felt sort of weird, I had to admit. I kissed Carol, remembering her name just in time.

'Come on in,' I said as they shuffled around, unsure of themselves, in the hallway. I turned all the lights on as we went into the living room, aware that they were looking around in alarm at finding the house enveloped in darkness. 'Didn't take you too long getting here, I hope,' I said.

'Wasn't too bad, I thought it would be worse,' Kevin said.

'Traffic was awful,' Carol said.

We sat in silence for a few seconds. 'Would you like some tea or something?' I asked.

'No, thanks mate,' said Kevin.

'Oh yes please,' said Carol. 'I'll make it if you like,' she added as I started to get up. Kevin nodded approvingly at her as she made her way into the kitchen and I sat down again. They must have planned for her to vanish every now and again, so Kevin and I could get some time alone together . . . to talk in manly fashion of what had happened, I supposed. I looked at my feet, surprised to find that I had gone to sleep with my shoes on. I really ought to think of something to say to Kevin to relieve him of his discomfiture, I thought, as my mind shifted into utter blankness. We had already talked about it . . . he was one of the first persons I called that day . . . was it just yesterday? Thursday, the twenty-seventh of August. How long it had taken for two days to pass.

'How are you coping, Rahul?' he asked gently. We were never gentle with each other and for one awful moment I wanted to burst out laughing and ask him to cut it out. But I merely nodded, still looking in amazement at my shoes.

'Where's Anjali?' he asked, looking around.

'She's still at that Social Services place. I saw her this morning.'

'Will she be staying there for a while . . .' he trailed off.

'No, I think it's meant to be a respite place . . . emergencies and things. They don't keep kids long term, I think.' He was silent and I added, 'Foster care didn't seem appropriate. Maya always had a thing against it for some reason . . .'

'What do you think you'll do?'

'Well, I don't think I really get to decide. Apparently, I need to have taken out something called *parental responsibility* . . . in court . . . to have a say in Anjali's future.'

'Which, you haven't?'

Jaishree Misra

'No.'

'Well . . . I don't suppose you were to know . . .'

Exactly Kev, I wanted to say, we weren't to know. Maybe other people are clever and wise about planning for all eventualities but we didn't, okay? I stayed silent, poor Kevin meant no harm.

'But they can't take her away from you, can they?' he asked.

'I'm the only dad she's ever really known,' I said, feeling a sudden weight descend inside me somewhere. A sudden vacuum seemed to have formed itself somewhere in my chest cavity.

'What about you, what are your immediate plans?'

'Me?' I hadn't thought that far yet. 'What do you mean?'

'I mean, you aren't thinking about going back to work straightaway, are you?'

'Well, it's the weekend now . . .'

'Yes, but after the weekend . . . on Monday . . . you don't think you'll be getting back to work, do you?'

I wished he wouldn't put pressure on me like that. To think ahead. To think at all. 'I don't know,' I said.

'Would you like a cuppa, Rahul? Kev?' Carol had reappeared in the doorway, wearing Maya's apron. Well, it was a communal apron really, and I remembered Carol having worn it once before when Maya taught her how to make biryani, but I wasn't very pleased to see anyone but Maya in it at the moment. 'Oh, I hoped you wouldn't mind,' she said, noticing me stare at the apron, 'but Kev picked me up from the office and we came straight here . . . I-I didn't want to spill anything on my suit. Oh God, I'm sorry . . . I just wasn't thinking . . .' She looked flustered as it dawned on her that she might have been insensitive and her normally brash voice had risen to a squeak.

'No, yes . . . I mean . . . no, of course, it's not a problem . . .yes, yes, I will have some tea . . . thanks . . .'

She vanished in a flurry of mortification and Kevin tried to pick up the threads again.

'I mean, why don't you take some leave, Rahul? And go to your parents for a while. Or even visit your brother in the US. He's somewhere in California, isn't he?

'San Francisco,' I muttered.

'Well, that's exactly the kind of break you need. Maybe they'll let you take Anjali as well. Supposed to be a great place, San Francisco, never been there myself.'

I hadn't either, although Maya and I had talked often about visiting Anil there at some point. Why hadn't I taken her goddammit? Carol came in with the tea. She wasn't wearing the apron any more, I noticed. She had done the tea properly, milk in a jug, sugar in a separate bowl—she had even found a tray cloth to cover our old plastic tray.

'Very nice, Carol,' I said, trying, really trying to appreciate the effort they were making for me. I knew it was hard for everybody else; in some ways, harder than it was for me because I was sort of entitled to wallow in my grief, while everybody else was expected to put up with my wallowing. Why couldn't I feel more . . . more *grateful* or something?

We sipped our tea, while Carol took over the conversation as she usually did, though this time she seemed to be trying to gee me up. Her words were all melding into one inside my exhausted mind and I could barely hear her as she prattled on inanely about something that had happened on the motorway. She was now going 'Parp–Parp' very loudly, trying to lighten the atmosphere with the tale of some errant lorry they had passed today. Maya had liked Carol, strangely. 'I don't have to make any effort when she's around,' she used to say. 'Don't need to talk, to *think* even. All I have to do, once in a while, is nod, I suppose,' she had added, laughing. While I thrashed on about what hard work Carol was and what appalling taste Kevin had always shown in women. Brittle, bottle-blonde, dim—each one of them unerringly similar to the previous one. And his whole process of falling in love was invariably such a dramatic event too, filled with relentless pursuit and angst and eventual noisy heartbreak. For some reason, it was always Kevin getting jilted. In all the years I had known him, I had never once known him to be the heartless jilter.

The room had gone silent and they were both looking at me now. Someone must have asked me a question.

'What? Sorry, I missed that . . .'

'Carol was just asking if you'd like to get your shopping done. You're nearly out of milk I believe.'

'And tea,' Carol added.

'There are probably other things as well,' I said, getting up. 'Yes, I suppose it's got to be done.'

I went into the kitchen, with both Carol and Kevin following me. Paper and pen to make a list—I knew Maya kept a little yellow pad in a drawer somewhere. There it was . . . with her handwriting on it . . . milk . . . bread . . . sandwich stuff . . . hara dhaniya . . . she had written, must have been on Wednesday evening. I ran my finger over her handwriting, feeling only the paper. I wanted to put the pad to my face, stupidly, and run it over my cheek, but Kevin and Carol were both behind me, opening drawers and telling me what else needed to be on the list. Sugar, Kevin was saying. Pasta, do you eat pasta, Carol was asking. I picked up the pen and started to write.

*

Tesco on a Friday evening was a bad idea. Cars were jostling each other for parking, giving an indication of the bedlam that lay within. I found myself walking up to the mangoes on their shelf near the door, as usual. I always chose one, a ripe yellow one for Maya while she raced off to get the essentials, milk and cheese and suchlike. It was only as I neared the shelf that I remembered I was not that fond of mangoes myself. They had always been Maya's treat, I did not need them today. As we made our slow journey down the aisles with our trolley, I was suddenly grateful for Carol's presence. 'Pasta!' she would trill, looking at the list, or 'Biscuits!' before going shooting down a crowded aisle with unerring precision, to return a few minutes later holding up the required object triumphantly. 'What's ha-ra da-ni-ya?' she asked at one point, stumbling over the Hindi that Maya had picked up from me.

'Er . . . it's green coriander . . . but . . .'

'Oh, that's back there with the vegetables, I think,' she replied.

'No, no, that's all right, don't go back for it,' I called after her, unable to explain that it was one of those Maya ingredients. She used it to garnish everything—daal, vegetables, curries. My cooking was never as elaborate as that. In fact, for a long time now, it was Maya who more or less ran the Indian Food department in the house, while I specialized in the Quickie Food stuff—stir-fry and pasta and beans on toast, that kind of thing. But Carol was already appearing around the corner, holding a small pot of fresh coriander aloft. That was the other thing—Maya would never have bought the thing in a flowerpot from Tesco. 'Far too expensive,' she would have said scornfully. 'For one-pound-twenty I can get three bunches from the Indian shop.' I took the pot from a beaming Carol, mumbling a thanks, and put it into the trolley.

*

After unloading the shopping bags back at the house, I helped Kevin fetch his and Carol's bags out of his car. Sandra appeared at her gate next door. 'Hi Rahul, are you okay? I'd called around to check on you earlier today.'

'I'd gone out to see Anjali,' I replied, stopping at her gate. 'Took her out for lunch to a café.'

She smiled. 'She must have loved that. How is she coping?'

'I think she's okay, Sandra. Although it's hard to tell with her . . .' I trailed off, my voice was going again.

Jaishree Misra

'Look,' she said kindly, 'if you do bring her back to the house and need some help with her bath and things, give me a shout, will you? You know I'm free in the evenings after work.'

I nodded. Unexpected kindnesses were having the awful effect of making me want to cry these days. I did not attempt introducing Kevin to Sandra because I could not trust my voice not to wobble. We nodded all around before Kevin and I returned to the house.

'Neighbour,' I said needlessly to Kevin, 'good friend of Maya's.'

'Seems nice,' he replied.

This was crazy. Kevin and I *never* struggled for conversation. On a normal day, he would probably have said 'big jugs' or 'does she have a licence to carry those'. Not 'seems nice' for God's sake. That wasn't the way Kevin and I ever talked. Beer, cricket, tennis, music, tits and legs—that was the stuff of our conversation. But I had never experienced bereavement before and didn't know yet that it had the capacity to change things forever. To reach into people's lives, turning things off, other things on, shifting everything this way and that. I didn't know yet that it was one of those oddest of things that would affect every single one of my relationships, sometimes for better, sometimes for worse. I didn't know yet that it had already changed me forever.

'Look, why don't you and Carol go and freshen up . . . showers and things . . . after that we'll go out somewhere for a drink and something to eat, shall we?'

'Good idea,' Kevin said, taking the bags upstairs.

I climbed the stairs to the study, wondering if I could call Anjali at her children's home to talk to her before she went to bed. The answering machine was flashing again and I bleeped it on my way into the toilet.

'Halloo, Rahul beta! Your mummy has just called me from India to tell me the terrible news! Beta, if you are there, will you pick up the phone please?' Aunt Bulwant's strident Punjabi tone was followed by a loud, sorrowful sigh before the phone went dead again. Why on earth did Mum tell *her* of all people? She was Mum's old Jalandhar schoolmate who had moved to Harrow after her marriage, more than thirty years ago. Big and brash, she had been full of motherly intentions towards me when I first arrived in England as an eighteen-year-old. Not that I disliked her or anything, but I always considered it wise to keep a safe distance from those of her ilk and had carefully managed that all these years, visiting her once a year or so, for Diwali or a family wedding or some such, if she pressed hard enough, or if Mum admonished me in her letters. Now, under these circumstances, I would never be able to shake her off. She would most certainly want to tuck me under that ample wing and keep me there. She had always seemed hurt by my aloofness, pinching my cheeks very hard and vowing to keep a closer eye on me every time she saw me—which only served to make me scuttle further away in fright. When I got my first job, she briefly reappeared for a while, attempting to introduce me to some niece of hers. 'Not for marriage or anything, beta,' she had boomed comfortingly, 'just to meet and see if you *like* each other, for going out and all, that's all.' I had fled from that scenario like a bat out of hell, needless to say. Some years later, after Maya and Anjali arrived in England, I took them down to meet Aunt Bulwant. To her credit she made no nasty cracks about second marriages and step-kids. She even laid out a lot of goodies—kaaju barfi and special Gujarati dhoklas—in our honour. Anjali took an enormous liking to her—and her food. And Maya had thought her quite nice too, but I still preferred to keep my encounters with Aunt Bull (as Maya and I called her in private) to a bare minimum. Now, nothing would shake her off my tail.

But I could put off returning her call for a while yet, I thought, pulling off my shoes and getting my towel out for a shower. The telephone rang as I was towelling myself dry. 'Shall I get it?' I could hear Carol call up the stairs. I closed my eyes at the thought of a

Jaishree Misra

Carol-Aunt Bull encounter, and having to explain a female presence so soon after Maya's death to a horrified Aunt Bull.

'No, no, I've got it,' I said, bursting out of the bathroom.

'Oh hello, Aunty Bulwant,' I said sheepishly as her unmistakable 'halloo' thundered down the line.

'Beta!' she wailed, 'what can I say to you! Such terrible news!'

I mumbled my agreement.

'*Tell* me how you are coping . . . Your poor mother, she is *so* desperately worried about you, beta!'

If I told her how badly I was coping, she would turn up here and cart me off to her house to lavish care on me, I was sure of that.

'I'm . . . I'm sort of coping, Aunty . . .'

'How can you be coping!' She was not taking any bullshit. 'I know you are just saying it. I know you can't be coping, you poor boy. Now you listen to me . . .' She was talking very slowly now, separating each word out from the next to make sure I really got it. 'I want you to just pack up and close your house and come out here to your Aunty Bulwant's house. Let me look after you and you can even go to work from here. Your uncle will not mind.' How could he—his silent presence only ever provided a kind of lugubrious backdrop to Aunty Bull's noisy life.

'Aunty, it's very kind of you, but—'

'But what?' Aggression and affection were difficult to separate out with Aunt Bull sometimes.

'I feel I need to be alone . . .'

'*Alone*!' She said the word as though it were worse than capital punishment. 'Alone! You should never be alone, not even for one minute at a time like this. It is worst thing to be, beta, you take it from me.'

How did she know—she had never lost a girlfriend, she had never even lost poor, silent Uncle Bull.

'Aunty, please don't mind,' I said, 'I'm really touched by your offer, but I can't take it up at the moment.'

'But I promised your mother I would look after you, beta!'

'I . . . I'm okay for now, really, I'll—'

'Then I'm coming there, to see you!'

No! I thought in alarm. I could imagine her taking stock of the situation and then calling Mum and Dad to tell them how messy the house was and how terrible I looked. 'I will, I will come over, Aunty. Next week, perhaps . . . I have two friends over for the weekend. So I'm okay for now, really. I'll come when they've gone, shall I?'

'When?' she demanded.

'Er . . . Wednesday?' I offered tentatively.

'Wednesday? Okay. I am having some people over that day, you see it is your uncle's birthday that day. So that will be good for you, to be with some people, enjoy some company.'

I could feel my heart sink. I didn't want to be with people and I didn't want to enjoy anyone's company. But Wednesday was a long way off. Anything could happen between now and then. I might even go and cop it in an accident!

'Yes, fine, Aunty,' I said, 'thank you for your concern. I'll see you on Wednesday.'

'I'll phone you every day,' she was calling out reassuringly as I hung up.

Bugger, bugger, bugger, I thought as I rubbed myself down violently. Damn, damn, *damn* all these kindly, well-meaning people who were trying to make things easier for me. I opened the wardrobe to pull out some clothes. I could hardly bear *Kevin's* company, how the hell would I cope with someone like Aunt Bull, for chrissake! I wasn't sure, of course, what it was that I did want. The first two days on my own had been murder as well. Anjali's presence merely made me want to put my head in my hands and weep. There was only one thing I really wanted—one thing, and that was being denied to me. What a goddamned, obstreperous, churlish thing life was! The temptation to take our other car and

Jaishree Misra

ram it hard into a tree or drive it right over Waterloo Bridge was overwhelming. I pulled on a shirt, tucked it into my chinos and zipped them up.

Kevin and Carol were both ready and waiting for me in the living room. Someone, Carol probably, had drawn the curtains and dimmed the lights. Did I imagine it or was the room tidier as well? Newspapers had been folded and placed in the wicker basket, the faded flowers from last week cleared away from the mantelpiece. I had noticed this morning that they had started to droop, letting off a sodden rotten stink. I meant to get rid of them, but didn't bother in the end. Sounds silly, but I didn't especially want to throw away anything that Maya had touched and arranged so recently. I was glad now, though, that someone else had done it; I certainly couldn't have kept them there forever. Poor Carol, I really ought to be more grateful. She could have spent her weekend in millions of more interesting ways than cleaning up after me.

'So where would you two like to go?' I asked, trying to sound cheerful.

'Whatever you say—whatever's convenient.'

'How about that Italian place up on the High Street? We'll be able to park at this time of night.'

'Sounds good.'

'Why don't you decide, Carol. What sort of food would you like to eat?'

'Italian's fine.'

'Or a pub, perhaps? Would you like a pub meal?'

'Italian,' Kevin was taking the decision, 'I think you'll like this place, Carol, not too noisy, great food.'

Maya loves it too, I nearly said, biting back the words just in time. I was longing to talk about her, but I was fairly sure that it would be really odd for everyone else. How would they arrange their facial features, for instance, while I rambled on about her? Would they look on with sympathy, or pity, or be able to *laugh* if

I remembered something funny? I suppose it would have been a relief to talk about her and laugh and cry quite openly. But I didn't think these poor people could cope with that. Not now, anyway.

We walked out to the car, Carol climbing into the back seat, Kevin next to me as I drove. The neon signs on Clapham High Street were flashing eerily at no one in particular. The evening stragglers had long since finished their shopping and returned to their homes. Only a few stray down-and-outs still hung around, some swilling from cans on lonely benches, others prodding for unlikely treasures in overflowing garbage bins. Maya hated walking back home after an evening out. I pulled in behind the row of parked cars skirting the roundabout.

The Pizzeria glowed its welcome as we neared it. Maya always went in and took a deep breath of the baking garlic air. Love it, *love* it, she would exclaim, eyes shining in delight. I was getting the familiar smiles and nods from across the counter where the breads and pizzas were being baked.

'Hello, sir,' the man at the front desk was saying, 'table for four, yes? Madame parking the car?'

'No, three,' Kevin said hastily.

But it wasn't going to be that simple. 'What, no Madame today?' He liked us and always flirted ever so slightly with Maya. Being Italian makes them think it's sort of *expected* of them, she would say to me, seeming annoyingly pleased to be flirted with.

He was still waiting for an answer and both Kevin and Carol were starting to look anxious. It looked like I would have to handle this. At least Hoo Fung's had given me some practice.

'No, no Madame today,' I said flatly. 'In fact, Madame won't be coming again. She's gone.'

Euphemisms. I hated it when other people used them but I was still not capable of the plain, bare truth myself. It was far too harsh for now—for him, for me, for everybody. He would probably think she and I had split up or something, but I was willing to allow him that comfort for now. We were shown to our table and settled ourselves down. I could see that Kevin and Carol were both looking rattled and wanted to say something to ease the situation.

'You want to try their hot dough sticks, Carol, they're excellent,' I said instead, burying my face in the menu that I didn't need to read at all. 'Wine . . . their house wine is excellent, Kevin,' I carried on brightly, aware that I was babbling and probably sounding very strange indeed. 'Why don't you two go for the house red, I'll have a beer because I'll be driving us back home . . . can't risk another accident, can we? That would be too, too droll for words, wouldn't it?'

Kevin and Carol were looking at each other, without looking at each other. I could sense their antennae tuning into each other in alarmed high-pitched bleeps. What a madman, they must have been thinking. And what did I care? Once I had sorted out something halfway decent for Anjali, I had no intention of hanging around. I could not see the point.

I woke up the next morning, surprised that I had slept. I had slept a whole night without once waking up in a cold, clammy sweat! Maybe it was because I had eaten a proper meal the night before. Maybe it had been the combination of wine and beer. I had tried being let off, but Kevin insisted he would drive us back home and so Carol and I polished off a bottle and a half of the house red between us. I remembered also drinking some Peronis and putting away a whole Siciliana, heaving with pepperoni and chillies, by myself. I was nearly asleep in the car on the way home, aware only that the High Street neon signs were still pulsating forlornly, announcing the distance left for home—the green of M&S signifying about three minutes to go, the blue of Go Hair and Nails, less than a minute. The car finally turned right at the flashing pink bottle of Save-On Food and Wines. Kevin must have helped me up the stairs and taken my shoes off. I was still wearing my shirt and chinos, with the buttons undone.

I would have to get up, despite the dull pain in my head. Kevin and Carol would be up soon—the least I could do was get them some tea. What a good egg Kevin was, my oldest friend in this country. I met him in my first week at university. We had both landed up in Durham, me fresh from India and him, a country lad from near Hexham. A common fondness for Led Zeppelin brought

'Pudding?'

'Yes, we'll think of something nice for pudding.'

'Apple pie!' she suggested, perking up.

'Good idea, or, even better, bananas chopped up into ice-cream!'

'Pink ice-cream.'

She was doing a deal. I paused to let her know I was considering her bargain carefully.

'Oh okay, pink ice-cream,' I said eventually.

I could hear her chuckling as she handed the phone back to the Australian worker.

'Well, that's one happy girl,' she said, adding, 'I've had a word with Susan, she said it's fine for Anjali to go home for a while tomorrow. What time would you like to come?'

Kevin and Carol had said they would be leaving first thing in the morning as they had to visit Kevin's mother on their way home. 'Eleven?' I asked. She agreed and I hung up. I did not have the heart to make the other phone calls and walked slowly down the stairs to the living room. Kevin had crashed out on the sofa, his cap pulled over his eyes. Carol was curled up in the chair, flicking through a magazine. We talked in whispers to allow Kevin his exceedingly noisy nap on the sofa. Or rather, Carol talked while my mind darted around to all the darkest, emptiest corners I could think of. Every so often, one of Carol's words or sentences would permeate my floating, serrated consciousness—'. . . *appalling*' . . . 'you wouldn't *believe* it' . . . 'I tell you I was just gobsmacked'— while I couldn't stop thinking of waiting in a crematorium queue to hand over Maya's smile to a man in a black frock coat.

The evening unravelled slowly, taking on misty edges, dissolving finally into empty silences. When the phone rang again, I dragged myself up the stairs, knowing it was probably Martin Cullen. I asked him to request the undertakers for the simplest function the crematorium would allow, telling him that I would pay for whatever it cost. He ran a couple of suggestions past me and I agreed that a bit of non-religious music with a reading would probably be most appropriate. I told him I had decided to attend it alone, as I didn't think Anjali would either understand or benefit from it particularly. If he thought that a one-man funeral was odd, he was kind enough to keep his opinion from creeping into his voice.

When I returned downstairs, Carol had woken Kevin up and had probably warned him of my deteriorating spirits. She had started to cook a meal, with Kevin providing occasional help. By now they knew I was not able to carry on the charade any longer and padded around me in whispers. Once again Kevin attempted to get me to book a trip to India, or America—'you need to get away from here, Rahul'—but even he had to give up after a while because I had no energy to do anything but agree to all his suggestions.

'Yes, I'll go to India, Kev.'

'Yeah, or maybe America.'

'Yes, once Anjali's sorted.'

'No, that's okay, I'll book it next week.'

His face was looking drawn now—it must have been a shattering day for him as well. But there was nothing I could do to help him; I was too far gone myself. Shovelling some of Carol's pasta down my throat to stop her motherly squawking, I tried to thank them nicely for the meal, but I'm not sure I sounded grateful enough. Carol wouldn't hear of it when I offered to do the washing up, and brushed me off with an affectionate swat of the tea-towel. I showed Kevin where the coffee percolator was and pulled out an old box of chocolate mints before asking if I could be excused. 'If you don't mind, I'll just go to bed. Suddenly I'm exhausted,' I said. And we all apologized to each other as I backed my way up the stairs again.

Kevin looked up at me anxiously and made one last attempt,

'Rahul, talk to me. Don't bottle things up . . .' But I had to get away, to my bed, to anticipate another sleepless night. How was I to say goodbye to her tomorrow? I didn't even know if I would be able to see her, or have to say goodbye to a goddamned *box*. I had forgotten to ask Martin about that. I knew roughly the routine in India, but this was England where I was fairly sure people were always put in boxes at funerals. And would I ever be able to tell if I was doing things the way Maya would have liked? That was important, wasn't it? Would she have wanted Anjali there? Would she want to stay forever rooted to this cold, damp place we had made our home for three years, the place that had finally killed her—wouldn't she rather go home to India? Was there any point in that, though, any blooming point at all? Who the hell would she be going back to anyway?

I hadn't prayed for a long time. I just wasn't the praying kind. That was for sissies and weaklings, all that stuff—Malayali mumbo-jumbo I called it just to annoy Maya sometimes. But that night, I got down on my knees, put my head on the bed and prayed. That's if you can describe the inane ramblings of a madman as a prayer. I just needed someone to tell me what to do next—or why I had to bother at all.

Outside, it had started to rain. One of those sudden summer showers when the day has been too hot, and grateful Londoners open their windows wide to let the cool spray in. I took off my clothes and lay down, feeling the spray land sweetly on my chest and on my stomach. Maya would have been coming into the bedroom around now, her face and neck smelling of some creamy thing, her teeth of toothpaste. She would curl herself up next to me, her face nuzzling my shoulder, her left leg entwining with mine. Sensing her mood, I would lift her nightshirt, exposing her breasts to the cool wet night and, as her nipples would go taut in the cold, I would begin to play with them, feel them strain against the softness of her breasts. Her eyes would close and she would stretch with pleasure and that's when I would slip her shirt off . . . gently, over her face and head and then with increasing urgency over her arms, throwing it off the side of the bed and to the floor. She would moan gently, her body moonlit, dark and light.

The empty space next to me on the bed was more pitiless than ever before. Pain stabbed at me and I made no attempt to stop the tears that were now coursing down my face. I wept as though I could never stop, like the rain outside, falling silently, unendingly against the windowpanes.

Jaishree Misra

_____

The sun hadn't risen beyond the large plane trees that lined our street as Kevin and Carol left the house the following morning. After waving them off, I walked back into the house, feeling surprisingly tranquil. Martin Cullen had called in the morning to say he had arranged for the undertakers to come at ten, which gave me an hour to get ready. I had prepared myself as I drifted awake early this morning, and knew what I had to put together. With uncanny calm I went through our CD collection and, with some deliberation, picked out Maya's favourite—a Lata Mangeshkar CD that I bought her a few birthdays ago. She listened to the *Tumhee mere mandir* track on it incessantly. She even had it taped to listen to it in the car. Might she have been listening to that in the car as her eyes closed on Thursday? *Stupid* thought. What did I need to know things like that for? I walked over to her bureau and pulled out a picture of Anjali and me, removing it from the silver frame in which it had lived for a couple of years. It was completely outdated—Anjali sporting her old hairstyle of bangs coming right down into her eyes; I wearing that old tartan shirt, leaning on a shovel, laughing at something Maya must have been saying as she took the photograph. How important it felt now to remember all those things we had said once and laughed at so casually then. She had never wanted to change that photograph in the frame, saying it was the day she remembered more than anything else. I can't remember what was special about the day, but she must have had some reason. I peered into the picture again, willing it to give up its secrets—it looked like any other English summer morning (or was it afternoon?), a bit like this one really, nothing special. It must have been her memory of whatever she had been saying to make me laugh like that. Anjali was smiling her artificial 'photo-smile', screwing up her nose to look cute.

I put it into the bag that already had the CD in it and took it out to the garden. There, I plucked a few sprigs of the lavender that Maya sometimes brought in to stick into her tiny silver vase on the bureau and put those into the bag as well. Then I went upstairs to the bookshelf and pulled out the book of Auden's poems Maya had bought after we had gone to see *Four Weddings and a Funeral*. She had cried inconsolably during the funeral scene in that film. Obviously. I should have let the title of the film warn me off taking Maya to see it. Funerals (and weddings, for that matter) were things we simply did *not* discuss, if we could help it. I was always overcome by a feeling of complete helplessness when I knew she was thinking about her own family and what had been done in her name at her grandmother's house. Helplessness. And rage. *Rage*.

It was hard to find out exactly how much she was wounded, because she talked so little about it. She talked about Kerala often enough, keeping track of what was going on there by getting hold of *India Today* and the *Asian Age* whenever she could. And so she would tell me, sometimes when I was only half-listening, that 'the LDF are back in power now, although it's a coalition government', or that 'the monsoons have failed again'—her voice full of sadness. I did try asking her once, when she talked of how hard the farmers would have worked all year round only to have their crops destroyed when the rains failed, whether she was thinking of her grandmother's fields and house. She was looking out of the car window, at the grimy council blocks, as she said softly, 'The waters of the kaayal used to grow all still and silent when they closed the bund off after a failed monsoon . . . it would become dark green, so dark that you couldn't look into it any more to search for tadpoles . . . and then, after a few days, it would start to smell like a dead thing . . .' before she stiffened her shoulders and fell silent. I never knew whether to talk about her past life or not. I had helped her escape from it and, I suppose, if I was to be honest, I was really never very sure if I had done the right thing in helping her leave Kerala. Once I even mulled over the thought that she might somehow blame me for all that she had lost.

And now . . . now all *that* was lost too. How strange! Why had she been brought to me so briefly? Had she been taken away from me because I had once taken her away from everything else she had been a part of till then? Was this my *punishment*? I felt gripped suddenly by the extraordinary yearning to return her to Kerala somehow. Something was telling me that that was probably what she would have wanted.

✳

At the hospital, Martin was waiting for me at the main reception, as agreed. I must have had some recollection of having met him on that tortuous Thursday—I knew his face as soon as I saw him. He came up to me and put an arm on my shoulder as he shook my hand. 'The undertaker's here already,' he said, as we walked briskly together down a long, white corridor. I remembered the smell of sickness and death from my last visit here. Suddenly, we were in a room . . . as I had thought . . . with a box in it. She doesn't like confined spaces, I thought, not able to look at the box at all. Someone else was now shaking my hand, saying something through a hot haze. 'I'm afraid I'll have to ask you to identify your partner again, Mr Tiwari,' the man said. I walked with him and nodded as he opened the box gently to show me just her face. There was no smile for me, of course, no shining warmth—just a waxy coldness, so unlike her.

Someone was holding my arm now, helping me away, down another long white corridor until we were outside in the harsh sunlight again. I found a big ball of bathroom tissues in my hand and didn't know how it had got there. When I had calmed myself down, Martin rubbing a spot between my shoulder blades, I got into his car. He drove, silently, for a long time until we had left the council blocks of south London behind, to reach a leafier part of outer London. I had never been to this part of town before. Then we were driving into a small car park, the wheels of the car crunching the gravel underneath. We got out and walked around the building to the front door. Everything seemed quiet and peaceful. Someone was filling in a form and handing it to me to sign. The man who had been at the hospital had already arrived. He must be the undertaker, I decided. That must mean she was here too.

After a short wait, I was ushered into a small chapel-like room. There were pews and a raised dais at the end of the room, with the box on it. Her box.

Martin asked me if I had brought the music and I took the CD out of the carrier bag I was still clutching tightly. He asked if I was ready and I nodded. I really needed to have it over and done with as soon as possible. He handed the CD over to the undertaker and then walked me over to the front of the room, to stand just in front of the box. I put the carrier bag down to take the book out of it. Straightening up, readying myself, I opened it to the page I had marked earlier. I looked at Martin and he nodded. Taking a deep breath I started to read . . . *Stop all the clocks, cut off the telephone* . . . my voice wobbling at first, before settling down to a calmness that surprised even me.

I didn't notice when, but the music had started to play softly as I was reading. Maya's music. I had never thought of it as anything but Maya's music because it wasn't the kind of thing I would have willingly chosen to listen to when she wasn't around. It rose up now into the high-vaulted ceiling, taking on a volume and a beauty it had never seemed to have when we listened to it in the house.

'Have you got anything else?' Martin whispered. I noticed, with some surprise, that his eyes were shining too, as if he had just remembered something terribly sad himself.

I dived into my nearly empty carrier bag again and carefully removed the lavender sprigs and the photograph. Martin nodded across to the box, indicating that I was to take them across. He didn't mean I was to put them *inside* the box, did he? I walked across and placed them on top, feeling for one moment the warmth of its wood under my fingers. Now, suddenly, I wanted to touch it properly, to hold it, for one moment. To put my arms around it and hold it, as I would have held her body. To hold it and put my head down on it and weep and weep, allowing my tears to soak into the wood and into where she lay. Please don't take her away from me, I was thinking as I turned and walked back to take my place next to Martin again. My invisible, inner turmoil was heaving and clamouring. This was a drum piece to end all drum pieces, hitting away inside me, threatening to smash everything to bits. I stood there, watching, as a set of rollers under the box started to move. Nobody had told me about rollers under the box. I looked on, surprised, wanting to shout at the deceit of it, as the box moved away from me now and towards a set of dark curtains hanging at the back of the dais. Before I knew it she was gone. Swallowed up by the curtains that rose obediently to receive her and then fell again into unruffled silence . . . almost as if she had never been there at all. Two years, nine months and a day wiped clean. Just like that.

Martin turned to me and put his arm on my shoulder, before asking if I wanted to wait in the chapel or outside to collect the ashes as I had requested. It would take some time to cool, he said.

Outside, I said, turning and leaving the chapel where the last notes of Maya's song were still playing softly.

Gnarled old trees watched silently as I sat on the grass and wept for what must have been a long time. Today I had remembered, in the calmness of my morning preparations, to put a handkerchief in my pocket and I used it to wipe my face and blow my nose when I had finished. Then I sat, with my back against a tree, and watched fat squirrels romp on the grass in front of me—as though the world were filled with secretly joyous things that only they were privy to.

I thought, as I had done many times in the last few hours, of that other ceremony that had been performed in the compound of Maya's grandmother's house, three years ago—on the banks of the water tank where she had played as a little girl. Here's the real thing now, I wanted to yell at the blameless sky. We heard of it when Maya had attempted to make contact one last time with her mother, sending her a photograph of the three of us as a last, desperate peace offering. Her father had written a letter to her in reply. She eventually translated it for me—it was in Malayalam— when I insisted that she do so, because her face had gone so white and her body so still. She told me that the letter had been written just to inform her that her parents had moved back to Champakulam after she had run away. Because her grandmother was very ill. And that a death ceremony had been performed. As was sometimes done when great shame and ignominy was brought on a family by one of its members. It took me a while to work out that the ceremony was done on her behalf, on *Maya's* behalf. She struggled to explain the concept to me. *Padi addachu pindam vekkal.* It means the death rites are done and the doors are closed forever, she whispered, shaking with the horror of it all.

So they did theirs then, three years too early. And I did mine today. They were able to shut their door quite effectively. Their silence proclaiming over the years how easy it had been to forget. I will never do that, Maya, I screamed inwardly, looking up at the sky again. I won't forget and I won't let them forget you either.

After a while, Martin emerged from the crematorium and walked across to where I sat. 'It'll take a little while more,' he said, 'but they have given me the cremation certificate.' He held out a brown paper envelope. I took it from him, staying seated where I was. 'You'll probably need that for customs if you decide to take the ashes out of the country. I know Hindus often do that to be able to float the ashes in one of their holy rivers . . .' he trailed off. 'Would you like to sit indoors with me while we wait?' he added gently. I got up and walked with him back into the dark interior of the chapel. We waited in a neat little office for what seemed like a long time until, finally, the undertaker came in holding another box, a much smaller one . . . with her ashes. He waited until I had got up and then handed it over to me. I couldn't blame anyone else for the absurdity of the situation. I had asked for it. I had wanted to be given her ashes to take her back to India. I had thought about nothing else last night and had decided that that was where she would have wanted to be. There had to be *some* reason for this ridiculous thing to have happened. That would be Maya's journey back to Kerala. With me.

Martin walked me back to his car and we drove home, with me holding the box on my lap. At the house, he asked if I would like him to come in for a while. He had been so kind, and I had no intention of hurting him, but I shook my head and asked to be left alone. He persisted. 'Could I call you a little later,' he asked, to which I nodded. I could understand, of course, his need to make sure I had survived the whole sorry business.

I walked up to the door, holding the box with one hand, while I pulled the keys out of my pocket. Now how was I to get the door open using just one hand? And was it okay to put the box down on the ground? Without a word, Martin was at the door, helping me. He took the keys out of my hand and opened the door as I continued to hold the box close to my chest. Then he gave me the keys and wished me goodbye again as I stepped into the house and closed the door.

I had to find some safe place to put it, which Anjali couldn't spot when she got here later today. Upstairs, in my wardrobe, the shelf at the top held only some old woollens that I hardly ever wore. I went into my room and opened the wardrobe doors. The cardigans were easily pushed to one side and I slid the box in. It amazed me how solid it had felt in my arms, considering its meagre contents. It was almost invisible from where I stood. I covered it with an old jacket until it could not be seen at all.

There were messages on the answering machine that I decided to ignore and I dialled the number of Anjali's home instead.

'Yes, hi, it's Anjali's dad. I'd said I would be picking her up to bring her to the house for the afternoon. Is it okay to come now?'

'Oh yes, hello Mr Tiwari, it's Susan Hill, the senior on duty. We were expecting you. Yes, it's fine to come now. She's been on window-watch for the past hour!'

'Okay, tell her I'll be there in ten minutes.'

I drove to the children's home feeling my spirits rise slightly. It had been a good decision not to take Anjali to the crematorium. She wouldn't have understood what was going on and could have got quite frightened by the proceedings. Or, even worse, *amused*, knowing the silly child. What if she had started to giggle at the sight of the box moving away from us on invisible rollers, for instance? I rang the bell at the home, feeling that familiar longing to grab her in the biggest hug I could manage. The door opened and she shot, like an ecstatic cannonball, into my arms. I laughed and hugged her, feeling unimaginably moved. This should be worth carrying on for. I felt a flash of guilt that it just didn't seem adequate at the moment. A woman who I presumed was Susan Hill was standing behind Anjali, smiling at us.

'Well, it doesn't look like she's going to ask you in for a drink, is she?'

'I don't suppose I need to come in though, do I?' I asked.

'No, not unless you'd like to. She can't wait to get out, certainly. Can you?' she said to the back of Anjali's head, which was already disappearing in the direction of the car, before turning back to me with a smile. 'She's really been straining at the leash all morning.'

'I'm sorry I couldn't get away earlier,' I mumbled.

'Will she need anything else from here to take home?'

'No, I'm sure I'll have everything she'll need at home. Well, thanks. I'll bring her back sometime in the evening, shall I?'

'Dinner's at about six.'

'Okay, sometime before then.'

Anjali was already at the car, trying to wrench off the door handle on the passenger side when I caught up with her. 'Whoa, whoa!' I said, 'let me unlock it first.'

She giggled as she made way for me, allowing me to belt her in before I walked around the car to get into the driver's seat. 'So, how's my Anjali?' I asked, looking at her.

'Where's Mum?' she replied.

I sighed. 'Anjali, baby, you must understand Mum's gone. Not coming back. Mum's–Gone–Away.' How many times would I have to repeat those horrible words before she would even begin to understand? 'Goddamn you!' I said suddenly and loudly, jabbing the keys into the ignition. Anjali jumped in alarm and I put a reassuring hand on her plump knee. 'I'm talking to Big Boy up there,' I said apologetically, 'not to you, baby.' But she was still looking puzzled. She didn't know about Big Boy up there, despite the fact that He had just played such a cruel game of dice with her life. I shook her knee and tried to be chatty. 'So, what colour ice-cream did you say you wanted today?'

'Pink,' she said promptly.

'Yummy! My favourite too . . . except I think we'll have to go and buy some. As soon as we get home, you go and check the freezer and, if we haven't got any, we'll walk down to Mr Save-On's and get some, okay?'

She nodded, smiling, and looked on with interest as she started to spot the familiar landmarks on the approach to the house. She sat up in her seat, wriggling with pleasure as I pulled into our tree-lined street. While I reversed the car into its usual slot, she peered out at Sandra's windows, but the curtains were drawn. 'Sunday,' I said to Anjali. 'Sandra must have gone to Brighton to visit her mum today.' Anjali tumbled excitedly out of the car, not bothering to mask her impatience as I fumbled with the keys, unlocking the house. When it was barely open, she squeezed herself in and then went bursting into the living room, hollering 'MU-UM!' at the top of her voice. She said it with such an air of undisputed confidence that for one brainless moment I found myself holding my breath, half-expecting to see Maya stroll out of the kitchen door, with a huge smile wreathed across her face. For a moment Anjali and I waited, listening to the silence. Then I could see understanding dawn on her face. Breaking into a slow smile she whispered to me, 'I know . . . she's hiding . . .' She put her finger across her lip to signal that, if this was the game Mum wanted to play, she was willing to go along with it. I watched her tiptoe up the stairs, feeling my insides melt in despair.

I walked into the kitchen to turn the kettle on and, for a few minutes, its comforting hissing and bubbling masked the sound of Anjali's footsteps upstairs running from room to room, still playing her desperate game of hide-and-seek. I was putting the milk back in the fridge when she reappeared in the kitchen, sidling along the wall with a sulky look on her face. 'Mum's not here,' she said before sticking her thumb in her mouth.

'Oh don't start that thumb-sucking stuff again,' I said. 'I thought you'd got over that habit.'

She continued to suck, silently. I squatted next to her. 'Shall we check the freezer for that pink ice-cream now?' She shook her head. 'Would you like a biscuit then? A BIG, brown, chocolatey one? Mmmm . . . *de-licious*,' I said, smacking my lips. She smiled, showing me buck-teeth with her wet thumb trapped in the gap between, and nodded. 'Well, let's get this out first and put it back where it belongs, shall we?' I said, gently pulling the sodden thumb out of her mouth and wiping it on the front of my shirt. 'There,' I said, putting her hand back by her side, patting it to make it stay and then getting up to look for the biscuits. I knew Carol had bought some chocolate digestives from Tesco and finally found them with the cereals. Putting two on a plate, I lifted Anjali on to the kitchen table and went back to making my tea. We sat together in silence for a while, with only the sound of Anjali demolishing the biscuits breaking the afternoon peace.

After she had finished, I dusted her free of crumbs and put her back on the floor. 'Shall we get those doors open and sit out in the garden for a while?' I asked, walking towards the patio doors. 'Go get your toys out too. You haven't seen them for a while, have you?'

She ran back and forth and up and down the stairs, seeming to have forgotten her earlier disappointment, bringing out long-lost friends one by one, greeting each of them with delight and checking for my approval with every new arrival.

'Horsie?' . . . 'Shall I get Barbie?' . . . 'Oh can I play my keyboard?'

'Yes, of course, you can play your keyboard. What's up with you—you don't normally wait for my permission!'

'No, no keyboard today. Uh-oh, where's my tapicorder?'

'Your tape recorder went with you to the home, didn't it? Never mind, you can use Papa's big player. I'll play some music on the big player, if you bring one of your tapes down.'

She ran off again, excitedly, returning with the tape of *Pocahontas*. I blew the dust off it and inserted it into the cassette deck, keeping the volume at a pleasant level, while her favourite song filled the room. Humming alongside, Anjali sat down to comb her Barbie's hair. I watched her for a few moments and then picked up the book on the table next to me. Maya had been reading it on . . . it would have been Wednesday night . . . after dinner and before we went up to bed. It was still lying exactly where she had placed it, on the little side table, upturned and open to the page she had been reading. Carol must have missed it on her cleaning-up spree. It was John Irving's latest, the cover said. *A Widow for One Year*. What was Maya thinking about that night? Could she have really gone to bed without even knowing that it was for the last time? How could such things happen without any warning at all? Events that shot people's lives up into the air, seemingly at random, blowing them to smithereens, making them completely unrecognizable as the pieces floated back to the unforgiving earth.

'Papa? . . . Papa! . . .'

'Yes, Anjali?'

'Papa, will Mum come for lunch?'

'No, Mum won't be coming for lunch, Anjali. But I can make you some when you get hungry.'

She looked doubtful. 'Don't look so stricken,' I said, putting on my hurt expression. 'You know I do terrific lunches. So what shall it be today?'

'You said, pink ice-cream.' She was starting to sound tremulous.

'Yes, that *after* lunch, with bananas chopped in too! But what do you want for lunch? Food?'

'Mmm . . .' She was thinking hard and I could see she was still trying to keep her tears at bay.

'Come on, think of all your favourite things,' I said.

After a few moments, she finally asked tentatively, her voice still wobbling, 'Fish 'n' chips?'

'Even you know we don't have fish and chips at lunchtime. It's much too greasy, Anjali. And you'll be getting a hot dinner at the children's home at night. You don't want two heavy meals—and on a warm day like this, do you?'

But Anjali not only wanted fish and chips for lunch, she also had no intention of going back to the home for dinner—or, come to think of it, going back at all. When exactly she had made up her mind on all these issues I could not tell, but I saw her lower lip extend itself mutinously. 'I'm not going back there,' she muttered darkly.

'What do you mean, not going back there, darling? You know you have to. In the evening, Anjali, you heard the lady say so . . .'

'I don't want ladies. I want my mum,' she said firmly.

'Can't you see for yourself, Anjali, Mum's NOT here and Mum will never BE here—okay?'

Anjali jumped to her feet and threw her Barbie doll at me, stamping her foot in anger. 'I WANT MY MUM! I WANT MY MUM! I DON'T WANT YOU!' she shouted.

Her doll had caught me on my shin bone and I could feel a surprisingly sharp stab of pain that made me suck in my breath. Trying to stay calm, I looked at her quivering figure and said, 'I don't want to have to keep telling you this, so I'll say it just one more time . . .' I could hear my voice rise hysterically and tried to remind myself that I was speaking to a child, Maya's child, just a *baby* . . . but my voice seemed to be taking on a life of its own and before I could stop myself, I was shouting, 'Mum's *gone*, Anjali. There's no Mum any more, okay? GONE! *DEAD*! SO STOP ASKING ME FOR HER. I CAN'T BRING HER BACK! SO PLEASE JUST STOP *ASKING*! I honestly can't bear it any more!' I stopped abruptly, with my face in my hands, rocking backwards and forwards with the agony of it all. Seconds later, shocked at myself, I attempted to scramble up to take Anjali in my arms and comfort her, but she had turned and run out of the patio doors into the garden. She can't go far,

I thought, relieved to remember that the garden gate would be locked. I went out after her, deeply ashamed at my outburst and called out for her. But the garden was silent, the bushes and the tree looking on reproachfully. I walked out, calling her name again and found her soon enough behind the garden shed. She was squatting amidst the long grass, copious tears rolling down her face.

'Anjali, baby, I'm sorry, come to Papa,' I said, going closer to her. But she leapt up again, running away from me, back in the direction of the house, screaming, 'Mum! Mum! I want my mum!'

It's my own bloody fault, I thought, running in after her. She wasn't in the living room and so I walked up the stairs to her room. I found her standing there, against the window, but the moment she saw me she started to scream again. Bending over, clutching her stomach, letting off long, breathless screams, as though terrified I was going to hurt her. I stopped in my tracks, and tried again to calm her by talking to her, by offering her fish 'n' chips, chocolate biscuits, her children's home, the ladies she didn't want, to stay here if she wanted, anything and everything that was within my power to give her. But she was having none of it. 'Papa go! I want Mum! PAPA GO AWAY! I WANT MY MUM!' Her face was twisted in confusion and grief and there was nothing I could do to help her. I backed out of her room telling her she could have what she wanted, that I wasn't going to hurt her, that I just wanted her to stop screaming. But the screaming carried on and I stumbled downstairs, trying to block out her screams and my own terror with my hands clapped over my ears.

After what seemed like an eternity, although it was probably only ten minutes, I could hear her screaming finally come to an end. Loud trembling sobs continued to float down the stairs for a while. I knew I ought to go upstairs and comfort her, but I was frightened of setting her off again. Instead, I stayed sitting on the sofa, my head in my hands, my limbs feeling too heavy with unshed grief to move at all. When people said that a sorrow shared was a sorrow halved, they didn't really have a clue, did they? Anjali's sorrow not just doubled mine, its innocent pain seemed to have formed itself into a searing dagger that was now hacking away at my own agony. There was an element of avoidance for me as long as she herself remained uncomprehending. Now there was no escape at all.

The *Pocahontas* tape clicked noisily to a stop as it came to an end and the house filled again with the heavy hush of silence. I listened to the stillness for a while, looking around at everything in the room that was exactly the way it had always been—the Ikea armchair against that window, the potted plant on its shelf, the books lined up obediently on the mantelpiece. It amazed me that I had actually managed to live in this house for three whole days since Maya's death without cracking up completely. Almost exactly three days, as the clock on the wall was telling me it was now half past one. How did I do it? How was I able to breathe the very air that my Maya had been deprived of? Plod on, as if there was some terribly compelling need to do so? There was no need, really. Anjali would keep me going for a while. But it was clear now there was only so much I could do for the child. For the first time since taking that impulsive decision to give Govind's address to the social worker, I felt relief rather than stomach-churning doubt. Now all I needed to do was wait for them to sort something out for Anjali so I did not have to worry about her any more. Then . . . of course . . . it was clear as day now . . . all I needed to do after that was end everything as quickly and painlessly as I could. There were plenty of ways in which I could do it—an overdose of paracetamol, hosepipe fixed to the exhaust of the car, perhaps both *together* to be absolutely sure. Painless repose was a very tempting thought indeed. Suddenly I was not frightened any more.

I got up and walked upstairs. Anjali was curled up on her bed, fast asleep. Her thumb lay flaccidly in her open mouth. I removed the plastic horse she was clutching in her other hand, setting off a flurry of renewed thumb-sucking, although she stayed sleeping, exhausted by her tears. I went upstairs and called the Faunce Way home to tell them about the afternoon Anjali and I had had so far. It was best to be honest, I thought. This was no time for faux parental ego stuff.

'Maybe she's finally realized that her mother's really gone, poor wee one,' a kindly Scottish burr said.

'Yes, probably,' I replied.

'Do bring her back here if she gets agitated again, we'll be able to handle it here, we're used to that kind of thing, you shouldn't be having to struggle on your own.'

'Thank you,' I replied, starting to weep again.

Unchecked messages were still flashing forlornly on the answering machine. There seemed to be hundreds—Aunty Bull (poor Aunty Bull, trying to be loyal to her faraway friend in the face of such unfriendly silence), Martin Cullen, my brother Anil, Kevin, David Watts from work, Pauline from Maya's work place, still demanding to speak to Maya.

I needed to call all those people back, but my energy levels had suddenly hit rock-bottom. I would try and get some sleep too, before Anjali woke up, I decided. I stumbled to my bed. Sitting on its edge, pulling off my shoes, I made a mental note to call Anil first and make sure he didn't book his tickets to come here. It was all getting clearer by the minute—all the things I needed to do after Anjali's future had been decided. It was all starting to feel oddly important as well. I looked at the closed door of the wardrobe. I had a pilgrimage to make. To Kerala. I would have to return Maya to it, having taken her away from it so long ago. And, in doing that, I had doors to open on her behalf. The doors that had closed with such finality three years ago would have to be prised open again. That's the least I could do for Maya. Take her with me on a pilgrimage of rage.

When I drifted awake, the front of my body, facing the open window, was feeling strangely colder than my back. Turning over, I found Anjali curled up against me. She must have woken up and then come to my bed. Her feet were tucked in between my legs and she had lodged her head firmly in the hollow of my back. She half-opened her eyes as I turned to face her and then closed them again when I put my arm around her. In her half-sleep, she heaved a wobbly contented sigh. 'Poor Anjali,' I whispered, putting my face against her hair. She smelt faintly like Maya did—perhaps it was the shampoo. Poor Anjali and her poor Papa, I thought, as I held Maya's sleeping child against me for what was probably going to be the very last time.

W hen Elizabeth Hawke called the following morning, I knew from the tone of her voice that she had something important to tell me. She opened up, thankfully, without too much preamble. 'Thanks for leaving Anjali's *biological* father's telephone number with my secretary on Friday evening, Mr Tiwari. I did manage to make contact with him over the weekend to tell him the sad news. He's arriving here tomorrow, if he can get a ticket . . .'

'*Tomorrow?*'

She must have heard my barely audible reply, but she carried on talking, swiftly, with what to me sounded suspiciously like excitement, 'Yes, tomorrow, Mr Tiwari. I'm sure you'll agree with me that the urgency and concern he seems to be showing are rather reassuring.'

'What did he . . . did you ask him what his present circumstances are, Ms Hawke?'

'Circumstances?' She sounded puzzled.

I didn't bother to mask my irritation. 'Yes, you know, whether he ever got married again, whether he's still single . . . we have had no contact with him for nearly three years. It's important to know what his present circumstances are, isn't it?'

'Oh, yes, I did ask him about himself. He didn't remarry. According to him, he was never divorced from . . . from Mrs Warrier.'

'Yes, that's true, which is why *we* were never married. He would never have given her a divorce, did he tell you that?'

'Mr Tiwari, we didn't go into all that.' I could hear the sigh in her voice. She was being patient with me now, stretching out her words to indicate she was really trying to understand my antagonism. 'We only really talked about Anjali, whom he's, understandably, very keen to see.'

'I never said he was unreasonable, as a father. I've seen him with Anjali, Ms Hawke, although it was many years ago. He'd never harm her, Maya said that often enough. That's the only reason why I gave you his telephone number.'

'Yes, of course, Mr Tiwari,' she said. 'He too seems very keen to do what's best for Anjali under these terrible circumstances.'

'Well, what will you do once he arrives here? The main thing is to get his permission to decide the course of Anjali's future care, isn't it?'

'Well, he was actually indicating that he might like to try taking her back.'

'To India?' I could feel myself lose control of my breathing again.

'Well, we'll obviously have a meeting once he's here, so that we can all voice our opinions on that, but he seems to think he might be able to care for her in India. Apparently, schools there are quite good too.'

'Of course, schools there are good, I went to one of them, for heaven's sake. But that isn't the point, is it? It's about her life *outside* of school hours. That would be the bigger concern, wouldn't it?' I asked, sarcastically.

'Well, he didn't go into the details, but I'm sure we can discuss all that once he's here.'

'I've got to say, I'm concerned that hasty decisions will be made on the basis of immigration concerns, rather than what's really best for Anjali.'

'Mr Tiwari, please rest assured that our decision will be taken purely on the basis of what is in Anjali's best interests. We are bound by the Children's Act to regard the child's welfare as paramount.'

'I'm also concerned that, just because I have no legal document that ties me to Anjali, you will not take my wishes into account at all.'

'Mr Tiwari, your care of Anjali in the past two and a half years—'

'Nearly three,' I cut in.

'Sorry?'

'Nearly three, Anjali's been with me more like three years, rather than two and a half.' I knew it was details like that they would use against me in the end. I could imagine them already trying to create a dossier to somehow write me out of the picture, to airbrush me out of Anjali's life. If splitting hairs was the way they were going to play this game, I wanted to be better at it than them.

'Well, it was closer to two and a half rather than three, you must accept, Mr Tiwari. I'm not being inaccurate really, am I?'

'Shall we say that depends on how you look at it, Ms Hawke.'

I felt a faint satisfaction that she had now lost her train of thought and waited while she tried to remember where she had been when I interrupted her. She took another breath and started again, 'What I was trying to say, Mr Tiwari, was that the years you had spent helping Mrs Warrier in Anjali's care puts you in a position of knowing better than anyone else what she is like and what her needs are. When Mr Warrier said something on the telephone today about Anjali being his child and not yours, I did remind him as well of this.'

Now I was out of my depth for a moment. 'Was that what Mr Warrier said?'

'Look, whatever might have happened between him and you three years ago is not my concern, Mr Tiwari. But it is important

Jaishree Misra

that you be able to sit together now and discuss the future of the child whose welfare you are both responsible for to a certain extent. I have already put that request to him. And I now ask the same of you.'

I was silent for a few moments before I said, 'Okay. Please let me know when and where the meeting will be held.'

'I'll call you once he arrives here, shall I?'

'Yes, do that please.'

I was about to hang up when she spoke up again, 'I've been in touch with the Faunce Way staff, and am aware that you've seen Anjali a couple of times over the weekend. Has it all gone well?'

Again, I wasn't sure whether this was a genuine enquiry or some kind of test. If it was a test, I suddenly didn't care if I was about to fail it by lying. 'Yes, it was all absolutely fine,' I said curtly.

I hung up, feeling my insides churn. Tomorrow, Govind Warrier was arriving here. *Tomorrow*. To stake his claim over Anjali. To taunt me over how short-lived my own happiness had been with his wife and child. *Biological* father. He too would be keen to remind me, like the Social Services Department had with their waggling fingers, that I didn't after all provide that all-important sperm or chromosome or whatever it was, which now gave him the permission to turn up here and place his orders. I wouldn't let him get away with that. I would resist, with every fibre of my being, anyone's attempts to take Anjali away from me. I would take the matter to court. I would meet my local MP. I would kick up such a shindig, they would reel from it for years afterwards. I remembered suddenly my own plans to top myself. Where on earth would that fit in with all these plans for Anjali? I was starting to feel so confused, I was getting nauseous. Bile was rising up in my throat, threatening to choke me with its bitterness.

Earlier that morning, I had tried to organize my plans to get to India, beginning by calling everyone who had left messages on my answering machine over the weekend. Even Aunty Bull. 'Yes, I do remember about Wednesday, I'll be there,' I reassured her, still hoping that some unmissable excuse would come up before then.

Anil was understandably anxious about my telling him not to come. 'But I've booked my leave,' he said, as the line from America hummed expectantly, waiting for a proper explanation from me. 'Why don't you come down to India instead,' I replied. 'I'll probably have to take Anjali there to try and sort something out for her and I'm thinking of spending a few days with Mum and Dad too. I'm sure we'll all appreciate your company then.'

What I meant to say was that Mum and Dad would need to have Anil with them when I finally got around to topping myself. If I didn't feel so wretched, I might actually have been amused at my rather dismal and furtive attempts at conjuring a half-baked plan to commit suicide. I seemed to forget every so often that I had that plan at all. Whenever I could seem to hold that thought for any length of time, my strategy was to first achieve for Anjali all the things that I thought Maya would want. Then I would make that trip with Maya's ashes to Kerala. After that I would spend a few days with Mum and Dad, then return to England and finally end my life here. If I had to do it, I was sure it had to be done here, in England. For one, I would be less likely to be found out and stopped. In India, I would be surrounded by people all the time and I was vaguely conscious that it would be far harsher on Mum and Dad than if they were to hear about it on a telephone. It was quite possible that days would pass before anyone would even notice my absence. You read those grim stories in tiny newspaper reports sometimes. Of poor hapless souls, generally very old, whose bodies were found only when the gas board broke in to find out why their bills had not been paid. It was hard to think that there was a time when that kind of a news report seemed to have emerged from some distant world, completely alien to mine. But it was the kind of thing that could happen to anyone, as I was just finding out. We were all, in the end, absolutely and indubitably alone. Mum and Dad would be shattered, I knew, but I couldn't hack this just for them. And, if I could get Anil to stay on in India after I had returned to England, he would be able to pull them through it. They would all just have to understand that life had truly come to mean so little to me—there couldn't be many people who managed to lose both a woman and a child all at once. Surely I would be forgiven for not being able to deal with that.

After I first came up with that line of thought, the veils in my head had started, quite amazingly, to lift. For some odd reason, it seemed to confer on me the kind of energy I needed to deal with all those previously postponed tasks. I spoke both to my workplace and to Maya's supervisor at the Women's Refuge this morning. I discussed leave arrangements with David Watts, explaining that I would need to go to India for a while. I even started to feel less angry with Elizabeth Hawke, beginning to wonder whether perhaps hers was a pretty unenviable task too.

But then she called and now there was the prospect of Govind's arrival in England. I had never really spoken to him properly, of course, except for that one brief meeting over the wall, in another age. But I had heard enough from Maya to feel that I knew him very well indeed. 'Perhaps he wasn't a bad man,' she had said recently, 'just misguided.' It seemed to me that, once removed from him, she had become far too forgiving of the mess he made of their marriage and her life. He had had the best years of her life and had left her with nothing at the end of it—nothing, except Anjali that is. I had had more years in number—or just about the same amount perhaps—and it just didn't seem fair now that he should have, so clearly, a bigger stake in Anjali. Not that I was sure he would see that as a boon anyway. It would certainly ensure he was never able to forget Maya who had bequeathed her smile so generously to her daughter. Seeing Anjali's nose crinkle so unerringly every time she smiled, had in the past few days brought

Maya back to me like something thudding very hard into my chest. Would Govind suffer the same fate? And should I really care?

I could never tolerate other people's self-pity and reminded myself sternly that what was far more important to consider now was Anjali, stuck in that ghastly children's home. Just about starting to discover that her mum had gone for good. Not overly keen on life at home with just her papa and her toys. The question was: would she find it easier to forget Maya in faraway Kerala? Would a fresh start give her a better chance? If I was not allowed to keep her, was it right to condemn her to life in an English children's home? Or with English foster parents? If I did persuade them to let me care for her, could I manage it? Without Maya? Did I even want *life* without Maya? 'Finish it, *finish it*, Rahul bloody Tiwari,' a voice inside me was shouting, 'finish the whole bloody mess off! Send Anjali off, two and a half years is hardly a lifetime, she'd forget you in a shot.' I had to admit it to myself at least—Elizabeth Hawke was right; it had been closer to two and a half rather than three years. But I really needed to know that, wherever she ended up, somebody would tell Anjali about this Papa-Unka person who loved her as much as he knew how.

But *Govind*? Was it right to be returning Anjali to the Govind Maya had run away from? Christ, Maya, what an unholy palaver to have left behind! What a goddamned stupid, uncaring, inconsiderate thing to do, going and dying on everyone like that! I looked despairingly out of the window, wanting to hurl something at the church spire across the road that was rising above the trees in its usual lofty fashion.

It was evening when Elizabeth Hawke called again. 'He's arriving on an Air India flight early tomorrow morning. He had some problems getting a visa, I had to call and speak to someone at the British High Commission in Mumbai to help him get it.' She was still sounding sort of breathless and excited. And it was still annoying me greatly that she should take such pleasure that it was all working out so nicely for her. She couldn't wait, I was sure, for Anjali to be handed over to him, and to be taken back to India, so that she could close the case. Put away Anjali's cardboard file in a steel filing cabinet, with the word 'Closed' scrawled heedlessly over it. But it wouldn't be, would it? Anjali would still exist, you know, I wanted to say, without the Mum she adored.

Elizabeth Hawke was still talking and I had missed half of what she said. '—he's been given permission to stay just two days. We'll obviously have to hold the meeting as soon as possible. Do you think you could come to our office at eleven a.m. tomorrow? I'll give you directions on how to get here, of course.'

I said 'yes' to everything, my mind still whirling. If he was only staying two days, he was almost certainly planning to take Anjali back with him, wasn't he? Two days! Does that mean I'll never see her again? Of *course* I won't—I was going to *die* anyway, wasn't I? It felt so obtuse to keep forgetting that! I sat in my chair, with my head in my hands, for a very long time. I was vaguely aware that darkness had, at some point, blanketed the world outside . . . that summer stars were trying to make a go of lighting things up . . . that my stomach, left unfed all day, had taken to emitting a loud gurgling chorus every few minutes. I had, somehow, to fight on—for Anjali's sake and Maya's. I had to try and face that meeting, try and concentrate on the task ahead, try to be Maya's voice at that meeting tomorrow. That was the least I could do.

*

I arrived early at the address that Elizabeth Hawke had given me— 1–30 Serpentine Court loomed out from the midst of grim council housing. A blue board confirmed that this was indeed the Social Services Department. A smaller sign indicated that the 'Children and Families' team were located along one side of the dirty grey building where a cement ramp led up to filthy glass doors. Fucking hell, was this where the futures of so many children were decided?

It ought at least to look like it was worthy of such important decision-making processes, I thought, peering out at the dismal facade through the windscreen of the car.

At about ten minutes to eleven, I saw Elizabeth Hawke pull up in her Ford Fiesta outside the building. I slid down in my seat as I did not want her to see me, but craned my neck to continue looking at her over the dashboard. She had a man with her— Indian, quite tall, balding. Govind. He had changed a bit. Something about the way he held himself. Either my memory of him was flawed or he had grown less ogre-like over the years. They hurried indoors and I noticed that Govind too was looking in barely concealed amazement at the derelict building he was being ushered into.

After counting, very slowly, to five hundred, I decided I was now not too early. I also did not want to give Govind too much of a march on me. Getting out of the car, I walked up the ramp and into the grimy doors that had swallowed them up. A harassed-looking woman was talking on a telephone at the reception desk while the other telephone on her desk rang insistently too. She threw me an annoyed look when I looked expectantly at her and signalled that I would have to wait.

'No, I've already told you, she's on leave today. No, her senior's in a meeting. I'm sorry, you'll just have to wait until she gets back. Tomorrow. I'm *sorry*, I've already *told* you, you can't speak to anyone else about it. If Marsha's your social worker, it'll have to wait for her. She'll be back tomorrow. Yes, I'll give her the message when she gets in tomorrow. No, there's no point calling later. Yes, he is her senior, but he's got a review to attend outside London after his meeting and won't be available. Yes, I'll *tell* her.' She clattered the phone down and looked at me as she picked up the other one that was still trilling unashamedly.

'I . . . I'm here for a meeting . . .' I offered tentatively, but she was already speaking into the other telephone. This time it was mercifully short and I tried to get in before one of her phones rang again. 'Meeting with Elizabeth Hawke,' I said quickly, 'name's Tiwari. Rahul Tiwari.'

She consulted a huge register on her desk and then got up to walk around to a door that she opened with a swipe card. I went in and waited to be told which of the many closed doors facing me it was to be. 'Number Three,' she said, diving back to answer the telephone on her desk that had started to ring again. The door marked 3 opened and Elizabeth Hawke walked out, seeming startled to see me. 'Oh, no one told me you were here. I was just about to fetch my senior from upstairs . . .' She looked uncertain about what to do next. 'Erm . . . Mr Warrier's here already . . . I suppose you could come in and meet him . . . give me a minute while I go upstairs and get Sandy Lockhart, my senior . . .'

I saw her run up a flight of stairs, looking flustered. Did she mean I was to wait for her here in the corridor, or was I expected to let myself into the room? Through a glass panel in a door marked 2, I could see a man with dreadlocks talking agitatedly to some other invisible occupant in the room. A small, bored-looking black child materialized in the glass panel, squeezing his face against the murky glass to see me better. His tongue and lips squeezed wetly and distortedly against the glass. I had no desire to be snooping on the lives of all the other families whose destinies were being decided today and gingerly opened the door marked 3 to walk in. Govind was alone and looked up from some papers as I went in. I could see recognition dawn on his face. He too had seen me just once, of course, but certainly knew now who I was.

Might as well be civil, I thought, as I stuck my hand out. 'Hello, I'm Rahul, you must remember me, Govind.'

He scrambled up from a saggy armchair, but did not take my hand. 'I told them I did not want to see you today,' he said, his fury apparent.

'Well, tough luck,' I said, choosing a chair from the assortment of different ones that had been arranged in a circle. A high-backed dining chair—it would be good to be perched above the rest of them, I thought. Removing a plastic wheel lying on the seat, I threw it into a box in the corner of the room from which broken bits of children's toys were spilling out. A jug full of water and a variety of glasses had been placed on a table in the centre of the room. Everything looked patched together or thrown together, or both. Govind was still standing, glaring at me.

'Look,' I said, 'I know how you feel about me. In an odd way, I can even understand. But all that . . . *all* that happened then needs to be put aside because of what is happening to Anjali at the moment. We just have to be able to sort her future out together now, whether either of us likes it or not.'

I could tell from the expression on his face that he was itching for a fight with me, but now he merely hunched his shoulders. Then he cleared his throat. Expecting him to say something, I waited a few seconds, but he was silent, only his eyes moving in his head, and so I carried on, 'Have you seen her yet?'

He couldn't avoid answering such a direct question, surely. 'Who? Anjali?' he asked finally. I nodded and after a pause he replied, 'Yes, at her nursery this morning.'

He had a heavy Keralite accent and hit all his consonants impressively. He looked uneasily at me and licked the edges of his lips nervously. Maybe he was wondering if he ought to be commiserating with me, I thought. Perhaps I ought to be commiserating with *him*—she had been his wife too, after all. It seemed more sensible to revert to the subject of Anjali.

'Did she seem okay? Surprised to see you, I mean?'

He cleared his throat again. Maybe England was overwhelming him—I remembered Maya telling me that he had never travelled abroad. Or it was more likely that I was the cause of his unease. He must have always thought of me as the villain who broke into his perfect life and stole his beautiful wife away from him. Certainly, he wouldn't have known of her unhappiness long before I even arrived.

We must have both looked relieved when Elizabeth Hawke came hurrying back into the room, followed by an older woman with short hair the colour of iron. She introduced first Govind and then me to the helmeted woman who was Senior Practitioner, Children and Families, Sandy Lockhart. Sandy shook Govind's hand and then mine. I could tell he was uncomfortable with this and remembered that in India women did not usually shake hands. Unless they moved in very westernized circles and met a lot of foreigners. I knew from all the things Maya told me that Govind was old-fashioned, full of conservative beliefs. Govind, oddly, seemed to be taking his cues from me now and scrambled out of his chair after Sandy had shaken his hand, when he saw me getting up from mine.

We sat down again and Elizabeth Hawke said it would be best to wait for Anjali's nursery teacher and the Faunce Way senior to arrive before beginning the meeting. We fell silent and Sandy Lockhart used the opportunity to voice her condolences over Maya's death. She looked vaguely at both Govind and me as she said it and I could see that she too was struggling with the question of whether an *ex*-spouse was deserving of a condolence or not. I nodded and Govind did too.

There was a flurry as three more women came into the room: Caroline, Anjali's teacher, whom I had met a couple of times; Heather, the head of the nursery; and Susan Hill from the Faunce Way home. After everyone had chosen a chair each from the assortment available, Sandy Lockhart began the meeting.

'We meet under very sad circumstances . . .' she said (while I inwardly closed my eyes at the thought of a speech). '. . . that of the tragic death of Maya Warrier in a car accident.' (Did she really need to be saying all this, I thought, we all *know* why we're here, for fuck's sake!) 'But the overwhelmingly important and urgent thing is to decide how best to organize Anjali's future, especially considering she is going to need care and protection for many years to come. Her father . . . her *biological* father, Mr Govind Warrier, has flown in from India as soon as he heard the news. And I think we must all appreciate the care and concern he has shown in arriving here so soon.' At this point everyone (except me) nodded and murmured their assent.

She then turned to me. It looked like I was going to receive a certificate too. *Damn*. 'And thank you too, Mr Tiwari, for having tried to do your utmost in making Anjali feel loved and cared for in the midst of what must have been terrible trauma for yourself.' I frowned at my shoelaces and blinked very hard. Please, *please* move on to the real business, I thought frantically and heaved a big sigh as I heard her say, 'Now, of course, we need to consider carefully and urgently Anjali's possible future, so can I please ask for your various suggestions, starting with you, Mr Warrier.'

Everyone turned to look at Govind who was now tightly hunched in his chair, seeming to want to vanish into the saggy upholstery of the armchair. 'I don't know . . .' he mumbled awkwardly. Then, taking a deep breath, he said, all in a rush, 'I think she should go back with me to India. That is her home, she should never have been taken away from there at all.' Having got the words out, he seemed to gain courage and proceeded to throw an angry glare at me again. It was clear that my plan to make a peace offering had been a bit fatuous. To Govind, I was still the enemy, even after three long years. It was clear that he had arrived so soon after the social worker's phone call because he had suddenly been presented with his best opportunity, not just to get Anjali back but, perhaps, more importantly, to take her away from me. Ideally, I suppose, he would have wanted Maya and Anjali back together. Not to make it up to them, necessarily, but merely to cock a snook at me. I was sure of it and suddenly felt very sorry at the ease with which I had succumbed to the pressure of handing his number over to the Social Services.

I was feeling weary again and had to drag my attention back to the conversation in the room. I caught the last bit of Anjali's teacher's question: 'How major would the changes be if she went to school there?'

'There are some very good schools there; she will only go to the best, of course. That should not be a problem at all,' Govind replied.

'Will she get admission straightaway?'

'Admission is no problem.'

'I think, we also need to discuss what kind of arrangements you will be able to make for her time *outside* of school hours, Mr Warrier,' Elizabeth Hawke was saying.

That was my question—I remembered having asked her *precisely* that on the telephone the other day!

Govind seemed a little stumped. Despite the earlier glare, I had it in my heart to feel sorry for the man. I had recently been subjected to a similar inquisition myself, without being given a chance to do my homework too. All eyes were still on him and he raised himself slightly on one arm to rearrange himself and buy some time before saying lamely, 'Time . . . can always be filled.'

My mind was wandering again . . . to Dad and his complaints about Indians and their time-pass abilities. The women in the room, all of whom had probably very meagre experience of the peculiarities of Indian time-pass, looked suitably nonplussed. It was my turn, I decided, to speak.

'Can I just say,' I opened up, 'having helped Maya to care for Anjali these past three years, I know just how time-consuming it can be. She is basically the sort of child who requires constant attention. I do believe there has to be a very clear plan as to how exactly this will be carried out.'

Govind glared at me again and said, 'It was not three years

but two and a half. And, if you could do it, so can I. I am her father, don't forget.'

'Well, you didn't seem to do very much for her in the first year and a half of her life,' I countered.

Govind looked like he might hit me. His face had gone a dark red and a muscle in his jaw was working nineteen to the dozen. I instantly regretted my hasty remark, but Sandy Lockhart had already rushed in to save the situation. 'Gentlemen, this is not the time for recriminations, I'm sure you'll agree. We're faced with this very difficult situation and really need to work together in the best interests of Anjali.'

Everybody nodded, except Govind and me. Now the Faunce Way person was speaking, 'I agree that there needs to be a very clear plan for Anjali's daily schedule in the evenings and weekends. She is one of those seemingly tireless children and has a lot of energy to burn up. We have to make sure it's put to good use.'

The head teacher turned to Govind and asked, 'Do you have anyone to help you with her upbringing, Mr Warrier?'

'My parents can be brought to live with me and we can also employ someone to keep an eye on Anjali. The maid who works for me used to be the one who looked after Anjali as a baby.'

So that girl was still there, Kuttan's sister . . . could I remember her name? Karthu . . . well, that was something. She had seemed kind and gentle. But the parents . . . I wasn't able to remember things very well, my head was feeling very fuzzy. I knew I had already been obstreperous enough and wondered if I ought to hold my tongue. But I could hear my disembodied voice float uncontrollably out of me, 'Please, I do think this needs to be clarified properly.' I turned to Govind and tried to look him in the eye without seeming confrontational. 'Are you sure your parents will be willing to take on the responsibility? I was always under the impression that they never saw too much of Anjali, that you did not encourage frequent visits or something?'

Govind was getting angrier with me by the minute. Barely masking his fury, he hissed, 'My parents, you are not to forget, are Anjali's *grandparents*. She was plucked away from all of us, *plucked* away. Now they are all waiting to see her again and you are saying that they will *harm her*!'

Three voices cut in, including my own, eager to mollify him:

'No, not *harm*, but it is a huge responsibility . . .'

'I only meant to say that getting back at *me* should not become the agenda that overwhelms everything else . . .'

'It's easy to get carried away in the present situation—with everyone wanting to help—but the long-term ramifications are enormous, Mr Warrier . . .'

In the ensuing bedlam, Govind heaved himself out of his sagging armchair and announced that he now just wanted to take Anjali and go. Saying something about having to get a ticket for her, he picked up his papers and left the room with Elizabeth Hawke in hot pursuit. I looked at Sandy Lockhart and shrugged.

'I do apologize for my part in this mess . . . I just didn't think he'd leave like that . . .'

She was surprisingly understanding. 'Well, these were the questions that had to be asked. You were in a better position to be asking them, having had some insight into Mr Warrier's family dynamics from . . .' She cleared her throat. '. . . Anjali's mother, of course. I'm just not sure we're really any the wiser about what exactly Anjali's future will hold. And that's a pity.'

Caroline, Anjali's teacher, who had gone all pink in the face spoke up, 'Would her staying on at Faunce Way have not been an option at all? She seems reasonably well settled there . . .'

Susan Hill responded with the expected. 'Faunce Way is really only meant for short periods of respite. We just can't afford to keep kids long term, especially as we're the only service of our kind in such a poorly resourced borough.'

'The only other option, considering we're looking at a period of at least twelve years, would have been foster care.'

'No, not foster care, certainly. I know Maya would have hated the thought of that,' I put in vehemently.

'And, of course, most important of all, we shouldn't forget that the decision wasn't really ours to take in the first place,' Sandy Lockhart was saying in a voice full of regret. 'There are no court orders on Anjali and so, as the only person with parental responsibility, her natural father really does have the right to make that final decision on her future.'

'What would happen if I went to court now,' I asked, sensing that Anjali's teachers were also waiting expectantly for Sandy Lockhart's reply.

She looked at me steadily, and I could see nothing but honest regret and sorrow in her eyes as she said softly, 'I'm really so very sorry, Mr Tiwari, but as Anjali's father is alive, and showing so much willingness to care for her, your own chances of getting custody . . . or even sharing parental responsibility are very, very slight. Access is another matter altogether.' She saw the expression on my face and nodded. 'Yes, but rather meaningless if she lives in India and you live here.'

At that point, Elizabeth Hawke came rushing back into the room. Her face was sweating and her dangly earrings were askew. She panted as though she had been running. 'Oh, Mr Tiwari, I'm going now with Mr Warrier to get Anjali's ticket. He's really quite upset. I came back to ask you if we could come to your house with Anjali after school so she can collect some of her things to take back to India with her. She'll also need to say goodbye to you, of course.'

Of course, goodbye, I thought blankly. Time to say goodbye to Anjali next. I nodded and Sandy Lockhart reached out a hand to place it sympathetically on my arm. She did not say anything, just patted it gently, while the room returned to silence after

Elizabeth Hawke had rushed off again. Then I got up, shook hands with everybody, and left without saying another word. What was the point any more? Outside, I walked slowly to the car, got in and drove back home.

I sat for a long time in Anjali's room, feeling myself go stiff on her small pink swivel chair. She would need at least two suitcases to take all her things—one just for her huge collection of stuffed toys, the other for clothes and shoes. She had better be taking everything, they might provide some comfort once she's far from here. I was sorry now that I had upset Govind, but his simmering rage at me, even after all these years had taken me by surprise. Maya had never been sure if her single letter to him begging him for a divorce went unanswered because he had always hoped she would return, or simply because he did not want to give her a fair chance with me. Now that I had met him, I couldn't tell either.

It was late in the afternoon when the doorbell rang. Elizabeth Hawke, who by now looked completely shattered, was holding Anjali's hand. Govind was lurking behind them. He nodded, but did not make eye contact as I let them in. Anjali launched herself into my arms in her usual exuberant fashion and started to wriggle when I took more time than normal to release her.

'Anjali's going to Indya!' she announced proudly.

'Yes, I know, I *heard*, you lucky girl!' I exclaimed, mustering up the enthusiasm from somewhere.

'Will you come, Papa?' she asked. I shook my head, not daring to speak.

'Shall we start your packing, Anjali?' Elizabeth Hawke asked brightly.

'Packing, yay!' Anjali shouted, racing up the stairs.

'We've bought a suitcase. I'll fetch it from the car,' Elizabeth Hawke said, going back to the door.

As the door slammed shut behind her, Govind and I looked uneasily at each other, old adversaries still circling each other suspiciously, irrationally. I decided to take the bull by the horns. 'Look, Govind, I'm sorry about the words exchanged at the meeting. I just felt I had to be Maya's voice, asking all the questions she would have asked.'

He seemed to start a bit at her name. Elizabeth Hawke must have been referring to her so far as Mrs Warrier. Did my uttering her name now bring her back to him too . . . vividly, over the years and over the miles . . . was *he* suffering too?

Suddenly he was speaking, and, oddly, without rancour. 'She was wrong about so many things. Always believing I had no love for her. It wasn't true. I never stopped loving her,' he said flatly.

'Well, I suppose it was just your . . . your *way* of showing love that she couldn't cope with, Govind.'

'What do you mean?' he asked.

'Your possessiveness, that's how she saw it.' He was silent, so I continued, feeling reckless, 'I feel you ought to know that we never had an affair while I was there, in Kerala. She was just someone I was trying to help. She asked me for help and I felt I couldn't refuse as a human being.'

He nodded, although I couldn't tell if he did believe me. Perhaps he too was starting to realize that, with Maya dead, angry was a pretty useless thing to be. 'It's all utterly meaningless now, isn't it?' I laughed. 'Almost as if someone up there thought this might make a pretty good joke, eh?'

He looked sharply at me, as though unsure of my bitterness. Then he said, although I couldn't tell if he was being sympathetic or not, 'Must be hard for you too.'

'Well, I'm losing Anjali too, whereas you're sort of getting her back . . .' He nodded in agreement, just as Elizabeth Hawke rang the bell again. I let her in and took her upstairs to Anjali's room. Anjali had already opened her wardrobe and pulled out a pile of clothes that were now strewn all over the floor. 'Oh, baby!' I remonstrated, 'just look at that mess! Let me do it.'

Anjali frowned at me, her voice rising up in a whine, 'I want to do my packing!'

'Come on, sunshine,' I said firmly, 'why don't you sit on your chair there and supervise, huh? You tell Papa what to do, and I'll do exactly as you say, okay?'

She considered this for a moment before saying 'Okay' in a matter-of-fact manner, and climbing on to her chair. I noticed Govind had appeared at the door and was watching us. Anjali ignored him completely, having crossed her arms self-importantly, getting ready to be my supervisor. 'Blue jeans,' she said imperiously, pointing to the pile of clothes on the floor.

'Yes, ma'am,' I responded, smartly clicking my heels.

Anjali giggled, with her hand over her mouth as I obediently folded her blue jeans and put them away in her suitcase. She then 'wiped' the smile off her mouth with the back of her hand before issuing her next order in stentorian tones, 'Orange dungawees.'

'Where are your orange dungarees, madam? Aha, here they are! Okay, next?'

'Red coat.'

'I don't think you'll need coats in Kerala. It's hot there, isn't it?' I asked Govind.

'She won't need any woollen clothes. It's always hot there.'

Anjali scowled at him. The red coat was a particular favourite. 'Red coat,' she said again, firmly.

Govind smiled at her and adopted a wheedling tone of voice, 'No, moley, it's very hot in Kerala, no? You don't remember? You don't need any warm clothing. Just take all your cotton things.'

Anjali was not amused. She obviously did not have a clear memory of either Govind or Kerala and was not keen to take orders from him, however cajoling his tone of voice. 'I want my red coat!' she yelled imperiously. Govind backed off hastily and threw a helpless look in my direction. Again, Elizabeth Hawke and I spoke up at the same time.

'Come on, Anjali, no shouting now,' she was saying.

'Look, my sweet, you take your red coat and you'll just melt in the heat,' I said, adding darkly, 'like that candle on the dining table downstairs. That's how you'll go . . . melllt . . . and then splutter, splutter, until you go out . . . pffft . . .' I ended dramatically.

Anjali giggled again and squealed, 'No I won't melt! I'm a *girl*, not a candle. I won't melt!' She was laughing and screaming loudly as I continued to hiss, pointing to her neck and to her head, 'There you are, see, you're melting already.' She grabbed at her neck to stop it from melting, rolling her eyes, pretending to be scared. 'Okay, so no woollies, right?' I said briskly and she nodded, still giggling. Govind let out his breath and I said, trying not to sound like I was delivering a lecture, but suddenly sounding uncannily like Maya, 'It's about choices, I suppose, or making her *think* she's making the choice herself or something. It can sometimes involve lots of convoluted explanations, though.' I laughed.

Once Anjali's clothes were packed, we surveyed the bulging suitcase. 'When did you acquire such a fine wardrobe,' I asked Anjali. She thrust out her chest as she strutted around the room, surveying her suitcase proudly.

'Well, we don't really want to leave your toys behind, do we?' Elizabeth Hawke said.

'Yes, I want my toys,' Anjali agreed, starting to gather her family of beanie animals together, stuffing them indiscriminately on top of her clothes and then attempting to squeeze her suitcase shut.

'Whoa!' I said, 'hang on, I think I have a suitcase.'

Elizabeth Hawke looked doubtful. 'Well, I don't see how we'll be able to have it returned to you . . .' she said.

'I don't need to have it returned,' I said brusquely. I went into my bedroom and opened the wardrobe to pull out the larger of my two suitcases on the top shelf. I threw a look at the shelf next to it. The box was not visible at all, but I reached my hand

Jaishree Misra

up among the jumpers and felt its smooth wooden finish. I stood there for a minute before closing the wardrobe door and returning to Anjali's room with the suitcase.

Anjali hopped around as her whole extended family entered the suitcase one by one, each of them accompanied by happy squeals and uncontainable excitement. Winnie the Pooh, Eeyore, Teddy, Barbie . . . I silently said my goodbyes.

By evening, Anjali's room wore a forlorn look. Only a few broken dolls and toys remained on the shelf, awaiting disposal. In the cupboard hung a few small outgrown clothes and her winter stuff was already stuffed into a large carrier bag ready to be run down by Elizabeth Hawke to the local Oxfam tomorrow. At Elizabeth Hawke's suggestion, Anjali started to say goodbye to everything else that was left in her room. Unable to resist the drama, she walked around the room, planting loud kisses on her chest of drawers, television, bed and chair. 'Bye-bye chair . . . bye-bye table . . .' I was sure even Elizabeth Hawke could see it had been an inane idea as I stood and watched Anjali, feeling irreducibly sad. Finally, she wandered over to me to put her arms around me.

'Papa, come to Indya,' she said in her affectionate voice.

'Not now, baby,' I said. My thighs, around which she had wrapped her little arms, were starting to tremble again. I didn't *want* to love her any more. It was all getting too unbearably painful. It would be far, far easier to let her go, as I had had to let Maya go. And then end it for myself too. She would be okay, without me. She would be with her flesh and blood, they wouldn't fail her. How long would it take—a year, months, maybe even just days— for her to forget?

'Come, Papa,' she said more insistently, something in my face suddenly edging her voice to the brink of tears.

I lifted her up and buried my face in her hair. 'Maybe later,' I whispered, as she wrapped plump legs around my middle.

Anjali pulled her face away and cupped my face between sticky little hands. She looked into my eyes with the direct gaze that she would no doubt outgrow in the next couple of years. 'Pomise?' she asked. I nodded silently and she wriggled her way back to the floor. 'I'm staying in a hotel tonight,' she added, beaming up at me.

Elizabeth Hawke made as if to comfort me, but I wanted none of her comfort and my glare stopped her in her tracks.

'Well, we'd better go then . . .' she said lamely.

'When's the flight,' I asked Govind.

'Tomorrow, nine p.m.,' he replied.

'Do you mind if I come to the airport to see her off?' I asked.

He shook his head and said, 'I'm taking her out tomorrow morning . . . to the zoo?' he looked enquiringly at Elizabeth Hawke.

She looked flustered and, without making eye contact with me, mumbled, 'Perhaps it's best you do that on your own with Anjali, Mr Warrier. It's important that you redevelop your bond with her before taking her back to India . . . that's less likely to happen if Mr Tiwari came as well.'

I don't think Govind was inviting me along exactly, but I was too tired to rise to any more bait now. 'I think you're right,' I said calmly, and then turned to Govind. 'I'll see you at the airport at about six-thirty, if that's okay.'

'It's from Terminal Three,' he said.

They left the house, rolling the two suitcases along. I did not offer to help and stood at the door, watching Anjali skip alongside them to Elizabeth Hawke's car. She tumbled into the back seat, her head still bouncing around visibly in the rear window, until she was restrained by the social worker and strapped into a booster seat.

It was probably a good idea for Anjali to stay with Govind in his hotel tonight. To help them get used to each other again, the Social Services lot must have decided. Knowing Anjali, it sounded like an excellent scheme to me too, although I wasn't sure what

I would have said if I had been consulted in making that decision. There would be all sorts of goodies to distract Anjali from the fact that she was with yet another relative stranger, a bouncy hotel bed to wreck, the delights of room service, that trip to the zoo in the morning. She would love it all, although room service would probably come out as her particular favourite. I hoped Govind would not give in to her every request for pudding. I had forgotten to warn him of her predilection for pudding! I ran up to the gate to catch them and tell them before they drove off, but the car was already moving down the road. Raising my arm, I waved frantically. Anjali, who had already freed herself of her booster seat and was now kneeling on it facing backwards, waved back, wearing a gleeful smile.

fifteen

Wallowing in grief must be the easiest thing in the world, especially when there's absolutely nothing left to live for. Anjali, stuck in her sordid little children's home, had kept me going for six whole days. Now that Govind had arrived to take her away, that was over too. I lay on my bed all of that Wednesday, looking at the sunshine create different patterns on the ceiling, listening to the phone ring and then stop ringing while different voices left various messages for me.

I thought about Govind and Anjali at the zoo and wondered whether Anjali would remember that Maya and I had taken her there once too. It must have been about two years ago. Anjali was tiny then, and behaved very badly in front of an ice-cream stall. I was sure she would be good today. Familiarity was what invariably bred that strange blend of contempt and overwhelming love in all of Anjali's personal relationships. She would be as good as gold today for Govind, still a stranger to her in many ways. Bereft as I felt, I still wanted it to work for them. I wanted, I *needed*, to know that Anjali was going to be all right with Govind. Please, please, please, let her be happy, I thought, even as the irony of having to be carved out of that picture to make it work stabbed right into me.

Sometime around five, I dragged myself out of bed and staggered to the bathroom. The figure that looked back at me in the mirror was virtually unrecognizable. Red eyes sat in dark hollows, my hair looked greasy and in need of a cut. I rubbed at the unshaven stubble on my chin and thought of how Anjali would complain if I felt 'poky'. Picking up my shaving foam, I started to lather my face.

An hour later, bathed and ready, I walked to the car and hurriedly got into it, relieved that there was no sign of Sandra or anyone else I would need to explain things to. The rush hour was just beginning to ease, and traffic was moving fast on the embankment. As I passed all of Anjali's favourite London landmarks, I wondered if she might be trying to tell Govind about them, suddenly worried that he wouldn't understand. If, for instance, she said, 'Battersea Dog', would he know that beyond that park was a dog's home that she often watched on a television serial? And if she said, 'Kinky Road', he would certainly never guess that she was referring to Kings Road where she and Maya sometimes went to buy Anjali's clothes, always stopping afterwards for a pizza? I felt terrible that I hadn't sat down with Govind to tell him all these things. He would need to know all these little details of Anjali's life to make it work. In the days that Anjali had struggled with language, Maya sometimes laughingly pondered if Anjali might be wondering why she was surrounded by really dim-witted people. Now, with Govind, who had none of the reference points, she would probably think she was stuck with one who was very severely dim-witted indeed. And then, if she threw a wobbly, he would never be able to manage, would he? I stepped on the pedal to get to Heathrow as fast as I could.

Earls Court was its usual mess of jaywalking tourists and cars parked recklessly on double-yellow lines. For some reason, the traffic had now ground to a complete halt. This was always the slowest part of the journey to Heathrow and I took a deep breath, drumming my fingers impatiently on the steering wheel, unable to see what was causing the jam. It would take at least fifteen minutes to explain all those things to Govind. He had said the flight was at nine. They would probably go through the security gates by seven if they didn't see me by then. I couldn't let them go without seeing Anjali just once again. Oh Jesus, why did I take so bloody long to shave!

Finally, almost at a snail's pace, the traffic started to move again and I shot forward. A cabbie waiting with his indicator flashing to get in front of me tooted his annoyance loudly. 'Fuck you!' I yelled as I pulled away, sticking an impudent finger up through the sun-roof. Once on the A4, I revved up, maintaining a risky ninety mph all the way to Heathrow, not heeding all the speed cameras on the way. The dashboard clock was showing a few minutes to seven as I sped into the Heathrow tunnel, its lights urgently flashing me on. Queues at the car park entrance, sticky button at the barrier, the slowest bloody barrier creakily going up—every damn thing seemed to be conspiring to hold me back. Pulling into the first parking slot I could find, I scrambled out, slammed the door shut and raced into the terminal building, remembering later that I had probably forgotten to lock the car.

They were by the Body Shop, Anjali with a brand-new pink purse slung across her shoulder, matching brand-new jelly sandals on her feet. She spotted me before Govind did, her eyes widening into little saucers. 'Papa,' she mouthed, breaking away from Govind's grasp, darting through the crowd and into my arms.

'Thank *God* you're still here,' I thought, forgetting for a minute that I did not really believe in that uncaring entity.

Govind's legs appeared next to us and I stood up again, lifting Anjali up in my arms.

'Sorry, I'm late,' I said.

'Well, I wasn't sure how long to wait before going through.'

'I was very worried you'd have gone already.'

'I wouldn't have done that. You had said you were coming.'

I nodded my gratitude. 'Has she been okay?' I asked.

'Well, she has asked about you a few times. She liked the elephant show at the zoo though.'

I squeezed Anjali who had already been set off into a flurry of disconnected words at the mention of the word 'elephant'. Taking in great big gulps of air, she was attempting to explain, 'Elephan . . . took the water . . . and phoooed it out . . .'

'She's trying to say that we saw an elephant blowing water out of his trunk, aren't you?' Govind laughed.

Anjali nodded. 'He was having his bath . . . like this . . . phooo . . . like a big, huge shower,' she said again, wrinkling up her nose, blowing loudly out of it, 'and, and, and, there was a tiny baby elephant too, really, really tiny . . .'

Maybe I didn't need to explain Anjali's elaborate reference points to Govind after all. It sounded as though he had managed fine today. I put her back on her feet and said admiringly, '*Nice* sandals? New, are they?' She nodded and pointed shyly at Govind.

He smiled ruefully and said, 'Winning back her affection did involve a few bribes in the end.'

'I recall many a timely bribe coming to my rescue too when they first arrived here.'

There was a slight pause before Govind asked, 'How long did it take before she accepted you as her . . . papa?'

I thought carefully for a moment before answering, not entirely truthfully, 'Oh very long. It's just a name that she uses. I don't think she really thinks of me as her father at all.'

'Did she ever talk about me?'

I couldn't tell if he was referring to Anjali or to Maya, but I replied, 'Of course, your name came up a whole lot. Maya was very keen to keep your memory alive for Anjali . . . she thought that was very important.'

He nodded as though a burden had been removed from his shoulders. After another pause, he said, 'Look, I meant to tell you yesterday . . . if you ever want to see Anjali, it can be arranged.

You can either come down to Kerala . . . or I can send her to you for a short holiday . . . when she's older . . . or something like that . . .'

'Maybe it's important she settles down with you . . . I don't know if seeing me might set off a chain of memories . . . but thanks very much for the offer. I do appreciate it.'

We both looked across at Anjali who had wandered into the Body Shop and was picking up and sniffing at fruit-shaped soaps. 'I suppose we are fortunate that she's so young. An older child would have been completely traumatized by now,' Govind said.

I nodded. 'I have rather wished, these past few days, for less understanding myself. How nice to be able to wander around, not really knowing what's going on . . .'

Govind looked at me and seemed to hesitate a moment before saying, 'You won't think so now, but, believe me, it will start getting better. Slowly, but surely. Even the worst pain can't last forever.'

The tannoy system had been announcing departures to distant places all through our conversation. The name Chennai was filtering through the crackling medley with some insistence now.

'Time for you to go, I suppose,' I said to Govind.

He called out for Anjali, who returned to him with her hands full of brightly coloured soaps. I watched him march her firmly back to the stall to return the pilfered goods. I watched in surprise as she obeyed him, without a murmur, colour coding the soaps expertly as she returned them to their baskets. I suppose the job wasn't *entirely* new to him—it was only about relearning some of it. He took out a large handkerchief and wiped her hands. First one, then the other. Gently, but firmly. Saying something to her that I couldn't hear, but she was now smiling up at him. As they walked up to me, I could hear him tell her to say goodbye to me. She lifted her arms, puckering up her lips to signal I was to be rewarded with one of her big ones. I lifted her up, allowing her to grab my face between unusually sweet-smelling hands, and plant a resounding kiss on each cheek and then on my nose as was customary. I wrapped both arms around her, bringing her as close to me as I could manage, trying very hard not to cry. She had survived her crisis in stoic rubber-ball fashion. I was determined not to make it hard for her now. Putting her down, I shook Govind's hand. We thanked each other—I'm not sure for what—and then I watched them walk away.

Down the ramp, up to the desk, showing their tickets to the man sitting there, looking back for one last happy wave, Anjali beaming from ear to ear, waving as though her arm would drop off . . . and then they disappeared through a door.

*

I sat at the wheel of the car, with my head on the steering wheel, weeping as though I could never stop. I have no idea how long it lasted, but the Terminal Three car park was dark and empty by the time I raised my head and eased my aching neck. Tonight would have been the best night to end it all. I could so easily drive from here to some cliff top, rev up the car and then launch myself off it, forever. But there was still that one last job to complete. I just had to hang on until I could get to India.

I started up the car, suddenly aware that I had probably run up a very large parking bill. Not that it really mattered. Nothing mattered, but I had to get out of this place where every few minutes a jet would roar overhead, taking someone away from someone else. I didn't want to go home, but I hadn't really planned to do anything else. I could go home and sleep, I thought, except that I knew sleep wouldn't come tonight.

I paid for the parking ticket at the main pay station using my card. The slip read £22—I had never known it to be any higher than £6 before. Wednesday, 2 September, it said. Maya had not been dead a week, and already I had lost Anjali too. What did life think it was up to, chucking me around in this way?

Wednesday—wasn't that the day I had been invited to Aunty Bull's? I knew she lived near here, I was sure I could remember the way to her house if I could get to South Harrow tube station. I couldn't tell if the sudden feeling overwhelming me was a desire not to be alone or a genuine wish to see someone warm and noisy like Aunty Bull. I also knew that if I did not show up as promised at her place, she would certainly come over to see me soon. I knew she would appreciate not having to traipse all the way down to Clapham in Uncle Bull's old beat-up Merc to see me. Mum would be happy too if I made the effort . . . and would hear about it tomorrow, no doubt. Yes, I would take the plunge. However painful the experience, I would go and see Aunty Bull tonight. Anything would be better than going back to the house, where I wouldn't be watched any more by those hundreds of beanie eyes as I walked past Anjali's room.

Signposts led me easily to Harrow. All I could remember was that the name of their road was Hill Avenue and that opposite their house was a cricket club. I would recognize the house from the outside, I was sure. I drove slowly past curtained windows that glowed warmly. Did all these people know how lucky they were to have warm, cosy, welcoming houses . . . and families . . . I wondered, trying not to feel craven with jealousy. Spotting Uncle Bull's old Mercedes, I slowed down until I spotted the house. The lights were on in all the windows, upstairs and down. There was definitely a celebration on. Did I dare chance it? After thinking about the alternative again, I parked the car and, taking a deep breath, walked towards the door.

I could hear the doorbell chime distantly and in a few seconds the polished front door opened, releasing a rush of loud music—some old Mohammed Rafi tune. A couple of curious children were blocking the doorway, giggling and shoving at each other, paying me scant attention once they had seen there was no smaller person attached to my side. Aunty Bull was looking out from the door of her kitchen. Spotting me standing on the doorstep, she bore down the corridor, arms outstretched, sari fluttering, a galleon in full sail. 'Beta! Darling!' she boomed, enveloping me in a huge, warm, perfumed hug. There was the faintest smell of kebabs about her, but I sank my face into her ample bosom, feeling it wobble and quiver sorrowfully. She was standing one step above me and I was trapped in her embrace until she drew away from me for a moment to whisper 'Beta' again, brokenly. Both our faces were wet and I sank mine again gratefully into her heaving chest, feeling suddenly gripped by the desire to see my mother again.

'Are you her son?' a little girl standing by the door asked me, as Aunty Bull and I finally drew apart.

'Yes, he is just like my son!' Aunty Bull responded gruffly, pushing the children unceremoniously aside with her ample elbow to take me indoors by my hand. She pushed the living-room doors open to reveal a crowd of about twenty people, some on sofas, some sitting on the floor. A man holding a harmonium on the floor seemed to be the centre of some attention. I mimed a namasté to Uncle Bull who was occupying his usual corner from where he was observing everything glumly.

'*Suniye, sab log*! I want you all to meet my son. Not my Ashu who is in Minnesota, but my *second* son, Rahul. His mummy and I were the dearest of friends in our schooldays. In Jalandhar. We were only six, imagine, when we first met! So he is just like my own beta, you see. *Yeh* Clapham *mein reheta hai*.' She said 'Clapham' pronouncing the 'ham' as in 'hamster'.

But, with that, mercifully, my introduction was over. I squeezed into a corner of the room while the man on the floor went back to playing his harmonium and all eyes returned to him again. Only one woman's eyes had widened when she heard me being introduced. I could see her now asking Aunty Bull something in urgent whispers and then covering her open mouth with a horrified hand. It looked like she was the only person in the room who knew what had happened to me so recently. I avoided her gaze from across the room and tried to keep my face expressionless as the man on the floor sang of some old celluloid heartbreak. A large, soft-looking woman moved along the sofa and patted it to indicate that the room she had created was meant for me. I eased myself in, feeling her pudding-like flesh softly give way. The singer was surprisingly good and I could feel myself getting lost in his music, sinking against the kindly softness of the woman next to me when she struck up conversation. I looked sideways at her, focusing on her lips caked in maroon lipstick, to make sure I could make out what she was saying through the cacophony of thoughts flying through my head.

'So have you had a drink, Rahul?' Without waiting for a reply, she clicked her fingers at a child lurking nearby and said, 'Eh, beta, bring this uncle a coke.' Then, turning to me, she asked, 'You will have coke?'

Aunty Bull had made off in the direction of the kitchen, closing the living-room doors firmly behind her. Fiercely sensitive about the smell of cooking in the house, Maya would have done the same thing. 'It's an Asian woman thing,' she would say, storming around the house with a hissing can of air spray. 'We take such pains not to smell of cooking—heavy perfumes, grimly closed doors—but invariably end up smelling of the last daal anyway. We might as well aim to smell of *fresh* food, I suppose, to be seen as a cut above little Bangladeshi kids from east end tower blocks trudging to school forlornly, trailing clouds of stale curry.'

The woman next to me had been successful in her mission of getting me a coke. The little girl had reappeared at her side, beaming from ear to ear, holding out a chilled can. For her pains she was rewarded with cheeks squeezed to make her look like a gasping fish and a loud 'mwoo' kiss depositing a huge slash of maroon lipstick on the little girl's forehead. As she wandered off, vigorously rubbing her forehead, I was given the coke with a flourish while my lipstick-ed benefactress settled down among mirror-worked cushions for a comfortable chat. 'So,' she said as though signalling we had a long session ahead of us, 'you are living in Clapham, eh?'

I nodded, sipping my coke, feeling the weariness of all the expected questions that would shortly descend on me: Who are you? Whose son are you? Do you have a good job? A mortgage? (The Killer) Are you married? And, if not, how can I get you to meet my daughter/niece/friend's daughter etc? She was sipping more delicately on her coke than I was, hers having been served in one of Aunty Bull's best lead crystal whisky glasses. I was swigging mine back ungracefully, wondering if I could get away with answering all her questions at random, with untruths. At that moment it didn't feel as if I would be able to summon up the energy even to link together a cohesive set of lies. I knew I couldn't survive her imminent quizzing and was wondering how to make good an escape, when I felt a hand on my shoulder. Uncle Bull's rheumy, sad eyes were looking down at me.

'Hello, Rahul beta, I wondered whether you might like to see my roses this year.'

I knew nothing at all about roses and had probably spoken no more than a total of ten words to Uncle Bull on any given visit. But I scrambled up from the sofa, barely able to conceal my relief. 'Sorry, Shamsher, to break up your conversation but, you see, this young man is an expert on prize roses . . .' he explained disingenuously to my neighbour on the sofa as we made our escape. She glared at Uncle Bull with scarcely disguised annoyance. Clearly there was a daughter or a niece for whom she would have liked to strike a deal tonight.

Despite not being the expert on roses Uncle Bull had so generously claimed me to be, it was the one flower I did recognize. I certainly knew their strong scent as we walked out into the back garden. It was hanging heavily and sweetly over everything, even masking the smell of food emanating from steamed-up kitchen windows. I inhaled deeply and Uncle Bull said, 'Yes, take in deep, big breaths of it. The aroma will help to clear your head of all your thoughts.' We walked across to a garden bench and sat down in silence, looking out at roses that I could only smell, and not see, in the darkness. 'I'm keeping the lights turned off so that no one else comes out and disturbs you here,' Uncle Bull said after a while. I felt a surge of gratitude to this old man who had never figured much in my thoughts before and who seemed so willing to allow me the silent companionship I needed.

We sat there while the moon came up over the hedge at the far end of the garden and watched it trail its gentle light over the flowers as my eyes adjusted to the darkness. I tried to work out what the original, daytime colours of the flowers might be. That purple one there was probably red, that golden one, white. They moved their heavy heads every time the night breezes sighed, sending out their heady aromas as if taking their cue from Uncle Bull's bidding to help me clear my head.

Somewhere far away Aunty Bull's voice was calling everyone to eat. After a while we could hear her strident call for Uncle Bull. 'Oho! Where has he gone at this time,' we could hear her say to no one in particular. He stirred next to me.

'She will be looking for me to help with the drinks . . .'

I nodded. 'I'm ready to go back in now, I think. Thank you,' I said.

He sighed deeply and said, 'I should have asked you about her, about how it all happened. But in some sense, there is no point, is there? Sorrow, my young friend, chooses some people, for some reason . . . and then stays, like a best friend. There is no point telling you otherwise. The earlier you are prepared, the better. She will always walk by your side now.' I thought he was referring to Maya, but he added, 'I too know sorrow, she is always there by my side, whatever I do, wherever I go. Get used to it, live with it, try not to let it infect everything around you.'

What was his sorrow? I wondered. I vaguely remembered Mum saying something about Aunty Bull having married a widower but I would not have dreamed of asking this normally silent man anything personal. After all, there was no point in talking about it, as he said. The sorrow was there to stay and that was the immovable constant.

We got up and went indoors where bedlam had broken out in the dining room. The table was surrounded by eager eaters—or the inimitable Indian queue, as Maya called it. Great platters of food were being set upon by plate-wielding warriors in saris and salwar-kameezes. Aunty Bull spotted me and decided to spare me the agonies of grappling for my food. Grabbing a plate, she heaped it generously with pulao, adding huge dollops of chicken makhani and matar paneer. 'Kebabs?' she mouthed across to me. I shook my head and she wobbled over, plate aloft, to where I stood against the wall, to personally deliver my dinner to me.

'Thank you, Aunty, you are so kind,' I muttered.

'Come on, no thanks-shanks from my own beta. I told you, you are *no* different than my son . . .' she said affectionately and then, embarrassed, she added more loudly, '. . . now I want to see you *eat*. Eat *nicely*, okay!' This last pronouncement was an order that I was strangely content to obey. Had my last Indian meal really been when Maya was still alive? I had reached the stage where I could not even remember when I had my last meal. As far as I knew, I had not eaten anything at all today. I ate slowly because I knew my empty stomach was very likely to revolt with the sudden introduction of rich food.

The lipstick-ed lady on the sofa had fought her way across the room to corner me again. Luckily, however, her plate of food was keeping her too busy for anything more than snatches of conversation. She was also having difficulty manoeuvring her plate around her chest that I could now see was of immense proportions, sticking out like a shelf before her. The silver fork in her right hand had a longer than average journey to make from her plate, around the shelf and up to her mouth, where the food had to be delivered delicately between those maroon lips. I did not have to worry about conversation any more. I ate slowly, watching the happy, shining, chewing faces around me, nodding occasionally at something the now-not-so-heavily lipstick-ed lady was saying.

When the meal was drawing to a close and Aunty Bull's large platters were starting to be scraped, showing their silver bottoms, a huge cake was brought to the table and a few of the women started to cluck around it, sticking candles in, getting them lit. 'Come on, ji, come and cut your cake, like a good boy,' one of the women called out, while the others sniggered coyly. Uncle Bull shuffled sheepishly out from the crowd and took up his place behind the cake, holding the knife unsurely. He looked at Aunty Bull and she gave him an encouraging nod. 'Go on, the guests are all waiting, ji. Blow out your candles first.' He blew out those sad cheeks, extinguishing all but one little flickering candle. Then he blew that one out as well, as everybody clapped and went 'Aaah' and started to sing. I slipped out of the room, wondering again what event had overcome the man now cutting his seventieth birthday cake. He had obviously lived with it a long, long time. Well, as long as I had known him anyway. So, it was possible to live with it, as he had said. But I knew already that I did not want to survive like that. Uncle Bull must have had his reasons for carrying on. Ashu, his son, perhaps. Maybe even the noisy, irrepressible Aunty Bull. But I was sure I had none. Mum and Dad would not be around very long—and they lived for each other anyway. My brother, Anil, had his own life in San Francisco and for the past year, going by his scanty email messages, an American girlfriend too. It felt that, with Maya's and Anjali's departures, I couldn't have been more alone in the world.

I opened the front door and let myself out into the silent night. Sleeping cars were glowing a myriad of dark, jewel-like colours. Window lights had dimmed and fallen asleep. Only Aunty Bull's house was still brightly lit, throwing its munificence a long way down this quiet street. The sound of Hindi film music was now soft, muffled by the closing of the heavy oak front door behind me. They wouldn't notice I had gone until much later. They would probably understand. I got into the car and slowly drove home.

There was only one more thing I had to do before leaving England. I had already booked my ticket to India—that took just one phone call. Then I called Mum and Dad and Anil, telling them I would fly to Kerala first, to immerse Maya's ashes, and then arrive in Delhi soon after. They sounded overjoyed, of course, and very relieved that Anjali's future had been sorted out. 'She will be better off with her own father, beta,' Mum had said gently. 'How would you have coped on your own . . . with your job and all . . .' Then, more eagerly, her motherly preoccupations came to the fore. 'I hope you'll be able to stay a nice long time, beta, before going back to England. How much leave do you have?' She sounded anxious suddenly. I muttered something in reply.

But before that long pilgrimage, I had a much smaller one to make, nearly as painful. I drove to it and pulled up on a single yellow line. A car behind me tooted, but I was already far away— in the midst of another busy, sunny afternoon just a week ago. Had it really been just a week? Who had cleaned the road and brought everything back to such innocuous normality? If the junction was not so perennially busy, I could have wandered around, looking for some other traces of her—something precious that would bring her back, if only for a fleeting moment. They had given me her things: her brown leather purse, that Citizen watch we bought from John Lewis once, now with a cracked dial frozen to that awful moment when everything changed forever. Twenty-three minutes past one. It was nearly that time now, just coming up to one o'clock . . . although I hadn't planned it to be that way. Despite the way I was feeling, coming here to observe a weekly anniversary would have been too ghoulish by far.

I looked at the busy junction, where cars obediently stopped and started again, jostling at the lights. What had possessed him to jump out at Maya like that? Like some crazed animal going in for the kill. Hitting her with unerring precision. The policeman had said they were not sure about a prosecution because he hadn't stopped and nobody had come forward with any information. At first I was angry that I had no one to blame, no one to fly at with my fists, shouting my horror. She had a scrape once before, two years ago, nothing worse than a dented bumper thankfully. On that occasion, the culprit was a young lad who had just passed his test, driving his mother's beat-up old car over give-way lines. They turned up at our door later, asking to pay privately for our repairs so as to avoid losing a no-claims bonus on their insurance. I gave them short shrift then but, for some odd reason, his was the face that reappeared now every time I wanted to feel angry with someone after this accident. His spotty face, nearly invisible through long, lank hair, and the Kurt Cobain song that Maya said was playing on his car stereo that day. Those were now coming back at me relentlessly, as if it might have been him returning to finish off his previously half-completed task.

Lunch-hour traffic was clamouring around me, everybody was rushing to or from some important assignment. Where was she going that day? Was she trying to get home for some lunch? Was there something else on her mind that kept her from concentrating? I knew, more than anyone else, that under her serene exterior ran an unhappiness so deep that even I could not reach it sometimes. I had to salve that pain even if it was the last thing that I did, wherever she was. I started up the car and drove home to do my packing.

I wouldn't need very much. Delhi and Kerala would be hot and muggy at this time of year. Didn't Kerala have its monsoon sometime around now? The box with the ashes fitted easily into my small shoulder bag. I wasn't sure I ought to be carrying it on board the aircraft. I certainly didn't want to be discussing it with a customs official at Bombay airport. I put it into my suitcase, covered it with my tee-shirts, a couple of shorts and one pair of jeans. Once I had done that, the suitcase did not look as painfully empty as before. I closed and locked it. There was nothing else that I would need. I wandered around the house for a few minutes and then, opening the suitcase and the bag again, put Maya's small sandalwood Ganesha and a few recent pictures of her and Anjali in, next to the box.

It was like being on autopilot, but I was going through all the paces unfalteringly—as if it was all being orchestrated elsewhere, leaving me to merely carry out the physical motions. Next, I had to call the mini-cab company down the road. The Air India flight was at eight-thirty in the morning. It was going to be an early start. I tossed and turned all night, not really expecting sleep to come. When the alarm went off, I was already awake and waiting with one weary hand poised over the clock to turn it off. By the time I had washed and shaved, I could hear the cab pull up outside the gate. I waved at him through the kitchen window to make sure he did not blow his horn. In a few minutes I was loading the suitcase into his car. 'Hang on a minute, mate,' I said to the driver, before going up to Sandra's door to drop a spare set of keys and an explanatory note through the letter box. I had written it last night, not wanting to go across and explain everything in person. It felt cruel to repay her kindness over the years with three abrupt lines, but it would have to do. It was getting very important to hold everybody off, *especially* the kindly, well-meaning ones. They were the ones most likely to rob me of my resolve and that, I was very sure, I did not want.

The drive to Heathrow should have had an air of deja vu about it, but the driver did not take my normal route. Instead of crossing the river at Chelsea Bridge, he turned left. I did not question him. I did not want to make conversation and have him ask me all the usual inane questions about holidays and going home to see the parents. Battersea Park was on my right now, and I felt sorry I could not get to see the pagoda gaze serenely out from across the river. As we crossed the river on Albert Bridge, I looked out at Chelsea rousing itself. The pinkness that had broken out over the river in the eastern sky had not trickled down to these salubrious western parts of the city yet. Tall town houses still lay slumbering darkly, their occupants still warm in their beds, holding each other. While I sped towards the airport with Maya's ashes in a suitcase bound for India. I was surprised at how little my self-pity had dimmed in the past week as I now felt its familiar prickle behind my lashes.

At Heathrow, I added a five-pound tip to make up for the silence of the journey. The driver gave me a big grin, pocketing the notes—strange how some people with such terrible teeth could produce the most magnificent of smiles. The suitcase felt unusually light for a trip to India. The last time I went, it was stuffed full of things for my parents: chocolates for Dad, household things for Mum, carefully chosen by Maya. I hoped they would not be expecting anything this time. I walked up to the Air India desk to be asked all the usual questions. Lifting the suitcase easily, I put it on the conveyor belt and, after it had been tagged, watched it wobble away until it was out of sight.

I went into the Body Shop where Anjali had helped herself to the fruit-shaped soaps three days ago, to buy her a small basket full. I could post them to her once I was in Kerala. I don't think I wanted to see her. Having met Govind, I was sure she would be as happy as she could get under the circumstances. I did not want to upset that delicate balance just as they were achieving it. How odd that, having finally become her papa (or unka on not very good days), I was back so easily to being a nonentity again. A sender of sporadic gifts. It was foolish to expect there would be room for an ex-stepfather in a kid's life, wasn't it?

Picking up a few large bars of Toblerone for Dad, I walked though the security gates. There was no point in hanging around on this side, with no one to see me off. Why did every other passenger seem to have at least one person to see them off? The flights to India were the worst—whole families turning up sometimes to see one passenger off. I would be far better off in the more equitable world on the other side of the security gates. The chap at the immigration counter wanted to know how long I was planning to be away. He must have been trying to be friendly, just making conversation, surely he did not need to know that. I said something about a quick visit to see my parents and he nodded approvingly.

The duty-free shops were beckoning with their glossy, shiny products on display. I sat on a thinly cushioned steel chair, closing my eyes and trying to block this bright, busy world out.

This was the bit I usually hated. The interminable waiting, once check-in and security were done. Maya often laughed at my furious pacing about—she could seem to sit so easily for hours together, leafing through a magazine. In this past week, however, I seemed to have learned, among other things, to float through distant mind-numbed worlds. I had acquired the art of *existing*. Of time-pass.

When the chap in front of me had finished nearly half his book, and the guy on the other side had read all his papers, rustling them about in barely contained irritation at this communal, enforced wait, I heard the first announcement for the flight. I looked at my watch and realized that I had been sitting on this hard steel chair for nearly two hours. Perhaps I had inadvertently learnt the art of meditation or something. I unfolded myself and stood up, feeling all my bones and joints object creakingly before beginning the long walk towards gate 29.

The flight looked like a busy one—air hostesses in saris had hands folded in falsely smiling namastés, and already looked faintly harassed. I put the bag containing the chocolates in the overhead locker and took my place. I had requested a window seat so that I could sleep (or pretend to sleep). My fellow passengers arrived soon after. A good-looking young Indian couple squeezed into their seats next to mine. Oh good, they would have eyes only for each other, I thought, and would consequently leave me alone, hopefully. After nodding briefly in my direction, they predictably put their heads together in a huddle, talking and laughing softly with each other. I leaned my head against the wall of the aircraft and closed my eyes. The pain was *still* almost unbearably bad. More than a week now, and it still took just a glimpse of someone else's happiness to bring everything flooding back at me. Would it never go away?

Surprisingly, I did manage to sleep, waking up only when the young man next to me touched my arm as the trolleys arrived with lunch. I must have missed the drinks trolley—perhaps it was just as well.

'Thanks, I suppose I could do with lunch,' I said, blinking away my sleep and accepting the small plastic tray.

'I'm always impressed by people who manage to sleep on board flights,' my handsome young neighbour said, smiling.

'Ah, a skill acquired after long years of practice,' I replied.

'Travel a lot then?' he asked.

'Often to Europe. To India, about once every other year, perhaps.'

Polite lunchtime conversation done with, he returned to his own tray and his wife, asking her what she thought of the lunch, talking and laughing in whispers again. I peeled back the foil wrapping to inspect Air India's offering for the day. They could usually be relied on to serve reasonably good food. At least, it would have authentic Indian flavours and be hot. Today it was chicken biriyani and palak paneer. I unwrapped my cutlery and sampled a mouthful . . . hmmm, satisfactory standard . . . and gulab jamun for dessert that would normally have been quickly appropriated by Maya and her sweet tooth.

I hadn't been inaccurate to the young man—we had been to India just once together in the past three years. Two years ago. We would have probably gone again this year, to see Dad. November, it would have been, in time for Diwali perhaps. Maya didn't like going back to India. 'Brings back too many things,' she said. In her case, it was probably because unlike me she really had no family to go back to. Although she accompanied me on my visit to Mum and Dad year before last, she did not want to go back to Kerala, understandably. She did not really want to talk about it either. So it lay there, like a still, sad pool between us. Never angry, never accusing. Just still and very sad and always there.

And now, I was going there to see if I could complete what Maya had not been able to do. Foolish. Quite mad. But, if this wasn't a time for madness, what was it? I felt quite overwhelmingly compelled to embark on this crazy scheme. For Maya's sake? Or because I wanted to ask questions that for too long had lain submerged? Because *I* needed to know why.

It was quite late at night when we arrived in Bombay and the city was a sea of neon and light as we descended over it. I had three hours to kill before getting my connection to Cochin. From there I knew I would have to get myself a taxi to get to Champakulam. I said goodbye to my young fellow passengers at Bombay airport. It is extraordinary how people seem not to mind striking up a conversation when they know they have only a few minutes left together. They said, as we waited for the aircraft doors to open, that they had recently got married and were returning from a honeymoon in London. 'London's a great city, really cool and happening,' the girl had said. 'You're so lucky to be living there.' I accepted the compliment graciously and wished them luck, watching them walk hand in hand towards the baggage collection area. I had to make my way to the transit lounge for another long wait, still questioning my sanity in embarking on this crazy journey.

I whiled away the hours at Bombay airport planning my words, harnessing my anger. By the time I boarded the early morning flight to Cochin, my nerves were taut and at snapping point. Could I pull it off? Did I still want to? They would be an old couple now. I had seen them just that once, over the wall, soon after moving into the house next door to Maya. Every fibre in my being was revolting at the thought of confronting an old couple, as old perhaps as my parents. Why was I doing this? Maya was *gone*. What did I have to gain?

Dawn was breaking as the A320 approached Kerala. The land below was lush green—very unlike the descent to Delhi where all one can see are stretches of brown, the odd river bed and, finally, miles of concrete laced by roads. Here, in the distance, I could see unreal purple mountains floating on a milky-grey sea of cloud. Perhaps it was mist. As the plane dropped, occasional toy houses appeared, their brown tiled roofs peeping out from amidst palm groves. Fishing boats were drowsing in their bed of blue and pink and, as we banked, all I could see, looking west, was the endless, shining vastness of the sleeping sea.

Finally, as the descent began, blue turned to green as the sea gave way to a carpet of palm tops rolling out interminably under the screaming engines. The lady in the seat next to me clutched the armrest tightly as the aircraft, swinging from side to side like a giant metal hammock, bumped onto the runway, juddering and screaming, trying desperately to stop. When the plane came to a final whining halt, she turned to me and, smiling sheepishly, said, 'Very bumpy landing.'

I nodded but could not bring myself to make polite conversation.

'You are a tourist?' she asked in a friendly voice, her trauma of the landing having been dealt with.

I nodded again. Yes . . . a tourist of sorts—visiting a tortured past like some crazed backpacker. I made no reply and my clenched lips had my hapless co-passenger retreat in abashed confusion.

The heat, although I was expecting it, hit me with its unwelcoming fury. Dense with humidity, it was more oppressive than anything I had known before. I could feel fatigue overwhelm me even as I trudged with the other passengers over the tarmac to the terminal. I looked in surprise at the building I was approaching. It looked new and oddly elegant—made to resemble a temple with sloping tiled roofs which were adorned with decorative eaves and finials. Inside, two young boys were hard at work at the conveyor belts already disgorging our baggage. Together they hoisted up suitcases and boxes, laying them in neat rows on the shiny new floor, their chocolate-brown faces and arms glistening with sweat.

'Thank you,' I said to the one who brought my suitcase in, not entirely surprised when he shrugged off my offer of a tip. I knew from my previous stay here about these people, on whom years of communist governments had bequeathed a kind of pride. 'Many people call it arrogance, especially when they organize themselves into unions and bring the entire state to a halt on bandh days,' Maya had said. There were a lot of things she told me about this state of hers, all of which were coming back to me now. It was the unsaid things, though, that had really brought me here. We should have been able to come here together, so she could have explained all this first-hand. We could have walked out into the shiny heat together, Anjali running along ahead, eager to meet her grandparents. That shouldn't have become such an impossibility. It seemed so wrong that Maya should have had that joy denied to her.

Outside the terminal, a sea of smiling brown faces was thronging at the railings, eagerly scanning our faces for those of loved ones bearing TVs and two-in-ones from Dubai. A tout approached me, offering me hotels, taxis and tours in broken English. He looked like a thug, but I needed to get to a hotel for a shower and some sleep before I could begin to think again. I followed him to his car as he walked ahead of me, grinning at the ease with which he had nabbed me.

'Good hotel. Any good hotel,' I said after getting into his car.

''otel Sea View very good, saar,' he said decisively.

'Five star?' I asked him.

He pulled a face. 'Why spend on five star, saar, too costly. 'otel Sea View best 'otel, saar, very good service.'

'No, no,' I replied just as emphatically, unimpressed by his desire to save me my money, 'take me to the best hotel in Cochin. Five star.'

He started up his car, cheerful despite losing his Hotel Sea View commission and said, 'I take you to Malabar 'otel, saar. Best 'otel in Cochin. On sea-front.' After five minutes, he started off again, 'I arrange trips for you, saar, best trips, backwaters, ayurveda, Kathakali, any trips, I can arrange.'

'I need to get to Champakulam tomorrow,' I said.

'Champakulam. Backwaters trip?'

'No, just Champakulam.'

'No problem, saar, I can arrange, what time?'

'How much will you charge?' I asked, not sure why I was bothering to ask. I had 25,000 bloody pounds saved up in my ISA account back in England, with no one in particular to leave it to. Did it matter what this man wanted to charge me for a bloomin' trip to Champakulam.

'Only five hundred rupees, saar,' he said tentatively, signalling his willingness to bring his rate down if I got shirty.

'Okay, ten-thirty, tomorrow morning,' I said, ignoring the grin that flashed my way in the rear-view mirror. I looked out of the window. Children were playing cricket in an open area next to a rubbish dump, using sticks for stumps. I watched the diminutive bowler perform a beautiful spin action as he came around the makeshift wicket in skinny bare feet, before the car turned a corner and they were out of sight.

Malabar Hotel was a graceful colonnaded building, heavy with creepers. A turbaned doorman with an impressive handlebar moustache took my suitcase out of the car, while I settled up with the driver. 'Thanks saar, thanks,' he was saying, bowing and backing away from me in delight at the generous tip. Bloody, mad foreigner, he was probably thinking as he drove away. I walked up the marble steps and entered the cool air-conditioned lobby with some relief. I didn't usually splurge on five-star luxury, and I now wished I had done this with Maya a few times. How she would have loved it. Soft music was playing and I could hear the delicate trickle of water somewhere. Even the smile on the face of the receptionist was a luxurious, wide, welcoming one. I was checked in, my passport scanned, credit card numbers were written down—nothing was a problem in a place like this.

I was taken up to my room by a bellboy, in a taller newer part of the building. As we stepped into the room, I drew in my breath at the beauty of the view. The window was an expanse of shiny blue, with sea meeting sky somewhere indiscernibly far away. A few catamarans with brown cloth sails were idling in tiny flecks of white in the blue-green sweep. Mid-morning heat was shimmering off the azure expanse outside, but inside, in this artificial world of opulent calm, everything was beautifully controlled and air-cooled. I suddenly had no heat, no dust, no fishy sea-smell and, dare I say, no London sorrows to bother me until I chose to step out of here again. I closed the door behind the bellboy and, ripping off my sweat-soaked shirt and trousers, threw myself on the soft, springy bed in immeasurable relief. In what must have been a few minutes, I could feel sleep overcome me. It was as though I hadn't known such rest in all of my tormented week.

When I awoke, the sun was setting, orange and lush. I ordered myself a mango drink with lots of ice and sat on my balcony, watching the Kerala sky turn all kinds of wonderful colours. What a beautiful land she had come from! Was it any wonder her eyes sometimes looked so sad and far away in the greyness of the city to which I had taken her? I crushed the ice cube between my teeth, unable to feel my old anger in the face of such unashamed loveliness. The flames of the setting sun that had engulfed the sea were now being slowly extinguished by inky black waves that gently lapped as the night drew in. Maya's beautiful land. I looked around, wondering why it had never seemed so beautiful on my last trip here. Now her palm trees were waving, her birds were flying darkly home to roost—it was almost as if she had whispered instructions to her world that it was to turn out in its best pageant tonight. Was it because—and how sad she would have been, poor Maya— we had finally, in a strange sort of way, come back to Kerala together.

seven teen

_____

The driver turned up at the appointed hour next morning, his car all polished and primed for the trip. 'You call me Mammookka, saar,' he said, baring all his teeth at me in the rear-view mirror. 'Everyone call me Mammookka.'

'Mammookka,' I muttered, practising the unfamiliar name. Names were a lot more straightforward in the part of India that I came from.

'Ikka means elder brother. You please call me Mohammedikka or Mammookka. Then I am like your elder brother,' he added helpfully, still baring his teeth.

Bugger it. My carelessness with my money yesterday had made this man adopt me as his brother now. I nodded, trying not to seem too friendly.

'You are going to Champakulam to meet some friend, saar?' he asked, looking at the address I had written on yellow sticky-backed notepaper, now pasted on his dashboard.

'Friend's parents,' I said, not entirely inaccurately. It had not been difficult finding the address—it was there, a hopeful little entry in Maya's neat handwriting, on the M page in her address book. Mr and Mrs Madhava Varma, Pulayil House, Meenampally Kaayal, Champakulam, Kerala. The only other place I had seen the address was on the back of that letter written by her father three years ago, disowning her forever. It might even have been less than three years ago. That was the last we had ever heard from Kerala.

We were driving over a long bridge now and I looked out at the same sea that had filled the window frame of my hotel last night. Those dirty brown catamarans were still idling on the water. Didn't they need to *go* anywhere, these little boats? This must mean there's enough fish for them right here in the bay.

'Mattancheri Bridge, saar, to come out of Willingdon Island,' Mammookka said, noticing me look out at the view. I wished he would keep his eyes on the road instead of watching me all the time in his rear-view mirror. I reckoned the journey would take about two hours. At the hotel reception they said it was about seventy miles. But, as Mammookka leaned on his pedal (and, with more enthusiasm, on his horn), I realized I hadn't taken the traffic into account. Nor the fact that Kerala seemed to be really just one endless village. I remembered that feature from the trip Maya and I had made to Padmanabhapuram Palace, when she first told me of her unhappiness. That world, and that unhappiness, however keenly felt at the time, seemed to have been reduced to nothing now. Nothing compared to the heaving, shredding sorrow of this week.

Just as we seemed to reach the end of a village or town where thatched roof houses finally thinned out, the next village would begin. Soon, another one would be upon us, developing from its sleepy edges into a noisy chaotic jumble of houses and shops, some of which had encroached so aggressively on to the road that it seemed to take all of Mammookka's steering power to keep from careering into them. Children darted across the roads without fear, while cars dodged them, their horns screaming abuse. Women, their colourful lungi-clad bottoms wiggling provocatively, carried this and that on their heads and cyclists wobbled carelessly through the melee.

An hour later, the yellow-painted milestones told me we still had about twenty miles to go. The heat was already oppressive and I wondered how bad it would get by the afternoon. My mind had already gone numb with all the thinking it had done since my arrival here. All the things I planned to say to Maya's parents had, in these past few hours, crowded in and out of my mind, angrily, despairingly. Now, before it even started, I was already tired. I felt a faint longing to finish it off soon, without lingering over it too much. The kind of thrill I had felt back in England—of finally meeting them face to face, of finally saying all those unsaid words, of assuaging Maya's unspoken pain—was starting to wear thin. 'Come *on*, Rahul,' I bucked myself up, as a sign welcoming us to Alleppey district flashed past. 'Don't chicken out now, not when you're so near.'

It really ought to have been dealt with while Maya was alive. But her propensity for remaining silent on the subject almost made me stop noticing her pain years ago. That I didn't use even one of the rare occasions on which she let her anguish show to comfort her in any meaningful way or help her sort the bloody mess out now felt like such a terrible burden to bear. I blithely assumed her ache would fade, and never thought, of course, that time would run out long before that would be given even half a chance to happen.

I wondered if I would first have to break the news of Maya's death to her parents before coming out with everything else. According to my calculations, Govind would have arrived in Trivandrum only a day ago. I had forgotten to ask him if he was still in touch with them and whether they knew of his trip to London. I could have called them on the telephone number I found in Maya's address book, or sent a telegram. But I decided I didn't really owe them that courtesy. After all, they said it first, didn't they? Translated for me by a shocked and white-faced Maya as she read her father's letter: 'Go and live your life in the way you have to. You do not exist for us any more. We will forget you ever existed, just as you

Jaishree Misra

will have to forget about us. The Maya, who was once a child of this family is now dead.' That was what they said. Dead. Well, now she *is* dead, Mr and Mrs Varma. Happy? I could feel my resolve harden again as we drove through a crowded, bustling town with a cheerful air—Alleppey. Champakulam was probably not very far now.

We seemed to be approaching a huge temple that was garishly decorated in red-and-green plastic bunting. The entire street—pedestrians, cyclists, everybody—appeared to be heading towards it. The car slowed down to an ambling pace, people overtaking us effortlessly on foot.

'Temble festival time, saar,' Mammokka said, before asking, 'You are Hindu, saar?'

'Yes,' I replied, 'not religious.'

'If you are Hindu, saar, you must visit this temble, Mullakkal Devi is very . . . very . . .' he couldn't find the word. I knew he meant 'powerful'. Maya had told me about her own childhood visits to this temple en route to her grandmother's house. I also knew, from my previous stay here, of the love and the fear their deities aroused in these people.

'But you must be Muslim,' I asked, 'with a name like Mohammed?'

'Yes, saar, but if I am driving through Alleppey I will always pay my respect to this devi. She is very, very strong.' Having said this, he slowed down, bringing the car to a juddering halt outside enormous temple gates. I watched while he put some money in a collection box at the door. I looked up at the towering structure. Maya must have been here many times as a child, every school holiday that she spent with her grandmother. I have a feeling that she always maintained her faith in these gods and goddesses, even after she left for England, despite everything. I remember her once shamefacedly owning up to sending a grateful postal order from England soon after she first arrived there. It might have been to this very goddess. The carvings on the temple were catching the bright sunshine, showing gods and goddesses, beasts and demons, the juxtaposition of good and bad, an earthly acceptance that one could not expect to have one without the other. Religious music was blaring on a loudspeaker. This . . . it was all this that had rejected her, I thought, turning away. I couldn't understand it. Everything I had seen in Kerala so far seemed so cultured, so civilized. Even this driver—a Muslim, stopping outside temple gates to pay his respects. That kind of respect would have been unheard of in the north of India where I came from. Why then, in the midst of this genteel, mannerly decency, did Maya's family oppose her chance of a new life so bitterly? They were educated people, living in the modern city of Bangalore. They loved their daughter, or so Maya insisted, *even* after receiving that letter— she obviously always hoped for some sort of reconciliation, in some distant time. I didn't argue with that, although to me it was clear that she mistook as love her family's desire to possess. I even stayed silent when she said she would try to send them a picture again when she had had the baby—when she was pregnant with our child and had started to plan way ahead of herself.

Ten minutes later, we were pulling up at a boat jetty. 'From here by boat to Champakulam, saar, best way. Mammookka come with you.'

We parked the car in the scanty shade provided by some palm trees and walked down the jetty to where a boat was already waiting, filling up with passengers. 'Waterbus, saar,' Mammookka explained. It was obviously some kind of a ferry service, calling at various tiny villages on the banks of the backwaters. Not quite a river, I thought, looking into the grey-green dank waters being churned up by the boat engines. I had heard of cruises on the backwaters and had planned a day-trip on my last visit to Kerala. Of course, that had never happened.

I could feel the eyes of the other passengers on me. Was I

another mad foreigner, wanting to examine their life for some inexplicable reason? Or was I an ex-Malayali, returning to seek his lost heritage from some distant uncaring land? Neither, I wanted to shout out loud, my rage starting to build again as we neared Pulayil House. It was engulfing me again. I needed to stay calm to say my piece. As I took a few deep breaths, Mammookka nodded in my direction, indicating that ours was the next stop.

As we disembarked, I heard Mammookka ask a passer-by for directions, holding the yellow sticky-backed bit of paper in his hand. The stranger was keen to know who we were but, on not receiving a reply, pointed to a gate not too far from the jetty.

As we approached it, I noticed how tall and rusty it was, the wrought-iron black in patches, the rest overtaken by rusty orange. It had a thick, unruly hedge trying to engulf it. The words Pulayil Veedu, carved into a piece of grey granite, were staring out at me from the rain-marked concrete gatepost. Pulayil House. My mouth was suddenly dry, my head spinning out of control. The *heat* . . . it must be at least forty degrees, I thought irrelevantly. Mammookka looked at me enquiringly as I reluctantly opened the gates.

'This is not house, saar?' he asked.

'I think it is,' I said feebly, finally lifting my arm to raise the latch. It fell away with a clang louder than I intended and the gates creaked open grudgingly as I pushed at them. A house revealed itself, large and imposing, overlooking the canal in front of it with an air of majesty. It was set back among some dense trees. Some of its window shutters were open; I could see net curtains fluttering through them. There was definitely someone around. I sucked in my breath and walked over soft sandy soil towards the house. The front door, polished dark wood, was closed. I spotted a doorbell and rang it once, and then a second time. Huge yellow blooms in a flower pot nodded at me cheerfully.

Footsteps approached the door on the other side and I could

hear bolts being slid open. The door opened and a woman of about forty looked out enquiringly. She wasn't Maya's mother, I was sure of that. Maya's mother was quite tall and slim, as I remembered her. Anyway, this woman was too young by my calculations to be her mother. Some other relative, perhaps?

'Er . . . Mrs Varma . . . Rukmani Varma?' I asked.

The woman's face cleared immediately, but still wore a puzzled expression as she said, 'Rukmani chechi does not live here now. She rented this property to us some years ago. You are . . .?'

'I . . . I met her a few years ago . . . in Bangalore . . . when she lived there, you know . . .'

'Ah, yesyes, when Madhavettan . . . her husband, was alive . . . that must have been many years ago! Three years at least.'

'Yes, I suppose it was . . .' I trailed off, but the woman's plump face, shiny with sweat, continued to look enquiringly at me. This is India, I reminded myself, people are *entitled* to know things here. I took a deep breath and hoped I sounded convincing. 'I was a friend of her daughter's. I came to Kerala for something and thought I might be able to meet Mrs Varma again . . .'

It still did not seem to be working. This lady with the stout, kindly face was more savvy and far more informed about Mrs Rukmani Varma than one would have expected. She frowned, dropping some of the red powder of the bindi on her forehead on to her nose. 'But she has no connection whatsoever with her daughter any more. You know that?' she asked.

'Yes, I had an idea there had been a split . . .'

'Yesyes, very sad it is, very sad,' she said, clucking regretfully, 'but if you have come to patch things up, it is no use. No use,' she repeated firmly.

'Oh no, that isn't my intention at all. I just wanted to meet her. You wouldn't happen to know where she is at the moment, would you?'

'Oh, after the sad business with Maya, you know, her daughter, and after her husband's death, she left here to go and live in the Bhagawati Kshetram at Tirunalmala. Here, in Champakulam, there is no peace, she had said to me when she rented us this house, no peace. "People will not let me forget about my daughter, too many questions, too many nosy people." So she went to devote her life to the goddess there. Sometimes she comes, but hardly ever these days. We send her the rent by postal order.'

'Could I have her address, do you think?'

'Yesyes, I can give you the address, but it is very far from here. At least five hours by car.' She looked at me doubtfully, but I stood my ground, still looking her in the eye. 'I will get it,' she said, 'you come in please.' She turned on the ceiling fan and waved me in. 'Sit down please.'

I stepped into the cool interior of the house. Maya's childhood holiday home—where she had come to see her grandmother every year. Or, more likely, where she was brought for everyone to see her. So that they could fuss over her and exclaim how much she had grown and how smart she had become. She had said her memories of this house had all been wonderful ones. I looked around the room. Everything looked shiny and immaculate. Polished arms of wooden chairs gleamed, flowery cushions on every one of them. A vase full of plastic orchids was waving its purple blooms in the breeze of the ceiling fan. A Sony television sat in one corner of the room, gleaming proudly, its top half draped in a piece of cloth on which was embroidered the figure of a Victorian Englishwoman wearing a bonnet. I sat down, noticing that a small figure had appeared at the door through which the woman had disappeared. Half hidden among the curtains, a little girl in tight pigtails stared out at me solemnly, retreating in confusion as I said hello. Older than Anjali. Shyer than Anjali, certainly. Maya might have smiled shyly like that at some visitor. Had she been a shy child? I had never asked. There were so many things I now realized I had never stopped to ask.

The sound of feet slapping in rubber chappals preceded the return of the woman, this time with the little girl attached somewhere behind her. She handed me a piece of paper with the address written on it. I glanced at it before putting it in my shirt pocket. She reminded me in a concerned voice, 'It is very far from here, at least four-five hours.'

'I'm sure the driver will know how to get there. I've hired him for the whole day anyway.'

She looked at me curiously. 'You must be very keen to see Rukmani chechi?'

There was the inflexion of a question in her voice. She really did want to know my business with her Rukmani chechi. I was sure that it was only because I was clearly an outsider that she had not asked me outright about the exact nature of my business with Rukmani Varma. I was damned if I was going to tell her, despite her helpfulness, and I was damned if I was going to let Rukmani Varma off the hook merely because I had another five hours to travel to get to her. Or because her husband had died. She had been as much a part of the whole business as he had been and I hadn't made the long journey to turn back at this stage. Getting up from my chair, I thanked the woman for her helpfulness and made for the door. She offered me a glass of water that I refused, explaining that I had a bottle in the car. I walked back over the sandy soil, feeling the heat filter furiously through the thatch of leaves and branches over my head. I hastily pushed aside the thought that I might be walking over the part of the compound where they had held their ghoulish ceremony for Maya so long ago. Turning to put the latch back on the gate, I waved briefly to the woman who was still standing at her door, trying to work it all out.

We had only a short wait, thankfully, for the return trip to the Alleppey boat jetty. I looked at the closed gates of Pulayil House one last time before getting on the boat. The second floor of the house was only just visible over the trees. Who would have ever thought I would make the journey here someday? The little girl had now materialized behind the gates, clutching the railings with one hand, the other holding a pigtail to her chewing mouth. Like a pretty little apparition reminding me hauntingly of why I was here. She was still gazing solemnly as we chugged away, her dark eyes shining in the sun.

In the boat, I turned to my companion, anticipating his next question. 'Mammookka, the person has moved from there. She's moved to . . .' I looked at the piece of paper before handing it over to him. He did not look displeased at what he read—more miles meant more money. This was, in cab-driver terms, a lucky break.

'No problem, saar,' he said cheerfully. I tilted my head out of the boat and watched the flow of the green waters below, wondering again at the vagaries of life. Maya's father was dead too. Did he ever feel a moment's regret for his daughter before he died? How meaningless rage was, really, in the end. His rage, taking light and burning in funeral fires back in the compound of that graceful old house, had come to nothing as well. What was the point in anything at all once the final fires were burnt?

Arriving back at Alleppey, we got into the now steaming interior of the car. I took a swig of water from the bottle bought earlier this morning, offering Mammookka some. He shook his head and washed his face at a roadside pipe instead. I leaned my head on the plastic headrest behind me, almost meltingly hot from the sun that was now behind us. I felt weak at the thought that I would, at this very moment, have been engaged in an unpleasant conversation with Maya's mother had she still lived in that house. Was it a blessing to have been given a five-hour reprieve, I couldn't tell.

'Saar, you will have lunch?' Mammokka was observing me again in his rear-view mirror, having left the crowded streets of Alleppey behind us.

'Lunch? Now? No, I don't think I can eat now.'

'Not now, saar. At Kalpakavadi, there is 'otel, saar. Very good 'otel, very nice food. After one hour we will reach.'

'Okay, after an hour will be okay.' I wondered if they did a good line in chilled beer.

'You eat frog legs, saar?'

'Frogs legs?'

'Very nice frog legs at Kalpakavadi, saar. Also chicken fry and all if you don't like frog legs,' he said reassuringly.

I could think of nothing worse than frogs legs and chicken fry in this heat and with my stomach already churning at the narrowly missed confrontation with Maya's parents. 'No food for me, thank you. But we'll stop so you can get some lunch and I can have a drink, okay?' This seemed to be a jolly decent prospect to Mammookka who proceeded to lean on his pedal again, a look of determined anticipation coming into his eyes.

An hour later, we were pulling into a tourist complex, with lots of pink buildings scattered around a large palm-dotted compound. KALPAKAVADI TOURIST INN, a large painted sign, faded and peeling, announced. Mammookka gratefully accepted the hundred-rupee note I held out to him before vanishing into one of the buildings. I wondered whether he would drink alcohol with his meal. Arrack or toddy from coconuts was the popular hooch here, I had been told. And there certainly would be no truly enforceable drink-drive laws, just as in Delhi. Not that it worried me particularly. I just needed to get to this place where Maya's mother was, so that I could get to say my piece. Then Mammookka and I could go and have a jolly good piss-up at some arrack den and drive his car off the nearest cliff into the Arabian Sea for all I cared.

I ordered myself a bottle of Kingfisher beer that was surprisingly cold when it was served. Taking a long deep pull, I sat back in the wicker chair, feeling infinitely better. Thank goodness for cold beer, I thought, thank goodness for the fact I had enough pound notes stashed away in my bank back in England to enable me to do all this. Just mine now—to be splashed out in exactly the way I wanted. Nobody else needed my money—not my brother, not my parents. I suppose I could look for a good charity. Right here in Kerala, perhaps? Now, why had that thought popped into my head just like that? This was the place that I ought to be feeling most resentful about. I took another sip of my beer, realizing that oddly enough I was actually starting to feel less torn about Maya now that I was here. This should have been the place to rip me into little pieces, the place we ran away from together. Since then, we had been to many lovely places . . . Lanzarote, Paris, even bloody Orlando. But this . . . Kerala . . . had never beckoned. It didn't want us and we didn't want to come and face its wrath. Or, if Maya did, she never let me know. I should be loathing every moment here, and wondered now why I didn't. Something seemed to be putting solicitous layers of soothing balm inside me everywhere as I looked around at the swaying palm trees, looking ridiculously top-heavy, each with its lavish burden of coconuts. Are you here Maya, I whispered, watching the trees break out into a chorus of nodding as a sudden breeze blew.

Mammookka turned up, looking jaunty and refreshed just as I was finishing my third bottle of beer.

'Eaten? Ready?' I asked.

He nodded, pulling up his dhoti and tying it expertly around his waist. Now he looked truly ready for action. 'You are not eating, saar?' he asked, gesturing with his chin to the table that held its shameful debris of three bottles, a glass and no plate.

'I'm not hungry at all. Too hot,' I said with a smile.

Mammookka, who probably had not seen me smile so far, grinned expansively. 'In the evening, saar, when it is not hot, I will take you to a best place to eat, saar. Eat and drink,' he added, looking again at the table, impressed probably with my propensity for beer.

'In the evening, Mammookka, you can take me anywhere. Once we've been to this place and I've met the person I have to meet, you can take me anywhere and I'll go with you. Then I'll be truly free.'

Mammookka looked puzzled, but still inclined to humour me. 'This place, saar, Tirunalmala, it is very nice. You have gone before?' I shook my head. 'Mountain and river, not many people, not like Alleppey. Very nice place, saar.'

'Well, then, let's be off, shall we?' I said, pulling myself out of my chair and dusting myself down, before following Mammookka back to the car.

Mammookka was right. The number of people and cars on the road were rapidly thinning as we drove away from Alleppey. As we hit a hilly area, and started to climb up narrow, winding roads, the numbers dwindled even more, until I could barely see one person every other mile. Some walked down the road, carrying bundles of twigs and other things on their heads, others just walked. Who were these people and what sort of lives did they have among these remote mountains?

eighteen

I t was nearly six in the evening and getting dark when we
 reached Tirunalmala, which turned out to be a small collection
of houses and shops with corrugated metal sheet roofs and the
red plastic bunting that seemed to festoon every town in Kerala
('Comminist gownment wins in elections, saar,' Mammookka
had explained). He pulled up now in front of a shop and I watched
him go up to the owner with the bit of paper I had given him.
Dusk was descending rapidly now and I could not see the face of
the man in the shop behind rows of soda bottles topped with tiny
fresh yellow lemons. But, from his expansive gestures, pointing
this way and that, I gathered that Mammookka was getting the
directions he needed. I was still feeling fairly calm, despite knowing
that I was now definitely only minutes away from meeting Maya's
mother. I rolled up the car window as I felt a sudden chilly breeze.

'Yes, saar, hilly place, very cold,' Mammookka said, climbing
back into the driver's seat. It wasn't cold, certainly not by London
or even Delhi standards, but the air here seemed definitely thinner.
It had the sort of purity that made you hear things you wouldn't
otherwise—the distant clanging of temple bells, the sound of
plaintive bleating as the goats were brought off their hill slopes
for the night, even the inner thudding of my own heart.

'It is very near, saar, ten minutes,' Mammookka said, turning the car in a screeching U, kicking up dust that rose in tiny glittering motes under the lone street lamp struggling to light up the tiny collection of shops.

We were now driving in the direction of the temple bells that were getting louder by the minute.

'It is also famous temple, saar, that man was saying, very strong, very, very big Bhagawati . . .' Mammookka shivered. For a Muslim, he seemed inordinately keen on keeping track of powerful Hindu female deities. I was silent as we turned off the main road on to what was almost a dirt track. The headlights of the car were throwing eerie shadows in the bumpy road ahead. The clanging was getting deafening.

'Evening time is time for main puja, saar,' Mammookka explained, raising his voice. 'People light up all lamps and you can hear bells, saar?'

'Yes, I can hear bells all right,' I growled.

After a few more bends in the road, everything seemed to come to a sudden halt. The road ended where a temple rose against the hillside, dark and looming, except for the inner sanctum that seemed to be ablaze with light. Mammookka brought the car to a sudden halt and as we stepped out, I noticed that he had dropped his mundu to cover his legs. What a strange Muslim, I thought again, following him to the outer door of the temple.

'You go inside, saar,' he said and clucked reassuringly as I hesitated. ''s all right, saar, you are Hindu. Mammookka wait here.'

'But I don't need to go into the temple,' I whispered back. 'I need only to meet this person, Mrs Rukmani Varma.'

'Yesyes, she is there,' he replied, gesturing inwards again with his chin. 'She lives in there, that shop man said.'

Maya's mother, living in a temple? I pulled off my shoes and lay them next to the other footwear that had been discarded at the door. They looked odd there, Nike size ten, nestling against all manner of rubber and plastic footwear, chappals and sandals, all at least three sizes smaller than mine. I had to bow my head to prevent it from hitting the dark, oil-laden beam of the entrance as I stepped in.

The clanging seemed to be reaching a crescendo and I could see a priest ringing a bell with one hand, using the other to wave a lamp with at least twenty wicks burning in it around the deity. He was chanting something that could not be heard above the clamour of the bells. The only face that looked at me was that of the deity herself—yellow and black with a red dot in the middle of her forehead. Her eyes seemed to bore into my face in what I would not describe as a friendly manner. Everyone else seemed to have eyes only for her. I scanned the crowd quickly, but could not spot Maya's mother through the pall of oily smoke that was now making my eyes feel sore. There were mainly women in the temple, but some men and children as well. Everyone, without exception, was gazing at the deity with hands folded in prayer, lips muttering, tears glistening. Who were all these people—there were at least thirty here—who had come to pray in this remote temple? The town I had seen did not look like it was big enough to house ten!

I looked around again and this time spotted her. Next to what looked like a side door to the inner sanctum. It was certainly her, she hadn't changed that much. Except that she was wearing the white of widows and now had very white hair, rolled into a small knot on her neck. It was odd, but she also looked like she had shrunk over the years, grown smaller and thinner. Her eyes were closed as she stood with her hands folded in prayer, swaying slightly as her lips muttered.

Suddenly I wanted to hold on to something and slid hastily behind a pillar. I could not believe I was here. In a clamouring temple, lurking behind a stone pillar, looking at Maya's mother! So far from home, so far from everything that was familiar to me.

I was mad, that was it, I had gone stark staring mad to have come all the way here. And for bloody what? To leap out at some unsuspecting old woman? To vent my wrath on her? Because I needed to be angry with somebody? Because her daughter was now *dead*?

I stayed behind the pillar and, as the chanting and the clanging slowly wound down and eventually stopped, I slowly shifted my weight to look again at Maya's mother. Her eyes were open now, but she was looking into the inner sanctum of the temple, hands still folded. Then she stepped aside, as the priest emerged holding a long brass hand-lamp that had some burning camphor on it. He pointed it at her first and she responded by cupping her hands around the flame before putting her hands to her eyes. I watched as the priest then brought the lamp around to where all the other people were and found myself being pushed to one side as they shoved at each other to do the same thing with their hands as Maya's mother had done. When I looked back at her again, I could see that she had spotted me. Recognition flickered faintly in her eyes. Strange that she should remember me from that one glance so long ago. But she wasn't looking at me now. Her eyes were behind me somewhere—I knew who she was looking for.

She stood absolutely still as I approached her through the crowd. Some people stood aside to let me pass, looking at me curiously. The priest had gone back into his inner sanctum and the crowd seemed to be dissolving away into the dark edges of the temple.

'Do you remember me?' I asked, although it was obvious from her complete, unmoving stillness that she did.

'Yes . . .' she said hesitantly. Then, taking a deep breath and looking beyond me again, she asked, 'Where is she . . . Maya . . .?'

Her voice was low and held tremors of age . . . or shock, possibly? She looked older and more frail than my mother, although she was probably around the same age. From so close I could see she had aged immensely since I last saw her as she walked into her daughter's house in Trivandrum. Her skin was papery and wrinkled. I was aware that I hadn't answered her as she looked more questioningly into my face and then took an almost imperceptible step back. For a moment she tottered slightly and, imagining she was about to fall, I stepped forward and caught her by her elbow.

'If we can sit down somewhere, I need to talk to you,' I said.

I followed her as she turned and walked out of the temple through a back gate, much smaller than the one outside where the car had been parked. She walked unsteadily, but again I wasn't sure if it was age or the effect of seeing me here so suddenly, a spectre from the past she had so determinedly put away. The path was dark and I found myself stumbling a couple of times. She suddenly seemed to remember something and stopped. Fumbling among the folds of her sari, she produced a small torch and clicked it on saying, 'Sorry, you don't know this pathway as well as I do.'

The weak beam of light showed a small footpath running along the side of the mountain. Beyond, along the edges of a distant hill, there was still light in the sky, the blue-grey of departing twilight. But here, on this little path, we seemed enveloped in murky darkness thrown down by the trees growing densely overhead.

'It is not far,' she said, just as we walked around a bend and I spotted the lights of a few small dwellings tucked into the mountainside. As we neared them, she pulled the end of her sari out and, using the key tied into one corner, opened the door to the first of the small terraced house. There seemed to be two or three others like it further along the row. She turned a light on as we stepped in. It cast a gloomy half-light over a room that was spartan but tidy. I stood unsurely in the middle of the room, feeling suddenly wretched again. I hated dim lighting. And this was not like anything I had expected from my encounter with Maya's mother. It would have been okay if she was still in that house in Champakulam, I could have dealt with that. But here . . . here was an old woman living like a hermit on the side of a mountain . . . why the hell did I come?

She sat down in one of the chairs, almost as though in anticipation of what I was going to say. 'Sit down,' she said to me. I seated myself gingerly on the edge of the chair opposite, still unable to say anything. 'Please complete what you were going to say at the temple,' she said, in a voice that was trying to sound stronger than before.

After a pause long enough for her to know I was definitely carrying bad news, I said softly, 'Maya's dead.'

The silence in the room churned noisily around me. It was almost as if my words, now that they had escaped me, were surging around, attempting to smother and choke both her and me in the half-darkness. Had she stopped breathing with the horror of my words hanging silently between us? I could hear the tick-tock of an alarm clock from the room next door. Far away, a couple of dogs howled an eerie chorus. I could feel anguish emanate from the small white figure in front of me, even though she had not said a word. How could I have imagined it wouldn't be there? After a few moments, the dim lighting showed me the gleam of tears coursing down her wrinkled face, but her voice was calm as she whispered, 'When . . . how . . .?'

'Car accident,' I said.

'Where is . . . Anjali?' She was stumbling over their names as though they had lodged unspoken in her throat for many years.

'Back with her father—with Govind. He came for her two days ago, I'm sure he'll be contacting you soon. I waited for them to leave before coming here . . .'

After a long pause, she asked, her voice still shaking, 'Why did you want to come and tell me?'

This was my moment. This was my chance to say that it was not kindness that brought me here. I did not make this long journey merely to break this news to her, couldn't she tell? The questions

I prepared during those sleepless London nights were still waiting unasked. My anger was still terrifyingly unquenched.

'I felt I had to come,' I said, trying to keep my eyes on her face. What I saw was a wrinkled old figure, rocking in her chair, as though that repetitive mindless movement could ease some of the pain. Was she truly all alone here? Where the bloody hell was her son? If there was someone, *anyone* here with her, I could have said my piece and left and have nothing more to do with her. My own ghosts would have been exorcized, in exactly the same manner as she had exorcized hers with Maya's death ritual all those years ago. And that would have been that. Perhaps if I had not experienced loneliness so recently myself, I would have done it. Even in a warm, bright London house, loneliness had stalked around like an evil being, suffocating and tormenting. How, in the darkness of this night, could I bring that on someone else? The mountains were too silent, the air too thin and cold.

'I've . . . I've brought her ashes,' I said.

'Is that what she—' She stopped. Then added gently, 'Thank you for doing that. I will speak to the priest about it tomorrow.'

'Tomorrow? I have to leave tonight,' I said, confused.

'Do not go at night,' she said. 'I will make a bed for you here. In the morning we will go down to the river and float the ashes. It is the most peaceful place in the world.' After a pause she added, 'It must all have been so hard for you . . . both so young . . . and Anjali . . .' Her voice broke again as she suddenly buried her face in her hands, her shoulders heaving silently.

I looked down at my shoes. For a while she continued to cry silently, barely audible over the noisy night chorus of crickets and other creatures. My own tears had been shed into my lonely pillow back at home, there seemed to be none left inside me now. I sat quietly on my chair, listening to the night come awake outside. Suddenly she dried her face and said softly, 'You wanted to take out some of your anger and sorrow on me, did you not?' There was no trace of anger in her voice, just that same tired tremor.

I looked at her. She had finished wiping her face and was now looking directly at me. I realized with some shock that somewhere in that countenance was a trace of Maya—something very tiny and subtle that I couldn't place at the moment. Not any of her features, more an expression, something in the turn of her head.

'My anger?' I asked. 'Yes, I suppose there was that. I just couldn't understand what happened between you and her. It seemed so unnecessary, somehow . . . And so terribly sad once she was gone.'

'Yes, it was unnecessary. I—I was upset with her father but I could not do anything . . . everything was going wrong . . . his mother's health . . .' she replied, sounding as though she was speaking more to herself now. 'How sad that we don't get second chances at being parents . . . we made so many mistakes . . . her marriage . . .' Her voice faltered before she took a breath and started speaking again. 'Govind was not the perfect man for her . . . but . . . nobody gets that. He was a good boy . . . he used to call me Amma too.'

She stopped speaking and held her throat as though trying to ease something clogging it shut. Slowly, she started to speak again, as though every word were an effort. 'How could she expect us to accept what she did to him, to Govind? Before she got married it was not that bad. I thought her father would not even forgive her that affair in Bangalore but, because she later agreed to marry Govind, he came to terms with her behaviour . . . but, again, and *after* marriage? It just became too much for him.'

'What affair?' I asked.

Maya's mother threw a wavering, uncertain look at me. 'I'm sorry . . . you did not know any of that?' she whispered. 'She never told you . . .' her voice trailed off and melted into the dark stillness of the night.

After an almost imperceptible pause, I replied, 'No, she didn't

Jaishree Misra

'. . . and, do you know what, even if she had, would it surprise you to know that I wouldn't have minded? I certainly don't believe in never forgiving people for their mistakes.' I could hear my voice rise pathetically and, suddenly, I was close to tears myself. But I ploughed on, 'What about your relationship with her, though? Didn't you ever care that it was destroyed?'

'*She* did that, not us. She went first, without even telling us . . . without saying a word. How could she do that?' She was crying again, more loudly now.

'Maya was frightened. She thought you would stop her. And she was desperate to go. She did not for a moment think that it would destroy things between you forever. She thought she could contact you and explain once she had got away.'

'Oh . . . but one word . . . one word to us before she left. We were with her less than a month before that and she did not say a thing. Of course, we blamed you—'

'I only helped her to leave when the time came. Initially it had nothing to do with me. Although I don't suppose anyone will believe me now.'

'If that is what you say, I will believe you.'

'It's true that I helped her to leave, even though I did try talking her out of it first. But she seemed so miserable and so helpless . . . and my own feelings were confusing me by then.' Now I was crying too. This was ridiculous. I had come here to *blame*, not to explain myself!

'But she sent a picture of all three of you, looking like a happy family. It broke her father's heart.'

'She thought you'd be happy to know that she was happy.'

'Govind had visited us just a week before that to ask if we had any news. We told him that we supported him entirely and could find no excuse for her behaviour. He left, looking so broken, so sad. And then, in a rage that I could not control, my husband called for the man to do the death rites. He had to vent his guilt, his fury on something. He could not bear that his old mother had to put up with all that shame and that loose talk in the village at her age. The shock killed her, you know . . . and then it took him too . . .'

'When . . . when did he die?' I asked.

'Six months after he conducted that terrible ceremony. I could see it eating away inside him. His mother had died before the monsoon. It was as if he was waiting for his mother to go and . . . soon after, he went too.'

'You never wanted to tell Maya about all that?'

'I blamed her. I blamed her for it all. I blamed her that I was now all alone while she had gone to have a happy life with you.'

The sound of her tears, bitter and anguished, filled the small room. I was silent. Wasted rage, wasted rage, my tired mind thought.

Finally, she raised her head. Wiping her eyes, she asked, 'Was she . . . was she happy?'

I could tell, from the way she asked, that she really needed to know that Maya had been happy. How odd that there should now be comfort in that.

I nodded. 'I tried to make her happy. I think a lot of the time she was. Not always, of course.'

She seemed to understand and said softly, the tears in her voice now receding, 'By the time I wanted to know that, it was too late.'

'It could never have been too late,' I said.

I was not sure she had heard me because she was still speaking in a faraway tone of voice, as though I wasn't there at all. 'I hoped for a long time that she would come. We could have comforted each other, but she did not come. It felt as if all she wanted was her new life with you. Slowly, my sorrow grew hard and cold. I had learnt by then to live without her. I felt there was less pain that way.'

'Yes, I suppose I can see that . . .' I muttered. Now I was talking to myself too. Then, looking at her I said, 'But, surely, after that . . .

did you not once want to write and make up? For months after that I think she still hoped there would be a letter or something.'

'Did she?' She sounded genuinely surprised. 'How I hoped too. Kept hoping there would be something . . . that maybe she would come again . . . that maybe you would all come . . . maybe to show me a new child . . .' She was crying again, but through her tears her voice, now choking with sorrow, kept coming as though she couldn't stop. 'For another year, I waited. Then the pain of that was too much, so I came here. So far that I thought nobody would find me. Then at least I could stop waiting.'

I got up and went over to her. Bending over her, I stroked her back, feeling my own tears salty in my mouth. She seemed terribly small and fragile, not at all like the tallish, slightly stern figure I thought I had remembered well. For a long time, she moaned quietly, finally giving way to sobs and then silence, disturbed only occasionally by a broken sigh. After a while, she straightened her back and took my hand in her dry, papery palm. 'Thank you,' she said before releasing it. She then got up out of her chair and turning to me said, 'Forgive me, you have travelled so far and I have not even given you a drink of water. I have some rice and curds here. Will you eat some before I make up a bed for you?'

I nodded. 'I have a driver waiting outside. I need to tell him we are staying the night.'

'He can also sleep here, in this room, if he does not mind sleeping on the floor.'

'I'll ask,' I said as she put her torch in my hands.

Letting myself out, I stopped for a moment to clear my head again. The stars were hanging heavy, unmoving and still. There was an incredible calmness about the night. I looked up at the inky sky, feeling the cool breeze brush my hot face, and closed my burning eyes for a few minutes. Maya's face floated into my consciousness. Already, her features were blurring and I felt the familiar panic that I might completely forget and never be able to recapitulate them at will. Are you watching me now, Maya, I asked softly. What mysteries did you carry with you, even when you were with me? I shook my head and took a deep breath. No, I didn't want to know her secrets, especially now that she was gone. We had been happy during our short time together—that's all I needed to know.

I began the walk back to the temple, reaching its small gate far more quickly than anticipated. I was probably already getting familiar with the rocky little path. The interior of the temple was quiet now, freed of its worshippers. The priest was sitting, wrapped in a shawl, making flower garlands using some red blooms. He nodded at me as I went past, saying something I couldn't understand.

'I'm . . . I'm staying with Mrs Rukmani Varma,' I said, feeling foolish to be speaking English here in this faraway place. But he seemed satisfied, nodding and showing me teeth stained with betel leaf in an accepting smile. I went out to the car and found Mammookka wrapped up in a heavy blanket and fast asleep on the back seat. 'Hello, Mammookka,' I said, shaking him by the shoulder. His eyes opened blearily and I said quickly, 'That's okay, don't get up, we're staying here tonight. You okay here or do you want to come in?'

He struggled up to a sitting position. ''sokay, Mammookka sleep in car, saar,' he mumbled.

'Food? Have you eaten?'

He nodded. 'Tirumeni gave me food,' he said, gesturing at the temple with his chin. I had to surmise that either the priest had given him something to eat or that the goddess herself had descended in one of his fevered dreams to personally deliver him sustenance.

'Okay, I'll see you in the morning then,' I said, removing my bag from the boot of the car. Turning back, I made my way through the temple into the dark pathway behind. I stood outside the door to the tiny house for a few minutes before knocking and opening

Jaishree Misra

it to let myself in. A bed had been made up in a corner of the room and small kitchen sounds were emanating from the room next door. I pushed my bag under the bed before walking over to the kitchen door and said, 'I hope you're not making anything, I'm not very hungry.'

She was standing over a kerosene stove, stirring something in a pan. 'Because I am on my own, I do not cook much,' she said. 'I hope you will drink a glass of Horlicks with your food, it is good for you.' She had taken a bottle out of a minuscule cupboard and was scraping in it with a spoon, adding bits of the sticky powder into the pan, stirring it all the time. 'If you take a plate out of that cupboard, you can help yourself to the rice in this dish. There is some curry and curds under that banana leaf. Pickles are in a bottle inside the cupboard.'

I busied myself, suddenly realizing how hungry I was. The prospect of rice and curds with pickle was strangely tempting in its simplicity.

'What about you? Will you be eating now?' I asked.

'Yes, I will. You start, I will join you.'

I took my plate back to the small living room and surveyed it as I ate. There was only one photograph on the wall and I recognized Maya's father. He gazed impassively at me and I wondered how it would have gone today had he still been alive. How easily he had taken out his anger and resentments on those he loved best. Would regret have grown out of that if he had lived any longer, I wondered.

She came into the room with two steaming mugs and placed one next to me and the other on the floor near her chair. It was her grace—*that* was what had been reminding me of Maya—a certain quiet grace. Then she went back in for her plate. We ate in silence, while the nightly chorus of crickets continued to chirrup outside. I was not sure whether she wanted to hear anything more about Maya. Her face was still drawn with pain, despite her busy air. If she had lived all these years without any news, perhaps it was better to leave it that way, I thought.

After finishing my meal, I washed my hands and my plate, using a mug to scoop water out of a plastic bucket. Maya's mother was back in the kitchen, closing things, putting them away in her little cupboard. She saw me looking around the fire-blackened room.

'You don't really need a fridge in these mountain places. The air is so cool.'

I was embarrassed. 'I hadn't noticed that . . . I was just thinking how different things probably were for you in Bangalore.'

'All the outward trappings,' she smiled. 'I didn't mind losing those. It was the other things, the important things, the love I had invested in all the people who left me one by one, my daughter, my husband—'

'Doesn't Maya have a brother?' I asked.

She smiled and nodded. 'Keshav is in boarding school in Ooty. I go to see him in the holidays, open up the house in Bangalore, so that he has a nice place to stay,' she said, looking around at our own bleak surroundings. 'Maybe that is a mistake too. I had wanted him to be far away from me . . . after Maya . . . scared of getting too close and then being hurt again or something. Maybe that's wrong . . . maybe one should never be scared of showing the love one has . . .'

I knew she wasn't really talking to me again. Her eyes had a faraway look for a while, until I spoke up again.

'How do you keep yourself busy here,' I asked.

'The temple and ashram keep me busy, not that I am very religious or anything.' She stopped and smiled again at the expression on my face. 'No, really, you don't have to be that religious to feel the peace here. There is peace for the soul in the mountain and the river. And work for the hands in the ashram. There's not much more I can ask for.'

'And if you fall ill or something?'

'The tirumeni . . . you know, the temple priest and his wife live next door. Also the woman who cleans the temple pots. There are enough people here, good, simple people. I try to be useful to them too. Inwardly we can be lonely, even when we are surrounded by family and friends, but we can never be truly alone as long as there are other people in the world.' She looked at me and then said gently, 'You look tired. Why don't you go to bed? I will finish my work and then I will go to sleep too. Tomorrow we have to be up early if we want to do the ceremony at sunrise.'

I used the tiny toilet outside the house. It had all the bare essentials, even a little faded mirror. I dipped my hand in the water stored in a plastic bucket in the corner. It was far too cold for anything more than just a quick splash on my face and hands and, having done that, I returned quickly to the warmth of the house. She was now in what was probably her bedroom. A dim light shone through blue curtains at the door. The lights in the kitchen and the living room had been turned off. I took off my shoes, unbuttoned my jeans and got into bed. The sheet felt clean and crisp although the blanket had an unused mustiness about it. I felt under the bed for my shoulder bag, the one I normally used for my trips to the gym after work. Through the thin leather I could feel the box containing Maya's ashes. I laid my hand on it for a while, wondering why the fires seemed to have stilled inside me somewhere. Relief that I hadn't vented my anger on Maya's mother flooded through me. Where had my rage gone? My eyelids were closing. The last thing I knew before I fell asleep was the whisper of soft breezes sighing through the trees.

*

I awoke to the clamour of birds and goats. Above my head was a calendar with the picture of a goddess on it. She was sitting on a lion and looked extraordinarily serene for it. Next to me was a tiny bookshelf. The Bhagavadgita, Vivekananda's writings, Sathya

Sai Baba's teachings, a small photograph album in old red leather. I pulled it out, blew the dust off it and opened it. They were all pictures of Maya . . . old black-and-white ones of a little girl at various stages of growing up, her features unmistakable even in the faded old pictures, even through layers of puppy fat. Maya wearing a tiny silk skirt and blouse, standing in some temple compound . . . Maya holding a terrified-looking kitten . . . another as a baby, sitting in a plastic basin, looking cross . . . a ten-year-old licking on an ice-cream cone, pure pleasure glistening all over her small face. And then there were pictures, now in faded colour, of an older girl, wearing a salwar-kameez, looking heart-breakingly pretty, her arm around her little brother. That would have been Maya sometime before I met her. One of her marriage, standing next to Govind, both of them wearing flower garlands, both of them looking slightly dazed. There were only two pictures I had seen before. One of Maya with baby Anjali in her arms—we had a copy of that in an album back in England. Maya must have had a copy of it in her bag or purse the day she left Kerala. I looked at the last one. I remembered the day it was taken with the clarity only a few beers could normally bestow—the date was there in a corner of the picture to remind me anyway. My birthday, more than two years ago, soon after Maya and Anjali had come to England. My cake was in the foreground, a cheesy-looking chocolate Lion-King from M&S, with a pink tongue lolling out. Behind it, I was brandishing a knife. Anjali, tiny then, was looking at the cake in eager anticipation. Maya . . . Maya looked gloriously happy for some reason, smiling up at me. Kevin had popped in on his way to see his mother and we had that impromptu party, took a few pictures and got slightly drunk. Maya had put it in an envelope along with her letter before giving it to Kevin to post, eager to let her mother know how wonderful her new life was, imagining she would derive happiness from her own joy, as she had always done. She wasn't to know, of course, of the journey it would make. Arriving first in Bangalore, redirected to Pulayil House in Champakulam to which her parents had already moved to nurse her ailing grandmother, a house still shrouded in the grief of her departure, soon to be the stage for three death ceremonies, one after the other. How its careless merriment would have stabbed in the midst of that pain. How strange that happiness in one place could so easily transform itself to anguish in another.

I reached down into the bag under the bed and pulled out the few pictures of Maya and Anjali that I had put into my suitcase back in London. I slipped them into the empty last leaves of the album. Maya's little sandalwood Ganesha was also in the bag. I took it out, wiped it down on the front of my shirt and placed it carefully on the shelf, next to the books. I heard footsteps outside and slipped the album back in its place. Maya's mother came in, taking off her slippers at the door. I could see, as watery sunlight trickled in through the open door, that her face and eyes were swollen and heavy with the weight of the tears she had shed last night. But she spoke to me calmly. 'I have spoken to the tirumeni about the ceremonies. He has called an eleyathu to get everything ready. An eleyathu is a priest who does the death rites. By seven we should be down by the riverside.' I got out of bed, buttoning up my shirt as she went into the kitchen saying, 'I will warm some water for your bath.'

She made me a cup of coffee, boiling the mixture of milk and water on the small kerosene stove again. In a corner of the kitchen, a steel bucket of water had an immersion heater stuck in it— water being heated for my bath. I drank my coffee, standing out on the porch of the house, looking up at the trees that now seemed to be abundant and trembling with chirruping birds. Then I carried the heated water into the bathroom. Mixing it carefully with the water in the plastic bucket which was now even icier than before, I washed myself, using a cake of red Lifebuoy soap that I found in a soap dish on the window sill.

Maya's mother had placed what looked like a brand-new dhoti on the bed. She seemed to have gone out again. I struggled with it for a while, tying it this way and that. I once wore a dhoti somewhat like this one when my parents organized a havan for Anil's departure to San Francisco. But I had Mum to help me then. As a last desperate measure, I removed my belt from my jeans and tightened it as much as I could over the dhoti. Then I left the house, closing the door behind me. Did people have to lock their houses in places like this? In London we turned on the burglar alarm even if we were just popping out for the papers.

Maya's mother and a priest were leaving the temple just as I arrived at its back door. 'Oh good, you are ready. We were just coming to call you to go down to the river.' She smiled down at my Nike trainers that were sticking out of the bottom of my dhoti.

'Not quite the picture of elegance, is it?' I said ruefully.

'I'm sorry, but people usually wear mundus for such things. It's all about auspiciousness I suppose,' she replied. The priest said something to her and she turned to me. Once again, her eyes had shaded over. 'Where is the box of ashes?'

I went back into the house and brought out the shoulder bag, carrying it in my arms, rather than slinging it over my shoulder as I normally would have done. They were already quite a way down the path and I followed, trying not to slip on the stones and twigs that did not seem to be bothering them despite their bare feet. As I turned a bend, the river unfolded before me, wide open and tranquil, shimmering peacefully in the dawn-light. Maya's mother walked up to the edge and took a few drops of water in her hand to sprinkle over her head. I stood on the cement step at the edge of the water, now holding on tightly to my bag. The priest came up to me, saying something I did not understand, finally taking the bag out of my arms gently. With an air of immense seriousness he took it into a little shack, emerging a few minutes later with the box, some banana leaves, a pan of red rice and little black gingili seeds.

Maya's mother turned to me. 'Will you be able to do some of the pujas? I am not allowed to . . . being her mother. And there is no one else.' I nodded and kicked off my shoes, uncertain of what to do next. Maya's mother gestured and I understood that I needed to take my shirt off. I handed it to her and saw that the priest appeared to be calling me down to sit near him on the last cement step against which the river water gently lapped. I stepped down, feeling my feet slip slightly on the step, slimy from its many years of contact with the river. The priest gesticulated for me to sprinkle some river water over my head, which I did, feeling small trickles run down my face. After I had settled myself next to him, he closed his eyes and started to chant some incantations, rolling the rice into sticky little balls, covering them with the seeds. He made a little ring out of strands of a palm leaf and asked me to wear it on the middle finger of my right hand. I watched him carefully, obeying his every gestured instruction, eager not to make a mistake.

It must have taken about half an hour, because we were still there as the sun rose, pale orange, spilling its warm rays down the slope of the mountain and into the water. As everything seemed to turn to light, he finished his prayers. Getting up from the step, he nodded at me to do the same and said something that Maya's mother had to translate.

'He wants you to immerse yourself in the river,' she said, sounding apologetic.

'I don't mind,' I said, getting up from the step. I took another few steps down and felt the cement steps give way to the river bed under my feet. The edge of my mundu was suddenly wet as the river water seemed to rush at me as though in welcome. I could feel it cling to my mundu and play with it, its currents grabbing at my knees, caressing my calves almost seductively. 'Be careful,'

Maya's mother said, but I just smiled at her reassuringly. I loved the water, had often surfed down the beaches at Cornwall. This was nothing. This gently rocking river was like a cradle by comparison to some of the seas I had frolicked in. I stepped out a little further, until I was nearly waist deep in the water, and then bent my knees. The water rushed over my head, blinding me, entering my consciousness as though tempting me to stay there forever. I held my breath for a few minutes, savouring the feeling of having been transported to another universe. Noisy but quiet, busy but soothing. I emerged as I felt my breath run out. As my eyes stopped stinging and the world formed itself around me again, Maya's mother was still standing on the steps, the priest next to her. The box, now covered with flowers, at their feet.

As the priest beckoned, I walked back out of the river and up the stairs, now dripping wet. We sat down again and I had to do some more stuff with the rice and the seeds, all the time dripping water over everything. Finally, the priest was saying something that I didn't need Maya's mother to translate. He pointed at the box and at the river and I knew that it was nearly all over. I bent down to lift the box, now opened and covered with flowers, pink and white, and lifted it to my chest. The flowers smelt sweet as I held the box close, carrying it down to the edge of the river. The priest was gesturing again, telling me to release the box into the river. I walked back into the river, until I was waist deep again, feeling the water lap at the bottom of the box that I was still holding tightly. I lowered it into the water, but felt it resist and attempt to float back into my arms. Then, as the water soaked into the box, I could feel it give way slightly and I pressed gently downwards with my hands, willing it to go. After a few more moments of uncertainty, it seemed to decide on the best path to take and I felt it sink into the grey-green depths. I reached out with both hands to see if I could still find it, but it had gone.

A few minutes later, a few pink flowers appeared over the

crest of the water, floating serenely downriver. But there was no sign of the box. It would appear again, no doubt, further down the river, washed up against a shore where it would be found by a child or some woman at first only intent on washing her clothes, upended and emptied of its contents. It would be taken back to their house as a curiosity, its 'Made-in-England' brass plaque and hinges exclaimed over. It would be cleaned and kept on display in a glass cabinet with smoky, streaked glass. Maybe it would be used to store rice or spices.

But its contents, so precious once, had merely darkened the water's surface for a moment, in the way that a pair of eyes shade over when saddened. Just for a few seconds, before it was shining clear again. Would I ever understand how a pair of bright eyes, the serenity of a smile, the warmth of a human body, her thoughts, her secrets, her touch, her kiss . . . all that . . . could merely melt into the rushing waters of a river as though it had been no effort at all. Did that mean she was now this water and a part of every sea? Would her name rise with the vapours to be whispered by winds and rustle every tree. Had she come to nothing or was she now everywhere and everything, my Maya?

*

For a long time afterwards, for most of the morning, the prayers seemed to go on. I could not tell if these were something to do with Maya or just the normal routines of the day. I sat on a rock, watching the mountainside come slowly to life as the day began. A girl, who couldn't have been much older than Anjali, walked past with three goats, expertly herding them together using a small twig and a peculiar clicking sound in her throat. I wondered what Anjali might be doing today. Had she remembered her old house in Trivandrum? And had she perhaps played that sorry little game of hide-and-seek all over again, still looking for her mum? Would she ever want to return to see me, I wondered. Would she have any memory at all of the life she had had with us these past three years? Surely it would fade. She was not even five yet.

Later, back at Maya's mother's house, I changed into my jeans again and threw the mundu, now soaking wet, into a corner of the room. She came in as I was nearly ready to leave. I went up to her and took her hand in mine.

'I have to go now, there's nothing more to be done, is there? No more pujas, I mean.'

She shook her head, her eyes still shining unnaturally. 'No, nothing more,' she said.

'I'll return to Cochin today and try to get a flight to Delhi as soon as possible. To see my parents, you know . . . they're worried too.' She nodded again and I continued, 'I thought about seeing Anjali, I have a little gift for her. Coloured soaps, she likes those. I'll probably give Govind a call from Cochin to find out how she's doing.' I paused and then added, partly to myself, 'Maybe it's best I don't call her actually . . . I don't know . . . don't want to be upsetting her, or Govind.'

She looked thoughtful. 'If you have the soaps here with you, maybe you can leave them with me and I'll try to give them to her. I can't even imagine that I might be able to see her quite soon. I will write to Govind and ask him to send her to me during the holidays. If he doesn't mind. She will like it here, the river and the temple. She can even come to Bangalore with me when I go to see Keshav. How they'll both like that!' She paused and looked directly into my eyes. 'Don't worry, I'll make sure you don't lose her love. I know how terrible a feeling it is to imagine you have lost the love of your own child.'

'Thanks,' I muttered awkwardly. 'She'll certainly remember you with no trouble, she often talked about her Ammumma-house.'

She looked at me, smiling now. 'Look, you must come too, to Bangalore, or here, whichever you prefer. When Anjali is with me. I promise you I'll make sure she doesn't forget you either, she must have been so fond of you . . .' I nodded. Maya's mother added carefully, 'You must carry on, living your life well; you are so young. You don't know what happiness awaits you. Please promise me that you will.'

I drew myself up and nodded again. 'Yes, I will,' I said. 'I will carry on, as you say. I suppose that's exactly what Maya would have said.' She smiled sadly. 'Goodbye,' I said. 'And thank you for helping me . . . I honestly didn't know where to go at first.'

'Thank you for bringing her back,' she said.

I turned and walked out of the house, closing the door behind me and turning to climb the path up to the temple again. There was no sign of the priest there, just a handful of worshippers, standing at the gates with hands folded in prayer. Mammookka was talking to a man who was selling flowers nearby. Spotting me, he bid the flower seller a hasty goodbye and hailed me cheerfully as he walked back to the car.

'Aha, now you are looking all right, saar, after bath and all! Good sleep? Saar you forget your bag?' he asked, gesturing to my empty arms in some consternation.

'No, that's okay, I've had to leave it behind,' I said, climbing into the car.

'Done, saar? Finished?' he asked.

'Yes, finished, Mammookka. Back to Cochin now,' I said resolutely. 'Maybe we can stop somewhere for some breakfast on the way?'

'Yes, saar,' he replied, starting up the car noisily.

'Oh, and if you can stop for a minute down where those shops are, I need to buy something.'

The Tirunalmala square was a hub of activity in the bright sunshine of the morning. It looked very different from the deserted space that I had first seen through the swirling evening mists. Mammookka pulled up outside the same shop from which we had taken directions on our way up and looked back at me enquiringly. I got out of the car, went up to the shop and asked if he stocked Horlicks. He pulled out a bottle from the back of a shelf, but I pointed to a larger bottle I could see behind it.

'Could you ask him, Mammookka, if that's the biggest bottle he has?'

As the man wrapped the two bottles in old newspaper, I asked Mammookka to request the shopkeeper to also have it delivered to Rukmani Varma who lived up at the temple. Mammookka broke out into another flurry of Malayalam and the man nodded, smiling, calling out to a young lad who looked like his son. Again, instructions were given as I paid for my purchase, adding a little tip for the boy who was already cycling enthusiastically up the hill with the little bundle.

Back in the car, as we slowly drove down the winding hill road, I could spot occasional glimpses of the river through the trees. It had not been visible the night we drove up, either because of the gathering darkness or because I had not known it was there. Had that been just yesterday? It was gleaming silver now in the sunlight, seeming to glint a smile, seeming reluctant to part, appearing and reappearing, as we made our journey to the main road below. Then, as we reached a sign for the national highway, the car turned on to the main road for the south. I looked back to get one last glimpse of Maya's river as it curved the other way, to make its final journey to the sea.

Jaishree Misra